BILLY BOB BUTTONS is the award-winning author of eleven children's novels including the Rubery Book Award FINALIST, Felicity Brady and the Wizard's Bookshop, the much loved The Gullfoss Legends, TOR Assassin Hunter, TOR Wolf Rising, the hysterical Muffin Monster and the UK People's Book Prize WINNER, I Think I Murdered Miss.

He is also a PATRON OF READING.

Born in the Viking city of York, he and his wife, Therese, a true Swedish girl from the IKEA county of Småland, now live in Stockholm and London. Their twin girls, Rebecca and Beatrix, and little boy, Albert, inspire Billy Bob every day to pick up a pen and work on his books.

When not writing, he enjoys tennis and playing 'MONSTER!' with his three children.

Felicity Brady
and the
Wizard's
Bookshop

Billy Bob Buttons

book 1
GALIBRATH'S WILL

THE WISHING SHELF PRESS

ISBN 978 1523216062

Published by THE WISHING SHELF PRESS, UK.
www.bbbuttons.co.uk Twitter @BillyBobButtons
Edited by Alison Emery, Therese Råsbäck and Svante Jurnell.
Front cover illustrated by Margarita Sheshukova.

For my wife who puts up with me.

Chapter 1

The Wizard's Bookshop

Down some steps, below a crumbling bridge, there sits a scruffy old bookshop. The plaster on the stone walls is bubbling and peeling, and the window is so grimy that you have to squash your nose up to the glass to peer in. If you hunt in the shadows, you will find a shabby brown door but if you push it, it simply will not budge. It will just growl at you, and creak, as if to say, 'STAY OUT! STAY OUT!'

But most people living in the small town of Twice Brewed know not to try the door for seeping under it there is always the stinking smell of rotting fish. They simply scurry on by, Falafel Pass curving along the river to the steps and the steps running up to the busy High Street.

Crouched under the bridge, her back rubbing on the stone bricks, was Felicity Brady. She stared up at the steps, gently lit by a rusty black lamp hanging over them. Whenever she heard somebody coming she would try to huddle even smaller, her tatty school satchel clutched in her frosty hands.

She had been hiding from the school bully and his gang of boys for most of the afternoon and her legs hurt from running. It was drizzling too and she was drenched to the skin. Even her school blouse under her duffel coat clung to her body, and her skirt and boots were caked in mud. Short boyish curls fell in wet rats' tails over her freckled brow, covering her frightened eyes and wind-scuffed cheeks. She was always being teased in school for being a bit of a tomboy, not helped by the crack in her front teeth, but her Aunty Imelda insisted she was very pretty. "Forget all them silly spots," she always comforted her. "Just your goodness oozing out."

Slowly, Felicity lifted her head and pushed the damp curls away from her face. It was then that she saw the bookshop for the first time; a door wrapped in shadows and a filthy window, scruffy books pushed up to the glass. As she looked, the glass seemed to clear, as if a soapy sponge was being dragged over it. She jumped, grazing her back on the jagged wall. Had she just seen a man's face gawping back out at her?

Somebody was coming. She bit her lip and wrapped her arms around her curled-up legs.

A man - well, Felicity guessed he was a man as he was so tall - was creeping down the steps. But there was hardly a sound. It was as if - as if he was floating!

She gasped and the man stopped. OH NO! Would he see her? She was huddled in a dark corner, in the shadow of the bridge, but if he got any closer...

Felicity let out a sigh as he spun around and glided over to the bookshop door.

Now his back was to her, she could just make out a long black cloak covering him. He was muttering something, it sounded like, "Apple crumble and...," she couldn't make out the rest. Then the door swung open and he slipped into the shop.

"If she's not down 'ere, you'll be in for a smack as well as 'er."

"I saw her go down here just now. Well, I think it w' Brady."

"It's a bit fishy down 'ere, in it?"

Felicity scrambled to her feet, her heart thumping with terror. She could run down the path by the River Cruor but she had been chased all afternoon; she was already worn out. They would catch up to her in a second.

She had to hide. But where?

Suddenly, Felicity discovered she was standing in front of the bookshop door. She looked at it in surprise. But how...? A stone bounced down the steps, kicked by one of the boys. Any moment, they would spot her.

In a panic, she pushed at the door but it just

whined back at her like a stroppy mule.

"Look what we have 'ere, lads. The new girl, Brady. Or is she a boy? Difficult to tell."

Felicity closed her eyes and rested her brow on the door. The wood was wet, a drop of water rolling down the bridge of her nose. A new town, a new bully, she pondered sadly. Reluctantly, she opened her eyes and turned to face them.

A boy stood in front of her, one leg bent, his hands stuck to his hips, a cocky grin on his spotty face. He was chubby, his v-necked jumper way too small for him, so he'd rolled up the sleeves to his elbows. Felicity gazed at his piggy nose and shuddered. He looked as if he'd been smacked in the face by a frying pan.

The other two boys had stayed over by the steps but Felicity could hear them sniggering.

"Trying to get away, huh?" The fat boy stepped up to her. "Snitch to your mummy?"

"Apple crumble and jelly."

His pals swaggered over. "What did she say?" one of them muttered.

"Apple crumble and som' in," mumbled the other.

"Custard."

"What?"

"I like custard with my apple crumble."

"Apple crumble and custard," Felicity yelled frantically.

"Off 'er rocker."

"Yep, I reckon. Go on, Colin, smack her!"

The fat boy stepped even closer, forcing Felicity to press her back hard up to the door.

"What y' playin' at?" he growled, his nose almost touching hers, his 'fish and chip' breath making Felicity want to gag. "Think y' a funny girl, do y'?" He lifted up a clenched fist. "I'm gonna whip y' bony..."

"Apple crumble and, er - whipped cream," Felicity shouted, and suddenly, as if the door had given up the struggle, it creaked sadly and swung in.

Frozen with fear, she lay on the cold damp floor. The door had slammed shut but Colin and his fellow thugs were kicking and banging furiously on the wood, trying to get to her. Terrified the boys might smash it in she got gingerly to her feet.

The shop was only dimly lit; a brass lamp perched on a chunky desk in the far corner casting shadows on the dusty books. Felicity crept over to a very old sofa. A rug lay in front of it, all patchy and wrinkled, and a brass tankard and a golf ball sat conspiring on a fancy coffee table. Felicity spotted the cold embers of a log fire and elaborate cobwebs hanging in the corners. She gulped. They were home to spiders the size of fists. But mostly, there were books. Many of them were piled in musty corners, others stacked on the desk, a few even stuffed down the back of the sofa; she could see the corners peeking out of the top. Sadly, they were all covered in dust, so thick Felicity could make tiny footprints on them with her fingers.

Wonky stools rested on the wonky floor, pipe ash spilled from ashtrays and a chandelier in the roof tinkled eerily as if a secret door had been left open.

It looked to Felicity as if nobody had shopped

here for years. Ooh, and the smell; she pinched her nose with two fingers. It was like being in a fish market on a summer's day.

But still, she felt sort of comfy, as if all her problems had been barred entry; as if she had lived here for hundreds of years and had always called it home.

Felicity crept over to the desk - the one with the oil-lamp perched on it - and closing her eyes to the monsters carved into the wood, she picked up a book.

'Out of Your Body, Out of Your Mind' by Professor E. Gomorrha, she read. Hmm, what a peculiar title. Then a second, 'If Sleeves Could Talk' by Randolph P. Plotinus, and a third, 'Well Gnome Surgery Tips'. Next, she picked up a book called, 'The Hush Hush History of Magic' and she opened it.

"Sorry, too many deep dark secrets in here," the book informed her calmly. "No kids, impsters or yoblins." It slammed shut with a bang, showering Felicity with dust. Then it jumped out of her hands and landed back on the pile it had come from.

She froze. Was it some sort of trick? She

peered closely at the book, but she couldn't see any strings. Was she being watched, she wondered suddenly. She gazed wildly around the shop looking for a hidden camera. Was she on TV being laughed at by half of England?

The door shook. One of the boys had kicked it, Felicity guessed, and over on a shelf on the wall a clock with splayed plump legs chimed the hour.

Then she heard a door creak open and slam shut and a green 'THING!' came scurrying out past the desk. It looked like, well, Felicity didn't know what it looked like, but it had on orange shorts and a stripy yellow t-shirt. On it was scrawled,

NEW IMP ON THE BLOCK

"Can I help you?" it peeped.

"Er..."

"No? OK then." It held up a gigantic cup for her to see. "Parched. Need a cuppa. Not stopped all day. Dusting. Dusting. Dusting."

Then it dashed by her, its eyes fixed on the cup clutched in its hands.

Felicity was torn between not moving and pretending this was not really happening and hiding just in case 'IT!', whatever 'IT!' was, should come back. She chose to hide.

She crept down a row of bookcases, a candle sitting here and there, lighting the way. Picking one up, she held it out in front of her. She wanted to escape from this dark and musty shop, but there was no way she was going to go back. Not if she had to face those boys. No, she would keep going. If she was lucky, she would find a back door or a window she could crawl out of.

She jumped, the candle in her hand wobbling, spilling wax on her shoe. What was that? A whisper?

 Felicity.

She swallowed as fingers of terror played up and down her spine. Slowly, she turned her head. But there was nobody there, just dusty books and flickering candles crackling at her.

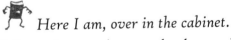 *Here I am, over in the cabinet.*

Like a lasso, the words dragged at her feet, telling her, begging her to turn around and to go back.

Find the key. Help me. Then I can help you.

The boys! Was it the boys? Had they found a way into the shop? Were they hunting for her and trying to scare her by calling out her name? She gulped. If they were, it was working.

No, she had to keep going. There had to be a different way out of here.

The floor creaked, making Felicity clench her clammy hands in terror, but no monsters jumped out of the shadows. She had come to the end of the row and to a very shabby door. It was oval at the top and the handle was shaped like a dragon's claw. Gritting her teeth, she grasped hold of it and pushed it down. She eased the door open.

The next room was even darker and she could only just see the rows and rows of dusty books. On the wall, just by her shoulder, she spotted a painting of a ghostly-looking man, a book open on his lap. Felicity stepped up to it and gulped. His left eye socket was empty and it looked as if claws had ripped his cheek to the bone. She screwed up her face as wax dripped from the candle and burnt the tips of her fingers. But there was no way she was going to drop it.

NO WAY!

Felicity crept on, her fear of lurking monsters making her hands shake and her mouth feel dry. The rustle of her skirt and her footsteps on the wooden floor seemed to bounce off the walls, giving her away. To try and stay calm, she browsed the books on a shelf as she passed them but then the books began to jiggle and hop and that did not help at all.

She heard shouting as she made her way down a row of books on love tonics. Felicity stopped, her ears pricking up. It sounded as if it was coming from the next isle just along to her left. Very gently, she rested the candle on a shelf, reached up and pulled down a copy of 'Charm Your Man'. On tiptoe, she peered through the gap in the books.

It was the chap in the black cloak. His back was to her, but he was so tall, Felicity just knew it was him. He was leaning over a table speaking sharply to a much smaller, fatter man, but his face was hidden too.

"Why do you keep refusing my offer?" the cloaked figure barked. "I mean, look at this place." He ran his finger over the top of the table. "Dust everywhere, books everywhere, but customers, nowhere." He bent closer to the other man and Felicity wondered if their noses might touch. "I am doing you a favour," he hissed.

"Really, Tantalus, you know this shop is not for sale, and it never will be as long as my old ticker keeps ticking."

Tantalus pulled away and sniggered, and at last Felicity saw him properly. He had short black hair and his face was gaunt, drawn back as if pulled by an invisible string. His nose was long, his lips thin and cruel-looking, and his eyes - they seemed to flash in rage like a tormented bull.

"So Galibrath, how is the old ticker? Very dusty in here." He sniffed the air. "A touch of damp too, I fear. Not good for a poorly wizard with..."

"I feel just dandy. Really, Tantalus, I'm touched but you must not worry. Now, I must be getting on. Ducks to feed, dogs to walk."

"One second. Mr Banks!"

There was a flash of green light followed by a

shuffling sound, but it was too low down for Felicity to see who or what was making it. Then a swollen canvas sack, knotted at the top, landed on the table with a clunk. It lay there.

"Gold," Tantalus explained. "Go loll in a hammock, sip Grogbog beer, chat up a pretty witch in a grass skirt." He had been pacing back and forth up till then, but now he stopped and glared down at Galibrath. "Just give me this shop," he seethed, his words sharp as a dagger.

Galibrath smiled. "Always good to see you, if only for the snap of a dragon's jaw. Now, can I lend you a brolly for your walk home? A spindlysloth told me the rain's not going to stop for hours."

Tantalus's nostrils flared and his jaw snapped up. Wondering what a spindlysloth was, Felicity watched tensely as they stared at each other.

They did not move.

They did not blink.

"Let's go, Mr Banks," Tantalus finally snapped, snatching up the sack of gold. There was a second flash of light, then Felicity watched him turn sharply on his heels and march to the door.

As he strode past her hiding place, she stepped back, her elbow knocking over the candle. It tumbled to the floor with a clunk, flickering out.

The footsteps stopped.

"Bats," she heard Galibrath say.

"What?"

"Bats in the roof. Hundreds of them. They like to hang in the rafters. They love the damp, you see."

"Huh!" uttered Tantalus in disgust, and he marched on.

Felicity heard a door open and slam shut and after that the man called Galibrath shouted, "Miss Brady, do you fancy a cuppa?"

Chapter 2

A Cup of Ladybird Spot Tea

Felicity sat on the sofa and fiddled with a loose button on her skirt. She kept her eyes lowered as Galibrath stood in front of her, looking a little stern and tapping his foot on a growling rug.

"I'm sorry if I got in the way," she blurted out at last. "You see, I was tryig to escape from this gang of nasty boys..."

"Ah, yes." He glanced over to the door. "I think they're still out there. They seem a little upset by your vanishing act."

Felicity smiled sweetly. "So, I hid in here," she whispered.

Galibrath crouched down. He looked at her and his face softened. "And how did you manage to get in?"

"The man in the black cloak - you were

talking to him." Galibrath frowned and pursed up his lips. "I was hiding under the bridge and I overheard him say apple crumble and, well, I couldn't hear the rest. So, I guessed and the door sort of - opened. Is that a trick, by the way? And that book over there, 'The Hush Hush History of Magic', it slammed shut; told me I was just a kid. Is it a sort of puppet? I didn't see any strings."

He rose and began to pace up and down in front of her, muttering and scratching his brow. They were back in the room she had first discovered. Galibrath had marched her there, his hand clasped on her shoulder, as if she was being led away to jail.

Felicity ballooned her cheeks; and so far, no sign of the promised cuppa.

He was not a tall chap, not much taller than Felicity, but he was much, much fatter. He had a jolly face but his skin was like a crumpled paper bag and when he talked his chins wobbled. His hair was curly and grey and his nose stubby as if he'd just walked into a door. He had on half-moon specs and a wrinkled gown which was dirty where it had dragged along the floor.

Billy Bob Buttons

"The man I was talking to," Galibrath turned and looked at Felicity, "you heard everything?"

"Oh no, well yes, I heard a little but I didn't understand..."

"Good," he cut in. "Better that way." Then he was silent and Felicity thought he looked rather sad.

"Is he a bully too?" she ventured, at last.

Galibrath forced a smile. "Let's just say he is not on my Christmas card list."

"Slug and daffodil tea?" a voice squeaked, making Felicity jump.

She stared goggle-eyed at the small olive-green 'THING!' which had just sprung up in front of her. He was the one she had seen carrying the cup and saucer but now his t-shirt informed the room,

I'M SMALL, I'M CUTE AND I'M HUNGRY

He had very big clockish-round eyes, a freckled face and pointy ears that leapt out from a mop of wild and wiry curls. His head was small and so was his body, making his long arms and legs look even longer. He now had on green

26

shorts tucked into his t-shirt, but his feet were bare, fuzz curling out from every toe.

He crossed his arms and patted the floor with his left foot.

"This," Galibrath looked at Felicity, "is Miss Brady."

"Felicity Brady." She smiled.

"Ah, yes, and this is Al, he's an imp and he's my - assistant." But Galibrath did not look too convinced of this.

The imp puffed out his small chest and bellowed, "My job is Assistant to the Head Wizard," he looked at Galibrath, "in Charge of Dusting," Galibrath chuckled, "and Tea Brewing."

"What a grand title," said Felicity. "You must be very important."

The imp looked pleased. "Yes, well, pays the bills." He grinned, showing her a full set of yellow crooked teeth.

"Tea," Galibrath prompted him.

"Oh yes. I have slug and daffodil, a bit of a kick to it but just try and dodge that. dorfmoron's eyeball, always served in a very big mug. There's, of course, goblin bogey," Al pulled a face, "and I have ladybird spot, warming, strong but wonderful for shock."

"Ladybird spot, please." It seemed the right thing to say.

"Bat's milk?"

"Er..."

"Go on."

"OK, but just a drop." The imp vanished, making Felicity jump and almost topple off the sofa. "WHERE DID...? HOW DID...?"

"So, how do you like my little shop?" Galibrath asked her, seemingly blasé to Al's vanishing trick.

"It's, er - brill'," she stuttered, still in shock. Then she sneezed. "A bit dusty though." She eyed a cobwebby chandelier and began to wish she was not sitting directly under it.

"Dusty! Well, yes, I suppose it is a bit. Protects the books," he added lamely.

"Poppycock," muttered 'The Hush Hush History of Magic', the cover lifting up for a split second. Startled, Felicity turned and stared at it. Galibrath turned too but his stare was much more of a glare.

"And I think your plant is a bit cold." She

nodded at a spiky cactus. It stood shivering in the hearth, where a crackling fire should have been.

"Cold!? Really, you think so?" Galibrath looked astonished and 'The Hush Hush History of Magic' started to shake as if it was trying to stop itself from saying anything that would get it into any more trouble.

"I don't mean to be rude, but the floor needs a good scrub; the window too - do you have any Jiff? And the sofa..."

"The sofa!?"

"It looks so old." She lifted up a lumpy cushion, the stuffing spilling out of it as if it had been involved in a pillow fight. With swords! "And er - maybe the stool over there needs a new leg," she ventured on, hoping not to upset him. "And who's the scary man in the picture on the wall in the next room?" Then, in a whisper, "I almost wet my knickers."

"That's old Gothmog," muttered Galibrath, his jaw hardening. "He's stuck to the wall. If I pull him off, the shop will probably collapse."

Felicity had a feeling he did not like this Gothmog-fellow very much. She screwed up her nose. "Is there a butchers next door?"

Galibrath sniffed. "Ah, yes, Al's Stink Charm. Keeps the riff-raff out."

The imp popped back up and handed Felicity a mug. "Thanks," she chirruped. Ooh, it tasted of rhubarb with a hint of cherry and really was very good. She started to feel a bit better. In fact, she felt oddly calm. Her mind had stopped turning cartwheels anyway and her knees no longer trembled.

Perched on the sofa, she sipped her tea and wondered what a charm was. And a spindlysloth. And a dorfmoron. She had never enjoyed novels of boy wizards and magic, but now she had been told off by a book, the rug on the floor kept growling, next to her slurping from an elephant-eared mug was a green imp, and the imp had called Galibrath a wizard.

"Can you do magic then?" Felicity blurted out. "Can you pull a rabbit from a top hat and flowers from your sleeve?"

Galibrath chuckled. "Rabbits, no. Flowers, yes, but only very limp daffodils."

"Do I know any wizards? Do any know me?"

"Oh, yes." Galibrath sat on the sofa too,

sandwiching the imp between them. "On Daffodil Way..."

"But I live there!"

"I know. On Daffodil Way there is a very powerful wizard called Mr Spindly. Wonderful chap! Always in the garden; enjoys growing monster turnips."

Felicity mind buzzed. She knew Mr Spindly, or she thought she did. He had just moved in next door. But Felicity had thought 'HE' was a 'SHE'! "But..."

"It's the long silvery curls." The wizard did not even blink.

"Oh." She sipped her drink. "So, if I ever upset Mrs - sorry, Mr Spindly..."

"You'd look in the mirror and 'HOCUS POCUS!', you'd see a slimy, yellow-spotted slug. But only if he wanted to," Galibrath added with a wink.

Felicity pondered this for a moment. "How do you know where I live and how did you know my name? A magic spell? Can you read minds?"

"It's on your school bag."

Felicity blushed. Then she had a wonderful

thought. She jumped up, spilling half of her drink on her pleated skirt. "Can I do magic too?"

Galibrath thought for a second, then nodded and waved his hand around the shop. "You just have to study the right books."

At that moment, the door flew open and a chilly wind whipped through the shop. A man walked in wearing a long snowy gown and a rubber glove on his left hand. A stethoscope hung around his neck.

"How are we all today?" he asked cheerfully, in a voice that sounded like rain pattering on a tin roof. "Any wheezing? Warty fingers? Aching toes?"

"Professor Dement!" Galibrath rubbed his brow and the imp snorted.

"Er, *Doctor* Dement if you don't mind." He put his stethoscope to Galibrath's chest and told him to cough. "Hmm. Dodgy. You look a little pasty. In the last twenty-four hours, have you swallowed a hedgehog or any other small rodent?"

The wizard's face dropped and he pushed Doctor Dement's hand away. "Would you like to buy a book?" he asked him coldly. He picked one up. "'Medical Magic, A History'. Hot off the press."

Felicity frowned. It looked a hundred years old.

But the doctor ignored him as he was too busy scribbling on a scrap of paper he had plucked off the desk. He stuffed it in the wizard's hand. "To be taken twice a day following meals." He glanced at Galibrath's belly. "No problem there. Have you considered going to Wizards' Weight Watchers? They meet every Friday in Funny Bone Surgery..."

"Doctor Dement. Can I interest you in a book?"

"A book?" He scratched at his head. "Oh, OK, if you feel up to it, I do need 'Well Gnome Surgery Tips'. I'm opening up one of the little chaps later and I'm a smidge, er - rusty."

Felicity pulled a face and the imp giggled, clutched at his chest and fell over on his back.

Rubbing his chin, Galibrath tottered over to a shelf and began to pull books out. "No, no, no - YES!" He pulled out a very fat, purple book and flipped it open. "'The Land of El-Roth and Queen Blasthoof, the Tyrant Who Rules It'.

No." He put it back. "No, no, no..."

Doctor Dement jumped up on the windowsill and drummed his fingers on the wooden top.

Scrambling up from the sofa, Felicity crept over to the desk - the one with 'The Hush Hush History of Magic' on it. She had a feeling she had seen - yes, there it was, two up from the bottom. She pulled the book free and took it over to the doctor. "Is this it?" she asked him.

He looked down at her and then at the book in her hands. "Why, yes. Excellent! Excellent! Do I know you? Any fungus problems? Itchy armpits?"

In a moment of madness, Felicity blurted out, "I work here."

"Fresh blood, hey? Ooh, that reminds me, got to be off. Scalpels to sharpen!"

Jumping down off the desk, he flipped a gold nugget to Felicity. She caught it. Then he nodded at Galibrath and marched out of the shop, the book wedged under his arm.

"Super!" bellowed Galibrath bracingly, clapping dust off his hands. "A happy customer."

"Yes," squeaked Al. "How odd."

"Why?" ventured Felicity. "Do you not get many?"

The imp rested his brow on his hand and rubbed his chin with a bony finger. "I don't think, no - remember Bella Bozolnoz, she popped in for a cuppa and, by gosh, a cuppa she had. She was very happy. Mind you, the cup was a little grubby and it had a chip in it, just on the rim, golly, that witch was a bleeder. After that she had a sneezing fit. All the dust you see..."

"Yes, thank you," Galibrath hushed him. "I think Felicity gets the picture."

Studying the nugget, Felicity spotted it had the word 'flupoon' etched on it. She handed it to the wizard. "He's a very peculiar doctor."

Galibrath chuckled and turned to the imp. "What was Professor Dement yesterday?"

"A plumber."

"Ah yes, he offered to fix the tap in the kitchen. Still dripping, must sort it. And the day before?"

"He thought he worked in a library. He wanted to put all of our books in order but they kept nipping his fingers."

Felicity was getting more and more confused. "He changes jobs every day?"

"Every day," echoed Galibrath. "Always a new job, never the same. He says it keeps him young. Stops him from going potty."

"Ha!" exploded the imp. "He's a nutty nutbar."

Felicity plonked her bum down on the sofa. "Is everybody who shops here bonkers?"

"Oh no," the wizard grinned wickedly, "not everybody."

The shop had one more customer that afternoon. A man with blond bushy hair and a rug rolled up and slung over his shoulder. He wanted a book on crystal balls - another wizard, Felicity guessed - but Galibrath couldn't seem to find it for him.

Why didn't he just put the books in order, she wondered, helping him to look. Or maybe they'd bite his fingers too? The other wizard had gotten angry and had sat on the sofa in a huff.

She walked over to the desk and began to hunt through the books piled up there. But it was so hard to see even with the oil-lamp burning. She leant over the desk and gave the lamp a shake. The flame swelled. Better, she thought.

What's this?

A card hung on the oil-lamp and on it, in big black letters, was,

THE SECRET SAYING OF THE DAY
Apple Crumble and Whipped Cream

So that's why the door had opened.

She chuckled. Galibrath must really love puddings, she thought. Maybe Doctor Dement was right. Maybe Galibrath should go to Wizards' Weight Watchers.

Felicity wriggled a finger in her ear. She could still hear whispering. It seemed to be all around her as if the books were chatting to each other. She had heard one book talk, 'The Hush Hush History of Magic', but could they all talk? Ooh, and were they talking about her?

There was so much more Felicity wanted to

know. Where did the imp come from? If Galibrath was a wizard, what sort of magic could he do? It was dusty and it was cold and it did smell of rotten trout. But a magic bookshop! She rubbed her hands in glee and wondered how long they would let her stay.

Skipping over to the desk, she pushed past a stool missing a fourth leg. A glass cabinet hung on the wall and it was from here that the whispers seemed to be coming.

In the cabinet there was a book. A big black book. She reached up...

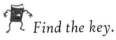 *Find the key.*

"Time to go, I think." Galibrath grabbed Felicity's shoulders and steered her over to the door.

She pulled up her sleeve and looked at her watch. "Oh no, my dad's gonna kill me," she freaked.

"Well, that'd not do at all." The wizard pottered over to the fancy clock ticking hypnotically on the shelf by the door. It looked very old and the face was gold and had a tiny window in it showing the day and the month. Plump legs splayed out from the corners and on the top it had a sort of crown, which might or might not be a handle to pick it up by.

"We call it The Clock by the Door. Very original we thought." Galibrath fiddled with the clock's hands and then, oddly, he murmured, "England." There was a thunderous banging on the door. "Now you'll be back in time for dinner," he announced, turning back and beaming at her.

Felicity looked back to her watch and her jaw hit her chest. The hands were spinning. The wrong way! "But..."

"Oh yes, the boys." The wizard closed his eyes and lifted his hand, and from his open palm a glowing orange ball popped up, flew around the room twice and then dived into Felicity's blouse pocket. It sat there shaking, as if it was really excited to be let out.

"It's called a sentinel. Don't worry," Galibrath handed Felicity her school bag and coat, "it won't hurt you; just a wizard's toy. See it as a sort of guard dog; if you need it, just whistle."

"Thanks." She took the bag and put on her coat. Then, the words tumbling over each other, she rattled, "Can I come back? I could help clean. Tidy up a bit. And I can dust."

The wizard grinned. "You know where we are," he said as the door shuddered. "Oh, and the password for tomorrow is 'Liquorice Swirls and Angel Cake'."

She looked over at Al and he gave her the thumbs up. Then she turned and grasped hold of the handle. "By the way, what's the name of the shop?"

"The Wishing Shelf."

Felicity nodded, murmuring the words. Oddly, they tasted familiar on her lips. "That's a wonderful name." She smiled, pulled open the door and stepped out of the shop.

Chapter 3

The Imp Rights Act of 1252

"From this world, I must be hidden,
Being spotted is forbidden,
By the wall, I'll be disguised,
Unseen by prying eyes."

A shower of silvery sparks fell on the goblin's head and he vanished, blending in with the stone bridge. Grumbling, he crouched down.

He disliked the land of England, apart from the shops. It was always cold and it was always raining. Already, his Calvin Klein shirt was soaked and he couldn't feel any of his eight fingers or his eight toes, and now a jagged stone was digging into his shoulder and he had pins and needles in his legs.

His boss, Tantalus, had told him to spy on The Wishing Shelf but he wasn't happy about it. He was getting sick of all the orders and the bullying. It might be OK with the wizard's trolls and imps but it was not OK with him. He growled. The bookshop window was so grimy he could hardly see anything anyway.

The goblin's name was Bartholomew Banks and he was evil, through and through. He even looked evil with beady green eyes and a warty chin. His nose was sharp, curved over like a droopy banana and there was not one curl on his glossy scalp. He was chubby too and when he talked his fat cheeks wobbled like jelly. But he did dress well, for a goblin anyway.

Why couldn't he watch the door in Eternus, he thought angrily. But Tantalus had given that job to his puffdolt, Cruncher. Banks snorted. Cruncher was an idiot. Probably snoring like a baby elephant by now.

The goblin sniffed, pulled a silk hanky from his trouser pocket and trumpeted into it. Then he saw that the sleeve of his shirt was all muddy. He looked down at his Gucci shoes. They were muddy too. Gritting his teeth, he stuffed the hanky back in his pocket.

This had better be worth it, he thought

bitterly.

All of a sudden, Banks felt dizzy and, swallowing bile, he slid the rest of the way down the wall, scraping his back. Somebody was shuffling time. But who? He heard a loud banging and he looked up.

There were three boys kicking and thumping on the bookshop door. Oooh, trouble at The Wishing Shelf. Tantalus will be happy. He watched as the door opened and a boy - no, no, a girl - a very boyish-looking girl, stepped out.

To the goblin's surprise, she didn't look scared and she didn't try to run away. She just stood there, hemmed in, as they crowded in on her.

There was a yell and the three boys jumped back as if they'd been stung. A glowing ball shot up in the air - a sentinel by the look of it - and dived at one of the boys, smacking him on the leg.

The boy lashed out, missed, then with a howl swung around and made a run for the steps. His chums dashed after him. But the orange ball was having way too much fun. It zoomed over the fleeing boys' heads and dropped down, blocking their way.

"Back! Back!" screamed the one in front. Too late, the other two slammed into him and they fell over in a tangled heap.

The goblin watched the ball pounce on them over and over. They were blubbering now and squealing like frightened pigs. Then the girl whistled sharply as you would to a dog, and the sentinel tore back to her and dropped into her pocket.

He watched her walk over to the jumbled mass of arms and legs. She stood over them, her hands on her hips, and Banks could see a gigantic grin on her face.

"If you ever lay a hand on me or any of my pals, I'll set my - it on you again," she warned them, "but next time I'll tell it to play a little rougher. Understood?"

The boys, still huddled on the ground, didn't answer. She crouched down. "Understood?" she repeated stonily. The ball popped out of her pocket and hummed softly. This seemed to do the trick.

"Yeah, yeah, whatever," one of them muttered sulkily. "Just keep that *thing* away from us."

"Good." She smiled and patted the boy's cheek. Then she stood up and ambled up the stone steps looking as if she'd just won the lottery.

Under the bridge, the goblin smirked. That was a turn up for the books, he thought. He wondered who she was. A witch? No, too young. An imp, perhaps? Al's bit of stuff? No, too tall.

But she did remind him a little of...

He shrugged, slumped back and began to whistle softly.

Every day after school, Felicity would run to The Wishing Shelf. Her mum and dad had seemed perfectly happy when she had told them she had got a job in a bookshop. They had even rung her Aunty Imelda to let her know the exciting news. "Remind her not to go in the cupboard," her aunt had told them. A very odd thing to say.

Felicity fell instantly in love with the old shop, even though she spent most of her time scrubbing floors and dusting books. She loved chatting to the imp and supping his peculiar teas, and listening to Galibrath's farfetched yarns of spins on flying carpets. Flying carpets! As if!

But the best part of working in a magic bookshop was meeting the wizards who popped in there. Not that many did, as it was almost impossible to find a book as they were scattered all over the shop. Even if they did find the one they were looking for, it was nearly always covered in dust and bat droppings.

But every time she dusted, it would fly up in her face and she would have a sneezing fit.

"What we need is the Hoover," announced Galibrath, coming to the rescue. "Al, can you fetch it?" He tossed the imp a bunch of rusty keys.

Al's eyes widened. "But, what if, you know?" he stuttered.

"He'll be sleeping."

"He never sleeps. You go. He worships you."

"Al," said Galibrath sternly.

"But..."

"Al!"

"It's because I'm an imp isn't it. I have rights you know. Section Two of The Imp Rights Act of 1252..."

"There is no Imp Rights Act of 1252. There is no Imp Rights Act full-stop."

"Well, there should be," he whined back. He dropped down onto his knees and clasped his hands together as if in prayer. "Please, please don't make me go," he begged. "Let Felicity go. She's new. She'll have fun. They can play Twister."

"Go where?" asked Felicity curiously.

Slowly, his eyes darting about the shop, the imp whispered, "The - cupboard - under - the - stairs."

"The cupboard." Felicity frowned. "You're scared of the cupboard."

"I'm not scared of the cupboard," squeaked Al crossly, still on his knees. "I'm scared of what's in the cupboard."

"Why, what's in it?"

"We have a monster in our cupboard," piped up the wizard dryly.

"He's huge," croaked Al, stretching his hands as far apart as he could to show how big he was.

"He is not huge," muttered Galibrath wearily.

"I'm the size of a teapot," squealed back the imp. "He looks huge to me."

The wizard mustered a long sigh and rubbed his brow. "Just go in the cupboard and fetch the Hoover; the one with the long nozzle."

"No! Not the one with the long nozzle!"

"AL!" Galibrath screamed.

"OK. OK. I'm going." The imp struggled slowly to his feet and, mumbling softly, trudged out of the room. "Fetch this, fetch that, a collar and a lead next and a bone to chew on. I should change my name, maybe Scooby or..."

Felicity followed him to the back of the shop and down a long corridor. There he stopped in front of a small orange door with five big keyholes but no keys.

"Space, I need space," he crooned, shooing her away. She took a step back.

She watched as he began to run on the spot, then he bent over and touched his toes - 3, 4, 5 times. The imp snapped his fingers and a very small dumbbell leapt out of his shorts' pocket and clanked to the floor. He picked it up and lifted it to his chest.

"One, two, three, a hundred," he puffed and then he put it back down again. "OK, here we go!"

The imp dug in his pocket and pulled out the key ring, on it lots and lots of rusty keys. He picked one out, slipped it in the top hole and twisted.

Felicity jumped as a bolt crashed back. Followed by another. And another. "Wow!" she gasped. This monster must be gigantic.

With a sad smile and a feeble wave, Al gently opened the door and peered in. Felicity held her breath but nothing charged out, so she whispered, "Maybe he's asleep."

The trembling imp shook his head. "No. He never sleeps. He's just playing with meeeeeeeeee..."

A furry paw shot out and grabbed Al by the neck, yanking him off his feet. In a flash, he vanished and the door banged shut.

There was a growl.

A yelp. And the door rattled.

Next there was a lot more growling and a lot

more yelping and the door went from juddering to full 'earthquake' shaking.

"What shall I do? What shall I do?" squealed Felicity, jumping up and down. She was about to run and fetch Galibrath when the door burst open and Al hurtled out.

"Help me!" he yelled to Felicity.

She ran over and together they pushed the door shut. Hastily, the imp turned the keys and one by one Felicity heard the bolts slam back.

"Got it," he wheezed, holding up a Hoover with a very long nozzle.

Felicity looked down at him and her eyebrows shot up. His curls were all ruffled and his t-shirt was in shreds. "Any - er, problems?" she quizzed him.

"No, no problems." Puffing out his weedy chest, he limped away, presumably to show Galibrath his prize.

Felicity watched him go and then turned to look back at the small door. She wondered what the monster looked like. She also wondered how her Aunty Imelda knew to warn her not to go in the cupboard. Crouching down, she put her eye up to the top keyhole, but it was very dark so she couldn't see much. Hold on! What was that? It was yellow and there was a black spot - no, it was gone, like a shutter coming down. Now it was back. What was it!?

Felicity yelped and jumped back.

It was an eye! A WINKING EYE!

She sat on the floor and watched in horror as the door shook and bulged out. It was trying to get to her! IT WANTED TO EAT HER! With a yell, she leapt to her feet and dashed back along the corridor.

"Start with the carpets, the rest can wait,
Weave round the tables in a figure of eight,
Destroy the cobwebs that dance from the beams,
Tickle the corners till The Wishing Shelf gleams."

On hearing the wizard's chant, the long nozzle swung up in the air like an angry snake. Then the Hoover sprang from shelf to shelf, diving under tables and jumping on top of stools, sucking up dust.

Felicity sat on the sofa watching it sniff in all

the corners. She decided it was just like a snooping dog.

She jumped up and turned to Galibrath. "Now we must put the books in order."

The wizard went pale, his chin drooping down to his chest.

"Come on." She tugged at the sleeve of his robe. "How can we sell a book if we can't find it?"

A hag, who had been on her hands and knees for three hours hunting for a book on 'mojo bags', ballooned her cheeks and mumbled, "Now y' tidy up! I got blisters on my blisters on my blisters."

But sorting out the books proved to be a very difficult job, as Felicity soon found out.

"RIGHT YOU LOT!" trumpeted Galibrath. Felicity looked around to see who he was shouting at. "I want you all to find a buddy and move back to your proper shelf. You know where you should be, so CHOP! CHOP!"

The books leapt up and began to fly around the shop. Felicity yelped and ducked to the floor; the room was filled with flapping and thumps as the books collided. "Not really what I had in mind!" she bawled over the din. She snuggled her head in her hands.

Finally, the flapping stopped and she sneaked a look up.

"What's next?" the wizard asked her, looking exceedingly smug.

Felicity stood up and frowned. She walked over to the wizard's desk and picked up one of the books lying on it.

"'The Hush Hush History of Magic'," she read. She looked coldly over at the wizard. "They flew around the shop and then they just sneaked back to the same spot."

Galibrath went red and one of the books shouted out, "I was born on this shelf, I'm gonna get worms on this shelf!"

"You tell 'em!" yelled the burly book 'My Milkman's a Mass Murderer, Full-Fat's a Killer', flapping his covers.

So each book had to be moved by hand, dusted and told sternly to stay put.

"You missed a bit, luvvy, up a little, there you go. Oooh, that tickles." 'A Witch Spotter's Book of Demons, Puffdolts and Goblins' giggled and squirmed in Felicity's hands.

She lay down the duster. "Now, where shall I put you? I know, on the witch's shelf."

"Oh no, you can't put me there," the book grumbled, her covers flapping wildly. "Such a peculiar lot, and I will never get invited to any posh dinners. No, no, no, put me on the reference shelf, that's where I belong, next to 'A Dictionary of Magical Names'. Charming fellow. Oooh and the leather." The book shuddered. "The thought of cuddling up to him for a century or two sends a shiver up my spine."

There were so many books in The Wishing Shelf, thousands of them, hundreds of thousands, full of spells and tips on how to fly magic carpets (so, magic carpets did exist!). There were books on goblins, ghouls and gremlins, and books offering advice on buying second-hand cauldrons. There was even a recipe for getting rid of spots in three easy steps, but to Felicity they did not look very easy at all. First you had to trap a troll and squeeze the pus from one of his warts and after that mix it with the blood of a dorfmoron.

"What's a dorfmoron?" Felicity quizzed the

imp, who was sitting on the sofa sipping from a cup.

He jumped up, splashing hedgehog bristle tea (his latest invention) on his knees. Looking warily about, he whispered, "Gigantic scary monsters," he took a big gulp from the cup, "all teeth and bad breath."

Felicity touched a glowing spot on her chin and sighed.

After three days The Wishing Shelf began to look much better; Felicity even fixed the dripping tap in the kitchen. The cactus was watered and put on a shelf near the window and a fire was lit. Even the rugs were taken out and beaten with a broom handle. But not too harshly as they yelped too loud.

The shop smelled good too, with the smells from the polished books and the scent of the hickory logs burning in the hearth - Felicity had begged Al to get rid of the fishy smell. Winter sunshine came in through the now sparkling window, and everything felt large, spacious and clean.

As they worked, Felicity chatted to Galibrath about The Wishing Shelf and all the old books.

Where had they all come from and how come they could talk?

The wizard smiled at her and picked up a book, 'Halloween, Pick a Frock to Shock'. He stroked it gently as you would a cat. "This shop has been in my family, the Falafel family, for a thousand years," he murmured, "maybe longer. And the books, well, they live here too. And drink, mostly Bicardi."

"Rum and coke," muttered the book in his hand.

"But, they can talk."

"Yes Felicity, they can. But they can listen too." He tapped the purring tome. "Full of tips on how to dress for a monster ball. But probably, if you ask it, it could tell you how to trap a Woolly Glumsnapper, the secret path to Shubablybub Sands, even why a dorfmoron is so very, very stupid. You see, every book in The Wishing Shelf holds a library."

"Yes, but, but – THEY CAN TALK?"

Galibrath tittered and tossed her a cheeky wink. "Well, I guess they have a lot to say."

Chapter 4

A Day of Shocks

Felicity stood back and folded her arms. "What do you think?" she called to Galibrath, who was sprawled on the sofa, reading a book entitled, 'Fishing for Serpents'.

The wizard stood up, his back cracking, and walked over to the window. He nodded and patted her on the shoulder. "I like the way you've, erm...yes, and I like, hmm, yes, very good."

It had taken her all morning to sort out all the books in the window. They had been full of spiders and covered in dust and cobwebs. She had picked out only the very best, with not a bent spine or a torn page in sight, and only books that did not crumble - or grumble - when you opened them.

She picked up, 'Halloween, Pick a Frock to

Shock' and shuffled it up to the glass. "Now people can look in and see what we've got."

Galibrath mustered a small grunt and rolled his eyes.

The door to the shop creaked open and a frosty wind swept in making the wizard's robe billow.

"See." Felicity stifled a smile and turned to the door.

The book in her hand fell to the floor with a thud. "Ow!" it grumbled.

Felicity took a wobbly step back for trudging in the shop, puffing on a knobbly wooden pipe, was a gnome! She shook her head and rubbed her eyes, but when she opened them back up the gnome was still there.

"Good day," Galibrath welcomed him. The gnome chortled a 'good day' back.

He wanted a book called 'Pruning and Potting Devil-Sting Creepers'. Felicity watched the wizard show him over to the gardening books in the back of the shop.

The gnome had a fat face with chubby cheeks dotted with red spots, and his big ears stuck out from under a droopy hat. His green trousers were all puffed out and his boots had curly tips and long rainbow-coloured laces. They dragged on the floor as he toddled along by the wizard, and he kept tripping up.

"How much?" the gnome quizzed Galibrath, after they had discovered the book hiding on a top shelf.

But the wizard did not answer. "Four silver flupoons," peeped the book.

"Two," countered the gnome.

"Three and I get a walnut shelf, no plywood, and I need regular dusting with a feather duster, not a smelly old rag."

The gnome grunted and nodded.

"Seen anything of the sun?" inquired Galibrath, wrapping the gnome's book in brown paper and string.

The tiny fellow dug in his pocket and handed the wizard the three silver nuggets. "Nope, been bucketing down all day," he grumbled. He took the book and stuffed it under his Mac. "Good for the garden, I guess."

Even odder, thought Felicity, peering out of the window at the winter sun.

She looked back and watched as they ambled

over to the door. They stopped there, Galibrath picking up the gnome and turning him to face The Clock by the Door. The gnome fiddled with the hands and croaked, "Eternus."

The clock wheezed and a spring went pop. Then the wizard dropped him back down. With a cheeky wink at Felicity, the gnome yanked the door open and slipped out of the shop.

Felicity bellowed a 'Richter Scale' registering yell. Standing in the doorway was a gigantic Wellington boot. It trudged away and Felicity saw imps everywhere, scurrying about under green and purple umbrellas. A lanky, floppy creature slunk by and...

The door banged shut.

She glared wide-eyed over at Galibrath. "W-what was that?" she spluttered. Her knees felt all 'jellyish' and not at all up to the job of keeping her up.

"That," murmured the wizard, relaxing back on the sofa, "was Eternus." He opened his book. "It says in here, Felicity, that krakor thunder serpents love to chase sticks!? Amazing!"

"Eternus!?"

"My land, well, not just mine, Al's from there

too - and the gnome."

Felicity scratched her head. The Wishing Shelf was a toy box full of wonders. "But where's Twice Brewed? How will I get home?"

"That was Twice Brewed, but in Eternus." The wizard grinned up at her. "Oh, and to get home, just tell the clock you want to go to Twice Brewed in England."

"The clock!?" Felicity looked over at it. "But you told me that it changed time, not..."

"It can do that too. Won it off a gypsy on a coconut shy in Mangbaloo. You see, Felicity, beyond The Wishing Shelf door is a maze of different lands, 10,452 to be exact and 10,452 Twice Breweds, all different; and to get to them - well, just ask the clock. But be polite or it might whisk you off to Twice Brewed in Slayaca. Not the most enjoyable of holiday spots, I can tell you."

Felicity felt like her head was going to explode. She screwed up her face and rubbed her eyes.

It was too much.

Just too much.

And then, A GIANT LUMBERED IN!

"JEEPERS!" she shouted, scampering over to the wizard's desk and hiding under it.

The giant looked - GIANT! Like a garden shed but with hands and feet. He was furry too, and it looked like there was a slice of bread tangled up in his beard. Dirty rags swaddled him: a tatty grey jumper and grey trousers full of rips and held up with twine. She noticed his boots were ripped open too so she could see his black, bunched-up toes.

 Felicity.

She jumped, banging her head on the desk. "Ouch!" she yelled, clambering out.

 Felicity.

A whisper in her mind, so powerful she instantly forgot even the giant.

 Turn around and look at me.

So she did. The glass cabinet. The one she had seen before, and the book. The big black book.

She took a step closer, gazing up at it in wonder.

"Articulus," whispered Galibrath. A shudder

ran down Felicity's back. "That is what they call him."

She turned and looked at him. "Articulus," she murmured, the word dribbling off her lips. It was as if she had been saying it all of her life.

The wizard grasped a small glass key that hung around his neck on a gold chain. He slipped it over his head and popped it in a lock on the glass door. He twisted and gently slid the door open.

Felicity, grab me. We can run away. Nobody needs to know. It will be our little secret.

But Galibrath will know.

Forget him. He's a crazy old fool. Nobody will matter once you hold me in your hands. I will protect you, I will help you be everything you want to be.

But...

No buts. Quick! Now! There is still a chance.

The whispers seemed to fill her mind. She watched in horror as her hands reached out for the book.

That's it, reach up. I am your destiny,

Felicity Brady.

"Sorry 'bout that." The wizard's words snapped her out of the trance. Her legs felt wobbly and her head was spinning. She clutched at the desk to stop from falling over.

"Don't worry, you should feel better in a sec." The wizard was still standing next to her but now he was cradling the book in his arms. "My blunder, I was too slow grabbing hold of the sly old boy."

The spinning seemed to be slowing now but her head still felt heavy as if it was packed-full of lead. "What happened?" she croaked.

The wizard's eyes darted around the shop. Felicity spotted that the giant was now trying to squeeze back out of the door, looking fearfully over his beefy shoulder at the book in the wizard's hands.

Galibrath looked down at Felicity. "This glass cabinet acts as a sort of magic wall, so when I opened the door I allowed Articulus to call out for a master." He gazed darkly down at the book. "Never be fooled by its sly temptations. Nobody can ever control Articulus. They would end up being controlled by it."

Felicity's eyes opened wide with fright. "But how can a book be that powerful? What can it do?"

Galibrath shifted the book until it was resting in the crook of his right arm, then with his left hand he began to very slowly thumb the pages.

The book was full of battling monsters. Cannons firing, slashing swords and dragons swooping down, belching fire. There were toothy goblins crushing wizards and trolls clawing out the eyes of hags.

Felicity turned away, feeling sick.

What powers did the book possess, she wondered, but there was no sudden flash of light and no six-eyed serpents reared up at her.

The only odd thing was a tiny fly that was hovering just by her left cheek. But a fly should fly, not hover!? Hold on! She peered closer. Felicity could just make out tiny wings beating very slowly up and down.

Her eyes were drawn to The Clock by the Door, and as she watched, she saw that the second hand was hardly moving.

Now the wizard was turning the pages much faster and the clock hands had begun to spin at an incredible rate. The fly had vanished and Felicity watched in fascination as the cactus they had put in the window began to grow, small flowers opening up to let in the light.

"Articulus can control time," mumbled Galibrath, slamming the book shut. "Speed it up or slow it down. Only the one holding the book and his followers can defy the power."

Felicity looked up at him. "Have you ever used it?"

Galibrath winced. "I am just the jailer and so was my father, Gooftwerp Falafel, and my grandpa, Douglas Falafel. We keep Articulus here in the hope that one day he can be put to work for good, not just for mischief. You see, Felicity, The Wishing Shelf is not just a magic bookshop, and it is not just the doorway to hundreds of enchanted lands; it is, most importantly, the prison for the most powerful and dangerous book ever penned."

He propped the book back up in the cabinet but as it left his grasp she could hear the same silky words in her mind. She fought hard to stay in control of her hands; gritting her teeth, she hooked her fingers in her belt.

Don't forget about me, Felicity. You know where I am now.

Galibrath slid the door shut and the words stopped. He locked it and hung the key back around his neck.

"War follows this book. Misery and the envy of others. He has been held in wicked hands too often. You see Felicity, any army led by Articulus will always crush the enemy."

As the wizard spoke he seemed to become more and more weary, as if talking about the book was draining him. "Come," he wheezed. "Time for a nice cup of tea." He ushered her away.

But as they walked through to the kitchen, she couldn't help but turn her head and look back at the book. Galibrath had just told her that the glass cabinet was like a shield that stopped the book from calling out for a master.

She felt confused.

For she could still hear her name being called over and over again.

Chapter 5

Rumblings at Hedes Spine

The goblin stuffed his hands in his pockets and ambled up the marble steps. He nodded at a puffdolt, one of Tantalus's guards. Slouched on the glass wall, the monster snorted back at him, picking a scab off his furry chin.

Banks was in no particular hurry. He knew that Tantalus would be pacing, his eyes to the carpet, his bony hands clutched behind his back. He smiled and flapped at a buzzing Smogly fly. Let him pace.

On stepping into the shop, an imp scampered up and bestowed on him a low bow. "Welcome to Hedes Spine Inc.," she squeaked. "The biggest bookshops in Eternus..."

The goblin kept on walking. "Where's your boss?" he barked.

The imp scuttled after him, scratching at the

mop of red curls on her head. "Mr Falafel? Well, I, er..."

"Forget it."

The imp stopped, stuck out her tongue and blew a raspberry. Then she skipped away.

The bookshop was gigantic, a glass-walled, glass-roofed monster crowded with bi-spectacled old wizards and hags in curly-tipped slippers. Many of them were perched on stools and stiff-backed sofas, chomping on muffins and slurping coffee, the rest stomped here, there and everywhere yelling at imps to "GET ME THIS!" and "GET ME THAT!"

Banks brushed by a pyramid-shaped fish tank chock-full of thrashing black eels, and, just next to it, a plant in the shape a volcano, a red spike erupting out of the top. Nonchalantly, the goblin flicked it and the spike toppled into the fish tank, skewering an eel.

"Ooops!" he muttered, stopping to watch his wiggly pals feast.

Dorfmoron pelts hid most of the stone floor and on the wall hung a picture of a decidedly haughty-looking Tantalus clutching a scroll. Under it stood a chubby imp playing a gloomy tune on a flute.

Banks picked up a book, 'Master Spells in Three Days'. He grunted. "Magic tricks," he scoffed, tossing it on the floor. Only The Wishing Shelf had proper magic, but that was damp and dusty and you couldn't find a thing in there. Up until now, anyway.

A small black book, covers flapping wildly, scampered across the marble floor. It squatted down in front of the goblin, blocking his path. Out of breath it wheezed, "A warm welcome to Hedes Spine, Mr..." The book stopped and chanted,

> *"To my contents first I turn,*
> *If a name I need to learn,*
> *I check my index for a sign,*
> *A certain letter underlined."*

The book stifled a strangled cough, gulped and swelled up.

> *"Skim through a page, and then I see,*
> *A B C D E F and G,*
> *Down the list I look for clues,*

Mr Banks, the name I'll choose."

"Mr Banks," the book howled, hopping up and down, gleefully. "Today, and only today, I am on," it shuffled closer, the spine stuck up in the air, "special offer!"

Banks mumbled a curse.

"You can buy me, 'A Hanky up a Sleeve, a Rabbit from a Hat' and get a bottle of krakor thunder serpent blood for free."

"Goodbye," Banks mumbled gruffly. Nudging the book out of the way with his foot, he walked on.

Coming to the back of the shop, the goblin climbed the steps to the top floor. He made his way down a dark corridor and knocked sharply on the door at the end.

"Enter," ordered a spiky voice. He strode in.

The goblin hated Tantalus's office. It was always gloomy and always smelt of mould. Black velvet curtains hid the windows and not a chink of light squeezed through. An oil-lamp sat on a cabinet just next to the door, but the soft haze could do little to light the murky room. Banks could just make out Tantalus crouched over his desk in a far corner of the office. The goblin frowned, wondering why the wizard was not pacing like he'd expected. He could see a little better now, so he walked over to him, looking up at the animal heads mounted on the walls as he went. Banks stopped and his stomach did a cartwheel. Tantalus had added a new trophy to his collection.

"Spectacular, is he not?" the wizard murmured silkily. "Had him stuffed by Fester Glumweedy himself."

Banks decided not to reply.

The wizard's eyebrows shot up. "You don't like to hunt, Mr Banks? You do surprise me. You being a goblin, after all."

"I prefer it when they can shoot back," Banks retorted sharply. "A tad more of a challenge."

Tantalus chose to ignore the jibe. He stood up from his chair and walked over to the goblin's head. "Killed him two days ago up in the mountains, place called, now what was it - oh yes, Boulder Dash Village."

Banks grimaced but held his tongue. The village had been his home and Tantalus knew it. He was just trying to bait him but Banks was determined not to nibble on the hook.

"Put up a tremendous struggle," Tantalus boasted. "He just did not want to die. But, of course, he had to, when I chopped off his head."

Banks faked a yawn and began to fiddle with a ring on his finger.

"Come now Mr Banks, a goblin of your reputation. You must have killed a hundred times."

"Never for fun."

Tantalus's cackling filled the room. "A gentleman goblin. I shall have to nominate you for the Hyperion Peace Prize."

Banks' head snapped around and he glared at the wizard, who wisely decided to push it no further. Drifting back over to his chair, Tantalus slouched down on it, winching his long, bony legs up on his desk.

"So, the old fool's finally got a bit of help," he muttered. "Won't do him any good. Too little and much too late." He raised his voice. "Wouldn't you agree, Mr Banks?"

The goblin stood silently on the other side of the desk. He looked perfectly relaxed, his hands hooked in his cow-hide belt, his left leg slightly bent at the knee. So Tantalus already knew. His puffdolt had stayed awake after all. Well, Cruncher couldn't have seen everything. Not from Eternus.

"Wouldn't you agree, Mr Banks?" the wizard repeated. There was an edge of menace to his words that demanded an answer.

Almost casually, he murmured, "She's swept up a bit, you know, dusted..."

Tantalus sprang up from his chair as if it were on fire and marched around the desk. "Dusted?" he sneered in the goblin's face. Banks grimaced as he got the full force of Tantalus's cheesy breath.

"Dusted," Banks echoed him, calmly. He backpedalled two steps and breathed in thankfully. "They've stocked up too and put the books in some kind of order. Lit the fire. Looks rather snug." Tantalus glared at him. "They've even got a copy of 'Halloween, Pick a Frock to Shock' in the window. Tricky to find; I was thinking of nicking it for my mum."

Tantalus began to pace. He often did this when he was angry and as he was angry most of the time he got through an awful lot of boot leather. But the goblin was not overly concerned. The wizard needed him, needed his talents, his connections. He would not dare to harm him. The wizard had over-stepped the mark before and Banks remembered with relish him begging him not to go. Yes, that had been a good day, a very good day indeed.

"Mr Banks, I don't need to tell you how important The Wishing Shelf is to me. I'm counting on you."

"The Wishing Shelf?" Banks murmured slyly. "Don't you mean the book?"

"Articulus. Yes, yes! I have customers, Mr Banks, powerful customers who would love to get their claws on that book, but that - that moron, Galibrath, refuses to sell it to me. Now this, just as he is down to his last bronze flupoon, almost on his knees. He would have begged me to buy that shop." He smiled nastily as he imagined Galibrath kneeling in front of him, pleading for his help.

Banks watched in disgust as a slither of spittle oozed out from Tantalus's lips and snaked down his chin. He looked away. Somehow the goblin doubted whether Galibrath would sell Tantalus a glass of pond water, never mind a book with the immense power of Articulus.

"I'm under enormous strain. Enormous! If I don't get that book soon..." He left the sentence unfinished but the look of fear on his face told Banks that these powerful customers were not used to being kept hanging around. "Who's doing this to me? A sorcerer? Hyperion's boys? I can send my trolls over."

"A girl," Banks said, simply.

"A girl?"

"Quite young, about thirteen maybe."

"Hmm. What sort of a girl? A fairy?" Tantalus slammed his fist down on the desk. "Bleedin' pests, flying around, poking 'oh so perfect' snouts in my..."

"No. She's human."

"Human!" roared Tantalus, tearing at his hair. "What are her magical powers?"

"I don't think she has any but..."

"But?"

"She is rather handy with a duster."

The wizard laughed wildly. "Let me get this right, Mr Banks. Are you telling me that my plans to take over The Wishing Shelf, to finally get even with that blockhead, Galibrath, and to get my hands on the most powerful book in Eternus is being thwarted by a spotty teenage girl, whose only talents lay in dusting?"

Banks seemed to consider this for a moment and then he nodded his head. "It would seem that way," he said soberly.

There was a soft tapping on the door.

"Come!" barked Tantalus.

A very small imp crept in and keeping his eyes glued to the floor, sidled up to the wizard.

"What is it?" spat Tantalus.

"Pr-Pr-Professor Plotinus is here for the book signing," it stammered, hopping from one foot to the other.

The wizard grabbed the poor imp by the lapels and lifted him off his feet. "I'm busy! Can't you see I'm busy?" He turned to the goblin. "Mr Banks, do I seem busy to you?"

"I would say incredibly busy. In fact, the most busy I have ever seen you."

"There!" shouted Tantalus. "I think we're all in agreement that I'm busy." The petrified imp began to make gurgling sounds, his legs kicking out frantically. Very slowly his face changed from healthy-imp green to unhealthy-imp blue.

"I think you're strangling him," Banks mumbled, nibbling on his nails.

Roughly, the wizard dropped the imp to the floor, spun him around and gave him a hefty boot up the bum. With a high-pitched squeak the imp shot out of the door.

"I think the time has come for me to pop back to The Wishing Shelf and meet this meddlesome girl." He marched to the open door. "What's her name?" he snapped.

"Felicity Brady."

The wizard stopped so abruptly, Banks half expected to hear the screech of rubber. "Brady, y' say!?"

"Yep," Banks muttered, casually fiddling with the strap on his Rolex watch. But he was watching Tantalus out of the corner of his eye. "You know her?"

"No! No!" The wizard attempted to be casual too but it did not wash with the wily goblin. "I just need to er, know, so I can put her name on the tombstone."

And with that, he stalked over to the door.

Banks watched him go. He didn't like to

admit it, but he had been impressed by this Brady-girl. He had sat under the old bridge and watched her sweep floors, wrestle with books and beat clouds of dust out of stroppy rugs. She had guts and Banks admired that. She reminded him of a girl he had known many years ago. But Felicity Brady was no longer his problem. Tantalus was the boss and his word was law.

For now anyway.

Chapter 6

Voodoo Dolls, Woolly Hats and a Very Rude Mirror

It was a Saturday morning and Felicity was very busy in the back of the shop emptying what could only be the junkroom. It had been jam-packed with odd bits and bobs, very odd bits and bobs and bits and bobs so odd she had no idea what they were. She had piled everything up in the corridor and written a list to show Galibrath, and then he could decide what to and what not to throw away.

So far, her list looked like this,

Wonky stools
Lamps (dented)
Growling rugs (mostly grey, I guess they get

old too!)

Rope (wriggling)

Rocking horse (rocking)

A pile of old newspapers called the Quill 'n' Scroll (dated 1827)

Set of golf clubs (most of 'em snapped in two, the rest wonky)

A voodoo doll (pin in eyeball)

A trunk (smells bad, probably has rotting body in it)

A golf trophy (on it the words Twice Brewed Charity Cup 1926, winners Galibrath Falafel and Hickory Crowl)

A woolly hat

A mirror (keeps insulting me)

Dragging the cobwebby stuff out of the junkroom, she wondered who she'd meet that day; maybe a goblin or a stroppy troll, or maybe one of Al's toothy dorfmorons or a puffdolt. Yesterday, she had spotted a snapshot of a puffdolt in a book. REVOLTING!

Oddly, the prospect of meeting so many gigantic, tiny, shaggy, bald, toothy and gummy monsters did not seem to bother her at all and she wondered why.

After two hours of hard slog she only had the very far corners left to check but to get to them she'd have to crawl in. Felicity, not surprisingly, did not particularly enjoy climbing into musty old junkrooms. She couldn't even see the walls; they were hidden in darkness, and her nostrils kept catching the whiff of rotting meat (even after the trunk had been taken out). She sighed. For the good of the shop, she thought staunchly, and reluctantly, she scrambled in.

Felicity felt her way along the wall, trying to ignore the cobwebs catching in her curls. She shuddered. It was freezing and darker than a coal pit. Suddenly, the tips of her fingers hit a hard, cold object making her jump and yank her hand away. Swallowing her fear, she reached back out, grabbed hold of whatever it was, and started to drag it out of the junkroom.

As Felicity got it closer to the door, she saw that it was, in fact, a very large gilt-framed picture. She rested it on the wall and curiously brushed off the dust with her sleeve. It was a picture of The Wishing Shelf, but how different it had been. The books were all smartly lined up, fluffy rugs lay dozing on the varnished floor, and there were wizards and hags everywhere, all of them laden down with books. She peered closer. She had just spotted, in front of the sofa, a very young-looking and amazingly slim-looking Galibrath. He was stood chatting to a very pretty girl, his hand resting on her shoulder.

"What y' up to?" Al quizzed her, tottering up and peering nosily into the junkroom. On his t-shirt he had scrawled,

SMALL BUT PERFECTLY FORMED

"I'm emptying this old junkroom and…"

"I can see that," butted in the imp, irritably. "I stubbed my toe climbing over all them old stools. But why?"

"Why? Well, it's full of junk, so I thought, y' know, if I got rid of it all we could store stuff in it."

"But it's full of stuff now." He glanced at the junk crammed in the corridor. "Well, it was."

Annoyed, Felicity looked back to the picture. "I discovered this in the very back. Guess who's in it."

Al rolled his eyes and peered over her shoulder.

"Who's the girl?" she asked him.

"Oh yes, that's er - no, no idea."

"Al!" Felicity eyed him sternly. "Tell the truth."

"The truth!" He smirked. "The truth is - I need a cuppa." He sprinted away, only stopping to snatch up the woolly hat she'd discovered in a spidery corner. "Ah ha!" he bellowed. "My old teacosy." He popped it on his head. "Oh, and Felicity," he shouted over his shoulder. "Did Galibrath not tell you that that junkroom there is a Never Ending Junkroom?"

"A - WHAT!?"

"Shut the door, and then open it," he called.

With a sinking feeling, Felicity did as she was told and gasped in horror. The junkroom had magically filled back up: wobbly stools, crooked golf clubs, even the old rocking horse, duplicating everything still in the corridor.

"Hey! Shut the door!" yelled the insulting mirror. "Silly girl. Terribly spotty too."

Defeated, Felicity sat cross-legged and stared

at the picture. The girl really was very pretty, young too, maybe only sixteen or seventeen. Her skin was dark and she had on a gown of sorts, a kimono maybe. Anyway, she looked very happy, but for the eyes: they seemed a little empty, almost lonely.

Felicity was about to put the picture back into the junkroom when she spotted the face of a boy peering over the top of the sofa. He looked very upset, his eyes red and swollen. She scowled. The eyes - where had she seen...?

"FELICITY!" Al's voice thundered out of the shop. "CUSTOMERS!"

"COMING!" she shouted back. She glanced back at the boy. It was the eyes. She knew those eyes.

"FELICITY!"

"OK! OK!" Annoying imp! Felicity got to her feet and, trying not to look at the mess in the corridor, ran to help.

Good news travel fast, particularly amongst

magical folk. After only a few days, the shop was overrun with wizards, imps and even the odd gnome all keen to buy books from the new and improved Wishing Shelf.

It was Sunday and Felicity had never worked so hard. Unfortunately, Galibrath had popped out and she soon discovered that Al, despite skipping here, there and everywhere, never actually did very much. So she coped the best she could, helping the imps hunt for Christmas presents and looking for fishing books for the gnome to look at.

All in all, she was having a wonderful day till a grumbling goblin marched in, his boots caked in mud. He marched up to Al and slammed a fat book on the desk. The poor imp jumped a foot off his stool. "Whoa!" he whimpered. "I almost wet my nappy,"

"This book 'ere is boring," the goblin rumbled gruffly.

"Boring" echoed Al, picking up the book and studying the title.

"Yep. The last chapter's so dull I fell asleep. There's hardly any blood in it - or sword play."

"'The Goblin Empire, from King Bollyhor-

Mimmy the Ninny to Queen Doolun-Tiddy the Old Biddy'," the imp read out loud. "It's a history book."

"I know what it is, but the fact is, the last chapter is ruddy boring."

"But, but," shrilled Al, looking very perplexed, "IT'S A HISTORY BOOK!"

"So," sulked the goblin.

"So," huffed the imp.

The goblin, a long shaggy pelt covering most of his scabby face, stared down at the imp crossly.

"I think what Al is trying to say," interrupted Felicity, hurrying over, "is that a history book is supposed to tell the truth, even if it is a bit dull. That's the job of a history book, to tell the story exactly the way it was."

"But, but..." the goblin spluttered, scratching his brow with a furry finger.

"Let's say you, well - not you, but this clever person, is doing a very important study," Felicity took a deep breath, "and he needs to know the name of a hill where, hundreds of years ago, a big battle happened. So, what can he do?" Al and the goblin exchanged a look. "He looks it up in a history book."

Al snapped his fingers. "Oh, yes." The goblin, baffled, kept his trap shut.

"There, in the last chapter, he discovers the name of the hill was Terrorside Creek. How exciting, he thinks..."

"But, but..." the goblin attempted to butt in.

"...but, in fact, it wasn't ever called Terrorside Creek. Ever!" Felicity began to pace, her eyes to the floor. "Y' see, many years ago, the old farmer who lived on the hill named it Honey Pot Knoll, but the author of the history book thought no, no, no, too pretty, too sweet, so he changed the name just to fit his story. Now, I think the poor reader would be very upset..."

"You can stop jabbering on," piped up Al. "He left."

Felicity's flow of words abruptly stopped and she looked up. "Left?"

"The goblin, he left, popped off, hopped the lily pad. I think he got a little bored." And so he had, taking the history book with him.

Felicity was on her knees hunting for a copy of 'A Manual of Flying Carpets' for a gnome when she first smelt it. She wrinkled up her nose. "Cor! That stinks!" she gasped. "What is it?" She turned to the gnome but he had mysteriously vanished.

She stood up and looked about. To her surprise the shop was empty. "Hello," she shouted.

The bookshop started to shake: the books, the stools, even the desks bopping up and down to the bass drum rhythm. A book slipped off a shelf and hit the floor with a 'Ooh, my spine! Need a chiropractor'. The door to the shop thumped the wall and a bald, flappy-chinned, aniseed-eyed, gummy-toothed, wobbly-chested monster in a purple leotard burst in. He (it had to be a he, it was so ugly) towered over her, smelling of the loo at the campsite Felicity had stayed at with her family in Skegness last summer. Felicity gulped. No teeth and the size of a cement truck; it had to be a puffdolt.

And there next to it, resting a casual shoulder on the monster's hefty left calf, was Tantalus.

"You must be Felicity Brady," he drawled, his

thin lips forming a shallow smile. He strode over to her, his hand outstretched. Fearfully, Felicity shook it. It felt cold and damp and she had to stop herself from snatching her fingers away.

"Well, let's have a look at you." He stood back and stared at her. Felicity shivered. She could almost feel his eyes burrowing into her, reading her mind and unfolding her secrets. "What a smashing looking girl!" he announced loftily. "And I hear you have been working wonders in The Wishing Shelf."

Tantalus's eyes darted around the room. "Where's all the dust? The cobwebs? The dirty mugs? For a moment we thought we were in the wrong shop, didn't we, Cruncher?" He looked over at the puffdolt, who was busy picking wax out of his ear and munching it. Cruncher grunted.

"Shall I go fetch, er - Galibrath?" Felicity spluttered, moving to the door at the back of the shop.

"But Galibrath is not here," Tantalus crooned smugly. "He's in Funny Bone Surgery having a check up."

"He is?"

"Let's not concern ourselves with him, shall we?" Flopping down on the sofa, Tantalus waved Felicity over to join him. "Let's have a little chat about you."

Felicity stayed standing. "About me!" she squawked in surprise. "What do you want to know about me?"

Al chose that moment to walk into the room, his eyes glued to a book he had open in his hands. Sensing something was wrong he stopped and slowly lifted his head. On seeing Tantalus and the huge puffdolt, he screeched, dropped the book and made a dash back to the door, but with a flick of Tantalus's fingers the imp froze, his face a mask of panic.

"Let him go!" Felicity shouted, finding her courage at last.

"Calm yourself. He won't come to any harm," Tantalus assured her.

Felicity looked at him indignantly. "I am calm. I just don't like seeing my friends being turned into mannequins."

Tantalus patted the sofa. "Come and sit. Relax. Don't be frightened. I'm not here to harm you, or your imp." He winked and smiled creepily. "Please," he whined.

Reluctantly, Felicity walked over and sat down as far from the wizard as she could. She reached for a cushion and placed it between them in the hope that it would protect her, like a child hiding under the quilt.

"Now, that's better, isn't it? A little more comfy," oozed Tantalus smoothly. "My name is Tantalus Falafel; no doubt Galibrath's told you my life history by now." Felicity pursed up her lips and began to fiddle nervously with the hem of her skirt. "Anyway, I own the largest bookshops in Eternus. Every one of them is wonderful, perfectly wonderful; tons of room, dust-free, every book in order, A to Z and all that. We even sell muffins, double-choc-chip. I pop to England now and then to buy them. The bakery over The Wishing Shelf."

Felicity had been wondering why he had been in England the first day she had seen him. Then, "I don't like double-choc-chip." She did really.

"We also have blueberry."

"Oooh, disgusting."

"Well, anyway, that's not important."

Tantalus's voice sounded a little strained. "What is important is that there is always a place for a hard-working, clever young lady such as you in Hedes Spine."

"You're offering me a job?" asked Felicity incredulously.

The wizard seemed to ponder this for a moment. "Yes," he said.

"But I already have a job."

Tantalus laughed. "This place," he sneered. "I mean, just look at it. How old is this sofa? And these books, full of outdated rubbish."

There were murmurings from a few of the books, though not quite loud enough for Tantalus to hear.

"But I enjoy it here," Felicity shot off. "This old sofa is perfect for a nap, and the books, well, they may be a little elderly but they tell me the most amazing yarns. But best of all, I love working with Galibrath. He's a good laugh," she looked stonily at the wizard, "and he's honest and good."

Tantalus was no longer smiling and his eyes blazed with anger. Felicity wondered for a moment if he had swallowed a thunder cloud!

He stood up, marched over to the puffdolt and whispered in his ear. Growling, Cruncher lumbered over to where the imp was still frozen, lifted up his dagger and held it there.

The wizard turned and stared down at Felicity. "Let me tell you a story. I once knew a gnome. Lovely chap, pretty wife, four children, now what were they called? Anyway, this gnome decided to open a bookshop. I asked him not to and like you he refused. Now he limps rather badly, his wife is no longer pretty and HE ONLY HAS TWO CHILDREN!" Tantalus walked right up to Felicity, towering over her. "DO I MAKE MYSELF CLEAR?" he bellowed, his hands flapping in her face.

A streak of silver light flashed through the shop, hitting Cruncher squarely on the nose. The dagger slipped from his hand and the puffdolt crumpled to the floor with a whimper. Tantalus hastily backed away from Felicity and lifted his hand.

"No, brother!" Galibrath stormed into the room and placed himself firmly in front of Felicity. He stared icily at Tantalus. "Still trying to filch all my staff. Once is OK, but twice is just rude."

"You," Tantalus hissed, his eyes murderous. "The time is coming when you will no longer be able to stand in my way."

"It is your hatred and greed that stands in your way, not me, brother."

"Don't call me brother!" Tantalus almost screamed. "Our blood ties ended the day you cheated me out of what was rightfully mine."

Galibrath shook his head sadly. "You gave Dad no choice."

"He had every choice." Tantalus's voice was full of venom.

"No! Your obsession with dark magic, your hatred of the old and the good - our dad knew, knew you could never understand The Wishing Shelf; what we were trying to do here..."

"He knew nothing. He was a fool."

Galibrath's eyes flashed. "Watch your tongue, Tantalus. The very magic that you hate, I control. With the knowledge I have gained from these books, I could destroy you in the blink of a cyclops' eye."

Tantalus threw back his head and laughed scornfully and Cruncher, sitting dazed on the floor, grunted and snorted. "You are just a feeble old man," the wizard cried, "and your power's pathetic, just like this silly girl." He flicked his fingers and a pile of books over on Galibrath's desk went crashing to the floor.

"HEY! I JUST PUT THEM IN ORDER!" stormed Felicity.

Galibrath stood stock-still, his palms resting on his hips. Then, very slowly, his eyes fluttered shut. Instantly, a black fog flooded the room, swamping every corner, every nook and every cranny. It felt, to Felicity, as if a giant's hand was trying to crush her. She felt like a grape being squeezed to make wine.

From the gloomy mist, ghosts erupted, swirling and spinning and filling The Wishing Shelf with howls and whimpers, sobs and yowls. Felicity clasped her hands over her ears and on the floor the puffdolt blubbered like a helpless baby.

"Stop this!" bawled Tantalus, his words brimming over with terror.

Suddenly, the ghosts vanished, the crying stopped and the fog faded away to nothing.

"Can you do no better?" sneered Tantalus. He

crept up to his brother, his teeth clenched, a snarl curling lips. "A few ghosts, the odd howl, why a six-year-old witch..."

A low rumbling put a stop to the wizard's jeers. The shop trembled, rugs growled and books crashed to the floor. Doors swung violently open and crashed shut and the lamp on the desk toppled over and smashed. Felicity, with frying pan eyes, gripped the sofa to stop from toppling over too.

In all the chaos, Galibrath boomed, "GET OUT OF MY BOOKSHOP!"

Tantalus gawped at his brother, his eyes awash with panic. Then the chandelier hit the floor with an ear-splitting 'BOOM!' and he dashed out of the shop. Cruncher, on seeing his master bolt, lumbered to his feet and clumped after him.

Chapter 7

A Falafel Feud

There were only twenty-five days left till Christmas and Felicity was rushed off her feet, draping tinsel on the oil-lamps, dusting the books and hanging baubles on a tree Galibrath had found for the shop.

Imps, giants, even a family of leprechauns dashed, slunk and lumbered in, hunting for presents.

"Orange elephants," demanded a witch with a twitchy eye. "I need a big book on orange elephants."

"Do you have any cookery books?" This from a gappy-toothed leprechaun, yellow laces in his sparkly boots. "I want to bake a wigglefinch tart."

Galibrath even conjured up a box of fairy lights, and when Felicity looked closely she saw that each light was a fairy, holding hands and blinking on and off.

Every afternoon, Felicity would dash out of the school gate and run to the bookshop, and every evening, thanks to The Clock by the Door, she would get home in plenty of time for dinner and to do her homework.

She had begun to tell her mum and dad a little about The Wishing Shelf - not the magical stuff, of course - and they had been delighted.

"'Bout time," her dad had barked at her. He was a sergeant in the army. "When I was a kid I worked on my dad's farm. Had to milk the cows every morning, crack of dawn, and I spent my weekends driving a tractor."

For once, they did not quarrel.

She was so busy, she never even found a chance to ask Galibrath about Tantalus and why Tantalus disliked him so much. She had been shocked to find out they were brothers. Galibrath was so kind, so gentle, and Tantalus, well, he was a monster.

Tantalus had told her that Galibrath had taken The Wishing Shelf from him; that he had let him down. She wondered why. What had happened? But she was too scared to ask and, anyway, the shop was always too busy. It was not until three days before Christmas, when she was in the kitchen helping Al iron his t-shirts, that she found out the full story.

"It was a long time ago," the imp mumbled. "I was in a nest, curled up in an egg when it happened." He kept his head down and seemed to concentrate even harder on his ironing.

Felicity folded a t-shirt and stuck it on top of the pile. "Al, is that the truth?"

"Yes." But the 'yes' sounded awfully feeble.

"Al..."

"Why do you want to know?" The imp looked up from his ironing and scowled. "It was in the past and it should be left there."

Felicity wedged her fists on her hips. "Galibrath let me work here - and he saved me from a bully's fists. A wizard wants to hurt him and I want to know why." She relaxed, letting her hands drop down by her side. "If anything were to happen to him..."

"Galibrath is a powerful wizard," Al retorted. "He hardly needs a silly little girl to protect him." He plonked down the iron and looked at her. "Look, I'm sorry, but..."

"If I understood why Tantalus detested him so much, perhaps I could help. Galibrath helped me. He saved me from a bully and gave me a job. So now I owe him."

"OK! OK!" The imp's face softened. "If you really want to know, follow me." He planted the iron on a hot ring on the stove - there were still a lot of t-shirts to do - and scuttled out of the kitchen. Felicity grimaced and chased after him.

"Where are we going?" she demanded. "Can't you tell me in the kitchen?"

"Nope. It didn't happen in the kitchen."

"But..."

"Come on. Keep up."

They marched into the shop, the imp walking crookedly like a crab, studying the books as he went. He stopped, squatted down and pulled a scruffy-looking book off the bottom shelf. Felicity watched him open it and begin to flick through the pages.

She felt like strangling him. Why did he have to make easy things, such as telling a story, so difficult? She began to tap her foot and make clip-clop sounds on the top of her mouth.

"Now, what do we have here?" The imp had

stopped flicking and was now reading, his head darting from side to side. He grunted, slammed the book shut and stood back up. "Nope," he peeped. "Keep up." And he scuttled off down a second isle.

Why couldn't he just tell her, she wondered, munching on her lip. Why was he looking in so many books? She heard a door creak open and slam shut. Gritting her teeth, she chased after him.

Four rooms and twelve books later, the imp jumped on a stool, reached up and with a cry of, "Got it!" pulled down a thin purple book with a scuffed corner. He smiled wickedly at Felicity and she glared back at him.

"So tell me then!"

"No."

"AL!"

"We have to go back to the front of the shop. That's where it happened. If we do it in the wrong place, it won't work."

Felicity crouched down and grasped hold of the imp by his collar. "WHAT WON'T WORK?" she yelled. Al chuckled, flicked his fingers and vanished, leaving Felicity holding a puff of green smoke. She shook her head. "Why couldn't Galibrath have got a chihuahua," she muttered, "or a tabby cat?" She stood up and trudged back to the front of the shop.

She discovered Al sitting on the wizard's desk reading the book he had found. He looked up when Felicity walked in. "What kept you?" he quizzed her cheekily, but Felicity just grunted and flopped down on the sofa.

"This is it, this is it," Al jabbered excitedly.

"What!?"

"You want to see what happened, then I'm going to show you." He peeped a squeaky kind of growl and began to chant,

> *"Bricks and boards your secrets yield,*
> *Conflicts of the past revealed,*
> *In picture clues the story's told,*
> *Wizard brothers, the scene unfolds."*

A ray of dazzling red light erupted from the wall in front of Felicity and brilliantly lit up the bookshop. She jumped to her feet in horror.

"Run for cover!" yelled a book, diving under the desk.

Too late.

A yellow ray burst from the letterbox; it shot over Felicity and she fell to her knees with a whimper. But there was no escape for her there, for on the floor a green fog was slowly rising up. Suddenly the room was a magical swirl of colours, blending and jumbling over each other.

Slowly, a human shape began to form.

"HELP ME!" Felicity bawled, doing a perfect impression of a hedgehog and rolling up in a tight ball.

"It's OK," the imp soothed her. "Sit up or you'll miss it."

"You must be joking! I'm staying here till you tell me what..."

"I am the youngest son and by wizardry law, The Wishing Shelf belongs to me."

That was Tantalus. She recognised the weepy drawl. Slowly, she pulled her fingers from her eyes. She could see two wizards standing only a few feet in front of her, but they did not seem real, like ghosts or a fuzzy picture on a TV that was not properly tuned in. Cautiously, Felicity sat up.

"Tantalus," one of them barked. He was older and much shorter, the skin on his face loose, like a big saggy jumper. "I cannot trust you..."

"TRUST!" Tantalus screamed. "You dare to talk of trust. It is I who cannot trust you. You sit all day in your lab playing with your chemistry set, or conspiring with that back-stabbing brother of mine to steal what belongs to me."

"You must earn The Wishing Shelf." This must be Galibrath's and Tantalus's dad, Gooftwerp, Felicity thought. "You must show me that you understand what we are trying to do here. You have never been able to do that."

But his stroppy son just scowled and showed him his back. Felicity watched him pace up and down the room, muttering and clenching his fists. He looked so much younger but already his brow was lined and his eyes were grey and sullen.

He stopped and turned on his father. "I have helped you in this shop for over ten years," he whined.

"Son, you must see, The Wishing Shelf is a responsibility few wizards can cope with. It is..."

"Yes, yes, I know," Tantalus scoffed him. "It is a doorway and a prison..."

Gooftwerp sighed. "But it is a sanctuary too - for all magical folk, where they can go and enjoy the wonder of words. It is not important to me, or to your brother, if a customer is rich or has a gaping hole in his boot."

Tantalus snorted. "You live in the days of dinosaurs. Don't you see? Bigger shops, newer books, we could be richer than any..."

"NO! That is enough, Tantalus. The decision has been made. The Wishing Shelf will become Galibrath's." There was silence as the father and son glared at each other. "But I will help you."

"Help me? Ha! I don't need your help."

"I will not turn my back on you. I am your dad."

"I have no dad," Tantalus spat back with such venom that Felicity felt a cold shiver run down her spine. Tantalus's father took an unsteady step back as if he had just been punched in the face. "Rejection hurts, hey? Welcome to my world."

Slowly, the two ghosts began to dissolve and Felicity got shakily to her feet. It had seemed so real, as if it had happened just now, not a hundred years ago.

"I - I think I understand now," she mustered shakily.

"Hold on," whispered the imp. "There's a second story to be told."

In a rainbow of colours, the shop was suddenly filled with wizards laden down with books, and just in front of the desk stood a very dapper-looking Galibrath, his hand resting on the shoulder of a girl, the very girl Felicity had seen in the picture in the junkroom.

"I do love you," she whispered.

"And I you." Galibrath kissed her gently, making Felicity blush. "But we must be careful. I cannot tell my brother yet."

The girl's face fell. "But why?"

"Because he knows The Wishing Shelf is to be left to me. He's jealous. He feels the whole world is his enemy."

"But I don't understand why we have to hide 'us' from him."

"Tantalus has always," the wizard rubbed his eyes and then looked around the shop as if trying to find the correct words, "had feelings for you," he mustered finally.

"But I have never felt..."

"I know, I know," Galibrath calmed her. "But now is not a good time. Maybe in a few months, when Tantalus has calmed down a bit. Then we can tell him."

Reluctantly, the girl nodded.

Suddenly the door to the corridor hit the wall and Galibrath's old dad pottered in, a camera clutched in his hands. "I need a picture for the Quill 'n' Scroll," he told the room, "so, say cheese everybody."

"CHEESE!" went all the wizards and the bulb flashed.

Felicity scowled. From behind the sofa she had just heard a low whimper, as if a dog was trapped there. Cautiously, she knelt on a cushion and peered over the back.

Crouched on the floor was Tantalus, or, the shadowy echo of Tantalus. His hands were clamped over his face but tears still managed to squeeze through his fingers. A bulb flickered on in Felicity's mind. It was not just about The Wishing Shelf or his dad's mistrust. It was about the girl. It had always been about the girl. Tantalus was jealous of his brother.

"Do you understand now?" The imp tottered

up and stood next to her. He slipped his arm comfortingly around her left leg.

"Yes, I think so" she choked, swallowing the lump in her throat. The reds, yellows and greens were fading now and the ghosts had melted away. The shop seemed dead and empty, like a theatre when the play is over.

"There is nothing you or I can do." He squeezed her calf. "The anger runs much too deep."

She nodded. "So, what I saw, it actually happened? Here in this room?"

"Every wall has secrets, every brick and every board has a tale to tell. You see, The Wishing Shelf is like a record sitting idly on a gramophone. You just need the right charm to wind it up." The imp smiled softly at her. "Cuppa?"

It all seemed so hopeless. How could two brothers drift so far apart and hate each other so much? What if things had been different, Felicity wondered. What if Tantalus had got the girl? Would Galibrath have become the monster?

She smiled feebly down at Al. "A cuppa

sounds wonderful," she murmured, and they ambled off back to the kitchen.

Chapter 8

A Power Drill and a Brass Trombone

"You look very handsome," declared Felicity, looking up at Galibrath and trying hard not to chuckle.

The wizard pulled a face. "I last put on this jacket for a gargoyle's wedding." He peered in the mirror and patted his swollen belly. "Put on a few pounds over the years," he chortled. "Too many crisps."

"Too many packets, more like," mumbled Felicity, but not too loudly.

He had on a banana-yellow shirt topped by a red and rather crooked bow-tie. Under his woolly jacket he wore a spotty-red vest, a gold watch dangling from the pocket. His blue flannel trousers must have shrunk in the wash as they only reached to his shins, showing one green and one faded pink sock.

And he smelled of lemon and strawberry soap.

He began to fiddle with the bow. "Let me," offered Felicity. She reached up and pulled it loose. "The trick is to cross longer over shorter and not to pull it too tight." She took a step back. "How's that?"

He glanced back in the mirror. "Wonderful," he roared, a mothball dropping out of his sleeve and bouncing along the floor. "Did they teach you that at school?"

"No, mum showed me. Dad's in the army, you see, so he's always going to a posh party or a ball, stuff like that and when mum's not in, I help him to get ready."

She picked up the mothball and popped it in the drawer of the desk.

The wizard patted her shoulder. "She did a wonderful job."

Felicity was a little nervous. Her mum and dad had asked her to ask Galibrath if he would like to join them for Christmas dinner. To her surprise, he had bellowed a "Yes" and "Should I bring a bottle of wine?". Her parents were very - ordinary really. She did not know what they would do if the wizard magically pulled a roast turkey out of her dad's army cap.

She glanced at her watch. "We need to be going," she muttered. It was a long walk from the shop to her house.

The wizard grinned. He put two fingers to his lips and mustered a long shrill whistle. The rug in front of the fire leapt up from the floor, zoomed over to them and hovered there like a dog begging to be taken for a walk.

Felicity stumbled back. "A flying carpet!" she gasped.

Galibrath chuckled. "Magic folk call them car," pause, "pets."

"Car-pets," mouthed Felicity, trying to imitate the wizard. "Why?"

"Well, they work similar to your cars: they go from A to B, they park, the newer carpets have even got horns. But they can be a bit 'doggish' too: they sleep a lot and they love to chase sticks." He patted the carpet. "Actually, this is more a flying rug and a little dog-eared at that, but it'll do the job."

He dragged open a drawer in his desk and pulled out a box and a bottle of wine, a red bow knotted to the neck. "Hop on."

Felicity clambered onto the rug and knelt next to the wizard. She clutched tightly to the sleeve of his jacket.

"Twisting and turning, spinning around,
To Felicity's home this carpet is bound,"

chanted the wizard. Then, he shouted, "England," to the clock. They floated slowly over to the door but it was still shut. Felicity tugged at Galibrath's sleeve, but before she could say a word, it sprang open and they shot off.

Felicity whooped in delight but clung on fiercely. It was the most wonderful feeling, like being on a roller coaster but better, much better - and faster too.

They soared up into the frosty sky over Twice Brewed. Brimming with excitement, Felicity peered over the lip of the flapping rug. She could see hundreds of tiny sheds and red roofs, swirls of smoke seeping from the chimneys. It was like flying over a game of Monopoly and Felicity grinned from ear to ear.

"This is so much fun," she shouted over the rush of the wind.

She felt surprisingly hot. When she had walked to the shop that morning she had been wrapped up in a thick duffle coat, but now, flying faster than a jet plane, she did not feel cold at all.

"It has very good heaters," hollered the wizard, as if he had just read her mind. Felicity nodded and shrugged. She had no idea what he was on about. But not to worry. She was on a flying carpet! Sorry, car-pet!

Felicity could see the tumbled-down castle on the top of the hill and canal boats chugging up and down the river. Twice Brewed had become a Lego town with a hundred toy cars crawling along on grey strips of plasticine. She only had to reach down, pack everything up and put it away in a box.

She wanted the ride to last forever, but all too soon they were hovering over her house. The old rug zoomed down to the ground and landed with a bump in the vegetable patch, just next to the shed.

"Wow!" gasped Felicity as she stood up and staggered off the carpet. Her legs still felt a bit wobbly.

She watched as it rolled up and stood on one end. The wizard tucked it under his arm.

"How...?"

"Crackers."

"Sorry?"

"Crackers." He held up the box he had taken out of his desk. "I made them myself. I read about them in a book, 'Festive Ideas, Christmas on a Shoestring'."

"No," said Felicity, shaking her head. "The carpet, the flying carpet. How did it - fly?"

"'The Secret to Magic Carpets', a fascinating read, the drawings really are very good. Third isle, fifth row, squeezed between 'Which Broomstick, A Buyer's Guide' and 'Swerving and Swooping', more of a children's book really..." He coughed and leant on the shed.

"You OK?" She rested her hand gently on his shoulder.

"Oh, yes, yes. A slight sniffle that's all. Can't seem to get rid of it." He sneezed. "May I borrow a hanky? I may be a powerful wizard but the 'hanky up the sleeve' trick is beyond me."

Hunting in her pocket, Felicity discovered a balled-up lump of tissue. She handed it to him and he blew his nose.

"Shall we?" he asked, looking pointedly at the door to Felicity's house.

She nodded.

Brushing off her hand, he walked briskly up the garden path. Felicity, still a little dazed from the trip, weaved after him.

"More sprouts?" Mrs Brady asked Galibrath.

"Oh, yes."

She spooned a large pile onto the wizard's plate. "Roast potatoes?"

"Just the one." She served him three.

They were sitting in the dining room around a large table hidden under a simple maroon tablecloth and a hill of food.

Mr and Mrs Brady sat next to each other and

across from them were Galibrath and Felicity. At the far end of the table, Felicity's baby brother, Samuel, was perched on a high-stool throwing carrots at the cat.

The wizard felt very comfortable at the Brady's home. They had greeted him with a pat on the back, a bowl of nuts and a very large glass of wine. Mrs Brady was very interested in The Wishing Shelf. Like Galibrath, she loved old bookshops and she told him all about the book she was reading and suggested he try it.

Pouring his wife a drop of wine, Mr Brady looked closely at the bottle and scowled. It was the wine Galibrath had brought and even though everybody but Felicity had had a glass it still seemed to be full. He shook his head and poured a drop more for the wizard. "So, Felicity says she loves working in your shop. She seems very happy."

Galibrath sprinkled salt on his three roast potatoes. "She's a great help; I don't know how we managed without her."

"We?" asked Mrs Brady.

"Oh yes, well, there's Al - he's an imp."

Felicity kicked Galibrath's leg under the table.

"Can I have some more turkey, please?" she asked her mum, desperately trying to change the subject.

"An imp?" queried Mrs Brady, shushing her daughter.

The wizard looked up from his food and grinned. "And what an imp he is. Always being silly. Playing tricks. Must pay him less, hey Felicity?"

"Er, yes," sighed Felicity. The wizard winked mischievously at her.

After a dessert of Christmas pudding drenched in brandy sauce, Galibrath produced his homemade crackers and they all pulled one. The bangs were very loud, more like small explosions really, and Mrs Brady had to open a window to let out the smoke.

The gifts they won were, not surprisingly, a little peculiar. Mr Brady won a power drill and Mrs Brady, a three pronged potted cactus. Quite how Galibrath had squeezed them into the empty toilet rolls was quite beyond poor Mr Brady. He looked at the drill in amazement and with a shake of his head, poured himself a second glass of wine.

"Thanks," said Felicity, pulling a face. She held up the big bag of yellow and green socks that had jumped out of her cracker. "Just what I needed - more socks to throw under my bed."

Galibrath beamed and blew loudly on the brass trombone that had fallen out of his.

To Felicity's surprise, the dinner was a wonderful success. Galibrath got on very well with her mum and dad and they, in turn, seemed to enjoy his bad jokes and farfetched yarns. After dinner, they sat by the fire in the living room and played cards - Chase the Ace, Gin Rummy and Knock Out Whist. The wizard performed a few card tricks confusing Mr Brady even more.

After the card games, Felicity's dad went into the kitchen to wash up and Mrs Brady began to clear the table in the dining room.

"Can I be of any help?" Galibrath asked, starting to get up from the sofa. "I'm a dab hand in the kitchen. I know this sp..."

"No, no. You sit there and relax." Mrs Brady smiled at him and left the room.

"I have something for you," Felicity whispered to the wizard. "A gift. It's in my bedroom. Stay here and I'll go and get it." She dashed out of the room and Galibrath could hear the thuds as she bounded up the stairs.

The wizard sat on the sofa and waited for Felicity to come back down. He wished his head would stop pounding and he rubbed at his eyes. He should be used to it by now. But it would go away. It always did. Though only a week ago, the witch doctor in Funny Bone Surgery had told him, rather harshly, to go on a diet. He snorted. How absurd! She was just confusing 'fat' with 'cuddly'.

He looked about the room. It was a very cosy house, he mused. A real home. He liked the way the sofa was drawn up next to the fire and the scattering of family photos on the cabinet. There was a lot of love here and he shook his head sadly. He wished his own home had been like this.

He glanced at the Christmas tree standing in front of the window. Perched on the top was a fairy, her fragile wings folded down over her back. He struggled up from the sofa and rubbed his aching neck. Been sitting down too long, he thought. Stretching his arms, he ambled over to the tree.

"You are a pretty lass," he whispered to the fairy, "but you must be a bit lonely up there all on your own." He stood still and listened. He could hear Felicity's mum and dad in the kitchen chatting about the bottle of wine they'd been drinking from all evening. It was still full. Galibrath chuckled. He must sort that. Quickly, he leaned closer to the fairy and whispered,

"Wrongly imprisoned and clasped to a tree,
From your trance awaken, I've set you free."

The fairy opened her eyes and very gently unfolded her wings. Gracefully, she rose up and floated a few feet in front of his face. "Thank you," she peeped, giving him a tiny curtsy. Then, in a burst of light, she vanished.

"Do you like our tree?" a voice called from behind him.

Galibrath turned around and smiled at Felicity. "Yes, I do."

"I helped to decorate it. I even chose the fairy to go on the top."

"What's that?" Galibrath hastily quizzed her,

stirring her away from such shark-infested waters. He pointed to the parcel in Felicity's hands.

"Your gift," she explained. She lugged it over to the coffee table where they had been playing cards. "Open it."

Feeling like a kid, Galibrath tore at the wrapping. He stopped, snorting in surprise. "Why, it's - Pickle Pumpkin!"

"Who!?"

"Oh, er - nobody."

"I found it in the junkroom. It was so dirty, so I cleaned it and polished up the frame. It took forever." She looked anxiously at the wizard who looked as if he'd been hypnotised. "You do like it, don't you?"

She watched Galibrath reach out and gently touch the face of the young girl in the picture. "My old dad took this," he murmured. "I forgot I even had it." Then, "It's the best present anybody has ever given to me."

The wizard covered his mouth with the back of his hand and coughed. "See you," he rasped.

"Bye," replied Felicity. "Perhaps, I should help you..."

Galibrath waved a hand at her. "Stop worrying. Just need to stretch my legs, is all. Go on in now, Felicity, before you freeze."

"OK, OK - boss!" She began to close the door, but stopped. "Thanks for the gift, and thanks for coming."

"Thanks for the invite."

"See you in a couple of days then, at The Wishing Shelf."

Galibrath nodded, rallying a smile and reluctantly she shut the door.

The old wizard grunted and rested his shoulder on the shed. The drums in his head were now enjoying the company of a trumpet and his throat felt as if a boa constrictor was wrapped around it, squeezing the life out of him.

Maybe he had been a bit rash giving Felicity the flying carpet tonight. It was a very long walk home. But how her eyes had shone and the picture had been such a lovely surprise.

Gingerly, he let go of the shed. Picking up the

picture and slipping it under his arm, he began to tramp slowly back to the shop. The street was flat, but it was like climbing a mountain; as if his boots were filled with lead.

He tripped, his dragging feet catching on a cobble. Gasping, he flung out his hands, dropping the picture and falling to the path. He rested there, his fists pressed to his brow. A full orchestra were going at it in there and now his hands and knees were cut and bleeding too. Sighing, he clambered to his feet, picked up the picture for a second time, and stumbled on.

Finally, he reached the shop and he staggered in. Dropping the picture on the sofa, he grasped hold of the banister and hauled himself up to his bedroom. Once there, he lay down and fell instantly asleep.

A dorfmoron, growling and spitting, brought the club crashing down but the wizard jumped back, stumbling, cutting his knee on a small rock.

He was being driven back, closer and closer to the cliff's edge. He cast a spell. "ROOTIFY!" Followed by a second, stronger this time, more potent but the monster brushed it away like an annoying fly.

The wizard stood on the brink of the abyss as the dorfmoron swung the club and Galibrath fell, screaming, plunging to his death.

Chapter 9

The West Wing of Lupercus Castle, Third Spire on the Right

The witch was perched on a stool next to a steaming, black cauldron and with a wooden spoon she slowly stirred the bubbling soup. Spices in fat glass jars were scattered on a table just next to her and a book was spread open on her lap.

Felicity watched her pick up one of the jars, sprinkle some silver powder in her hand and fling it into the pot. Gently, she stirred it with the spoon. Instantly, a cloud of yellow gas shot up from the cauldron and drifted across the kitchen. Felicity held her breath and pinched her nose with her fingers.

"A really good potion always smells a tad

nasty," the witch mumbled. The cauldron started to tremble and jerk, belching out a sunset-red fog.

"It smells like old socks," spluttered back Felicity. She was having difficulty holding her breath and speaking at the same time. "I bet it's yucky to drink."

The witch chortled. "Good medicine always tastes ghastly too," she lectured her. She began to study the book on her lap.

She was very tall, much taller than Felicity and her skin was smooth and soft. Not a wart in sight. She had brown, wavy curls and her eyes were a deep green. Over her purple dress she had on a simple orange apron and her legs and feet were bare. She was much too pretty to be a witch, thought Felicity.

She had floated through the door two days ago, followed by four grumbling imps laden down with books, jars and one huge black cauldron.

The imps had since vanished.

She spent most of her time in the kitchen, mixing potions and muttering spells, and every so often she would dip a cup into the steaming pot and carry it on a tray from the kitchen and up to the sick wizard. Felicity didn't know her name and she was too scared to ask. It seemed, or so Al told her, that she was the best witch doctor in town.

"This is masterwart," she announced, holding up a purple-filled jar. "Tricky to get hold of. Grows around the left wisdom tooth of a shubablybub." She counted three drops into the cauldron. "And this is catmint." She held up a second jar. It was brownish-looking and peppered with pink blobs. "Good for fever and dry skin. Oh, but never try it if you think you might be pregnant; if you do, the baby will be popping out a month or two early."

"Not likely," muttered Felicity. "Do you think I look fat then?"

The witch chuckled and added a splash of this too. "It's important to get the ingredients just right or Galibrath will be growing horns." She smirked. "Though, I do know the remedy for that."

She picked up the book from her lap and flicked through the pages. "Now, where is that - oh yes!" She stopped flicking and began to read the open page. "Stir in the frog's eyes, crush the eucalyptus, add one tablespoon of spikenard, cook gently until the potion thickens." She put the book back down and began to search the jars for the ingredients she needed.

"Is that a cookbook?" Felicity asked.

The witch looked up. "This is 'The Jumbo Book of Mumbo Jumbo'. It is full of recipes; tells me what to add, how much, when to stir. Just like any cookbook, I suppose, but the ingredients are a little more bizarre." As if to prove the point, she picked up a jar of frogs' eyes and dropped six of them into the cauldron. It growled and belched out a second cloud of red fog.

The witch plonked in the rest of the ingredients and then picked up a ladle and dipped it into the bubbling broth. She put it to her lips and sipped. "Mmm." She peered into the cauldron, thoughtfully. "Something is missing."

She looked at her collection of jars. "Maybe a drop of sandalwood. No, too rich. Mugwort, perhaps, but then, a little boring." She reached over the table and picked up a small jar hidden at the back. "Spearmint! That's what it needs.

Good for kissing too." She winked at Felicity and added a sprinkle to the cauldron. She took a second sip. "Perfect. Do you want to try it?"

Felicity shook her head staunchly. If it smelt of her granddad's old slippers, it was bound to taste of her granddad's old slippers.

She watched Galibrath's nurse dip a cup in the bubbling soup and place it on a silver tray. She bustled over to the door.

"Will it help?" blurted out Felicity. "Your tonic there. Will it help Galibrath to get better?"

The witch stopped and turned back to look at her. She smiled at her kindly but it was the kind of smile people give when they tell you that your dog has been run over, or that you have failed to get in the netball team, or that you have to move house. Felicity swallowed. Her throat felt tight as if a hangman's rope was coiled around it.

"Try not to worry," the witch told her. "Galibrath is a powerful wizard. His mind is strong, his will even stronger and my potion will help."

Felicity watched her go. She wasn't allowed to see Galibrath. He was too ill, she had been told. The cauldron spluttered and yet another reddish cloud rose up. She shot it a dirty look, put her hand over her mouth and darted out of the kitchen. Then she wandered off in search of Al.

Felicity found him in the front of the shop talking in whispers to a very scary-looking creature. It was small, not much bigger than the imp, with grey, leathery skin and a swishing, scaly tail. Long wings were folded down over a humped back, the tips just grazing the stone floor, and a fat snout sprouted out from a wrinkled face over a line of jagged teeth.

It looked very fierce.

Felicity watched in horror as a clawed hand slid out from under one of the wings and rested on the imp's back.

"Al, are you OK?" she asked, running into the room. They turned and looked at her.

"Yes." Al frowned, his eyes a little vacant. Nothing unusual there. "Why shouldn't I be?"

"I, er, just thought, erm...," stuttered Felicity.

"My name is Geoffrey," the creature crooned in a soft voice. He held out a clawed hand. Felicity looked at him in surprise. He was very well-spoken and sounded more like a country gentleman than a...

"Geoffrey is a gargoyle," Al announced.

"Oh." She shook the claw. "Lovely to er - meet you."

"Nice to meet you too." His claw was surprisingly soft and not at all unpleasant to touch.

"Geoffrey is an old friend of Galibrath's," Al continued. "He heard that he was not feeling too well."

"I was wondering if there was anything I could do," the gargoyle offered kindly. "Galibrath was a great help a couple of years ago when I was having a spot of trouble with a troll."

"Oh," Felicity mumbled for a second time. She still had not got used to chatting to the peculiar folk who visited the shop. She was never sure whether she should shake their paw or pat them on the head.

"It was a terrible time," the gargoyle sighed. "The troll wanted to chisel me off my spire. I'd been there for almost two hundred years, I would have had no place else to go."

"How did Galibrath help you?" asked Felicity, finding her voice at last.

"He sold me a book, now what was it called...?"

"'Crouching in Corners and Lurking under Windows. A Gargoyle's Rights'," the imp peeped up, helpfully.

"Yes, yes, that was it. Saved the day. The troll did not even know what a book was so I read out the bit on chiselling laws and that was that. Now every gargoyle in Eternus has a copy. We owe Galibrath a lot. He even held a speech at my wedding. Anyway, if there is anything I can do to help, just ask. Al here knows where I live."

"Yes," piped up the imp, nodding. "The West Wing of Lupercus Castle, third spire on the right."

Geoffrey smiled crookedly, and slowly turned around. He seemed to be having a spot of trouble gripping the stone floor with his taloned feet. "Cheerio," he called, rocking over to the door.

Felicity waved at his grey stony back.

The books were oddly quiet in the shop, many of them crouched in corners, whispering and nudging each other. The 'Witch Spotter's' book even plodded over to Felicity and asked if there was anything the books could do to help. She assured her there was not.

"Deary me, you look so pale. Can I cook you up a steaming bowl of toadstool and gooseberry soup?"

"No, honest, I'm fine." Felicity managed a feeble grin. "It's just that, we..."

"I know. Try not to get too upset," the book comforted her. "I can have a bit of a pep-talk with the other books. See that they dust and keep in order."

Felicity nodded her thanks. "That would be an enormous help."

The book waddled off back to her shelf, but then stopped. She spun on a corner to face Felicity. "My granddaddy - never met him, of course, why, he was around oh, three hundred years ago - he always used to say, 'There's no point in worrying about things you can do nothing about'."

"But, maybe there is something I can do."

The book nodded gravely. "Yes, yes, look on the bright side. My granddaddy used to say that too."

The shop was extremely busy; magical folk visiting day and night to wish Galibrath well and to bring him presents. Felicity loved it when a fairy had fluttered in and draped a 'THINKING OF YOU' banner over the stools and round and around the sofa. Later, a crowd of giddy impsters had stomped in with 'Get Well Soon' cards they had made in school.

On Friday morning, a sobbing giant lumbered in carrying a huge bunch of grapes. He stood in the middle of the shop, large tears rolling down his cheeks. Felicity worked on trying to comfort him as Al ran around catching the tears in a big red bucket. After seven cheese and pickled eyeball rolls and nine gigantic mugs of slug and daffodil tea he stopped blubbering and was calm enough to speak.

"I 'erd 'alibrath ain't too 'ud," he boomed, as he wiped a bogey on his sleeve.

"What?" said Al.

"I says, I 'erd 'alibrath ain't too 'ud!"

The imp scratched his head and looked to Felicity for help.

She sighed. "He says, 'I 'erd 'alibrath ain't too 'ud'." Al walked off in disgust.

And then Tantalus popped in.

"Where is he?" he hissed, glaring down at the cowering imp.

"Get away from him!" Felicity yelled. "Why don't you pick on somebody your own size?" She stood on her tiptoes and worked on looking as tall as possible.

Tantalus looked down at her and sniggered. "You're a thumb taller than a garden gnome," he sneered. Felicity pursed up her lips as the wizard turned and glowered back at the imp. "Where is he? No fibs now. Remember I could eat you for supper and I wouldn't even have to chew."

"B-b-bedroom," the imp stammered, keeping his eyes tightly shut.

Tantalus walked briskly to the door, but Felicity blocked his way, her arms folded, her face a stony mask.

"Why do you want to see Galibrath?" she

seethed. "He's sick, so let him be."

"MOVE!" spat Tantalus.

"NO!" Felicity shouted back. She was good at shouting. Her P.E. teacher had told her so. Her legs felt all mushy and she had to clench her hands to stop them from trembling. "I'm not scared of you, you - bully!"

"Really!? Well, you should be." Like lightning Tantalus's hand shot out and swept Felicity off her feet. It was like being hit by a double-decker bus and she fell roughly to the floor. "Kids today, no manners, no manners at all." He marched from the room.

"You OK?" Al asked, skipping over and helping Felicity to her feet.

"Yes, I'm fine." She rubbed her bashed elbow. "Really, I'm OK."

"You must be mad," the imp scolded her, shaking his finger in her face. "He could have put a spell on you and turned you into a vampire bat - or a lump of chewing gum on the bottom of a dorfmoron's boot. He could have killed you."

Felicity looked at the open door. "I wonder what he wants with Galibrath. You don't think he'll hurt him, do you?"

"Perhaps he'll conjure up a bunch of flowers for him," Al suggested.

She threw him a sour look.

"I think I'll pop in the kitchen and put the kettle on. Fancy a cuppa?"

But before she could utter a word, the frightened imp flicked his fingers and vanished.

Felicity stood silently in the bookshop. She had no idea what to do. She was scared too, very scared, but how could she let poor Galibrath handle Tantalus on his own? He was too poorly. She would just have to go up there and help him. But she had no clue how.

She crept out of the room and down the corridor, past the Never Ending Junkroom and the cupboard with the monster in it. Stopping at the foot of the steps, she looked up. But it was so dark at the top. The landing was a jumble of shadows and her imagination could see all sorts of monsters hidden in the doorways. Gritting her teeth, she started to climb, one step at a time, gripping the banister to help steady her hand.

Finally, she got to the top and the landing. She could see the door to the wizard's room; it was slightly ajar but oddly she could hear no sounds. Her heart skipped a beat. Perhaps Tantalus was strangling Galibrath right now in his sleep! So she rushed to the door and flung it open.

Chapter 10

Yellow and White Daffodils

Tantalus was standing over Galibrath's bed watching his brother sleep. To Felicity's surprise, the wizard's ashen face no longer looked angry, and his eyes seemed only to mirror a terrible sorrow.

"My old brother's not looking his best, is he?" he whispered.

"Why do you worry?" Felicity shot back, hotly.

Tantalus lifted his head and turned and looked at her. "There was a time, many years ago, when I loved my brother," he murmured wearily. "But people change. Things are spoken that can't be unspoken."

"You turned your back on him."

"No, he turned his back on me. He took The Wishing Shelf away from me." The wizard shook his head sadly. "I can never forgive him for doing that. Not even now when he is knocking on death's door."

"You're lying," seethed Felicity. "YOU'RE LYING!" She felt tears welling up in her eyes but she blinked them away fiercely. She was not going to let Tantalus see her cry.

The wizard marched over to her, his eyes flashing. "This old fuddy duddy is dying and very soon The Wishing Shelf will belong to me." Felicity looked up at him in horror. "And when it is, my first job will be to sort 'Staffing'."

"Give it a rest, Tantalus," boomed a strong voice.

Felicity nearly jumped out of her skin. Standing by the door, only a few feet away, was a man with the reddest beard she had ever seen. He was very skinny, like a string bean, and he was tall too, even taller than Tantalus so he had to stoop so as not to hit his head on the ceiling. He had on a kilt, a fluffy sporran and long socks and sandals. Curiously, he held a red-spotted umbrella in his left hand.

"Hyperion!" Tantalus exclaimed, looking uncomfortable. "I didn't hear you..."

"Obviously," uttered Hyperion coldly, glowering at Tantalus. He took a step closer to the other wizard. "What are you doing here?" he growled.

Tantalus smiled feebly. "Why, not happy to see me?"

Hyperion grunted. "I'm about as happy to see you as a skunk at a lawn party. Now, what do you want?"

Surprisingly, considering the tartan kilt, he did not sound Scottish at all.

"I was just visiting my poor, sick brother. He's terribly ill you know." Tantalus dropped his gaze and looked slyly at Felicity. "If anything were to happen to him..."

Felicity snorted in disgust.

"Now you have seen him, you can go." Hyperion slapped the umbrella on his open palm, the tip sparking ominously. "No doubt you are needed in Hedes Spine. Some poor wizard who needs swindling."

Tantalus mustered a false laugh and licked his lips. "You must be joking, of course," he whined. "What a jester you are, Hyperion."

The wizard stared at him. "Of course I'm

joking," he deadpanned, but his words were drenched in scorn.

Like two boxers just before the bell, the two wizards glared at each other. Felicity looked from one to the other and nervously took a step back. She felt so helpless. She just wished they'd go; let her sit and hold Galibrath's hand and listen to his farfetched yarns.

Over in his bed, Galibrath uttered a low grumble. Tantalus threw Hyperion a sickly sort of smile and turned to Felicity. "I'll be seeing you soon, Brady," he muttered. He leant a little closer and whispered in her ear. "Very soon." Holding his robes tightly around him, he brushed past Hyperion and walked stiffly away. Felicity let out a sigh of relief.

"Did he frighten you?" asked Hyperion, turning to Felicity.

"He'd frighten a red-horned devil."

"But you stood up to him."

Felicity thought for a moment. "Tantalus is a bully," she said soberly. "You have to stand up to them. If you don't..."

"If you don't, they'll never let you be."

Felicity nodded.

"My name is Hyperion." They shook hands.

"Hi, I'm Felicity."

They walked over to where the old wizard was sleeping. Next to the bed was a small wooden cabinet, on it a bubbling cup of tonic and a crystal vase full of yellow and snowy-white daffodils.

Felicity scowled. Maybe Tantalus had conjured up flowers after all.

"So, how's my old chum doing?"

Felicity shrugged her shoulders. "Not too good, I think, but nobody will tell me why he's ill." She looked up at Hyperion. "Can you tell me?"

"Do you think it will help?"

"My dad told me to always face up to a problem, but how can I if I don't know what it is?"

There was a silence. "You must never tell another soul. Do you understand?"

"Yes," Felicity said solemnly. "I promise."

Hyperion looked down at the sleeping Galibrath. "Fifty, maybe sixty years ago this old wizard worked for WANDD. That's W-A-N-D-D."

"WANDD - what's that?"

"Wizards' Army vs. Night Demons and Dorfmorons."

"Night demons, what are they?" asked Felicity curiously.

"Demons," said the wizard matter-of-factly. "They come out at night."

"Oh!" Her face reddened. "Sorry."

Hyperion kept his voice low and his eyes kept darting around the room. "Galibrath was an agent and a good one, my best in fact."

"He worked for you?"

"Yes, but it was a long time ago." He smiled sadly. "We were much younger. We cared about nothing and everything. We lived for adventure, to fight evil. Nothing could hurt us. We thought we were invincible.

"Galibrath was tracking a dorfmoron in the Trimmel Mountains, far across Eternus. After three days of climbing and hunting in caverns, he cornered it. It was quite a battle and Galibrath had to use all his strength to defeat it. But it left him exhausted and drained of all his powers." Hyperion sighed wearily.

"But how...?"

"He was attacked, but not by a demon or a dorfmoron. No, a thing far more lethal, so powerful that Galibrath, being so tired, could not fight it."

Felicity held her breath.

"Giants' flu."

"Flu!?" That didn't sound so bad.

"No, Felicity. Giant's flu. Did you know, and not many people do, a bad case of it will put a fully grown giant on his back for a month. You can imagine the harm it caused to a wizard the size of Galibrath."

"But that was years ago," mustered Felicity, confused. "Why is it attacking him now?"

"Galibrath is an old man," Hyperion said, gently. "He has been fighting this for over half a century but now, well - he hasn't the strength to fight it anymore. I'm sorry, Felicity."

"I'm not dead yet, you know," uttered a croaky voice. They looked down in surprise. Galibrath, his eyes half open, smiled up at them feebly.

"Look who's up!" Hyperion exclaimed. "How do you feel?"

The wizard grunted and sat up slowly in the

bed. "Terrible," he muttered. "I must have drunk over a gallon of tonic. Disgusting stuff. No idea what she puts in it but I think I'm growing horns." Felicity puffed up his pillows and he lay gratefully back down.

He looked so frail. He seemed to have lost most of his fat and he looked drowned in his baggy pyjamas. His once round face was now thin and bony, and loose folds of skin hung from his cheeks and chin. Bloodshot eyes peered out from deep craters and lines of pain were etched deeply into his pale face.

"You look much better," Felicity fibbed awkwardly, spotting he still had the key to Articulus's cabinet around his neck.

Galibrath snorted. "I lost a lot of fat, anyway. The witch doctor in Funny Bone Surgery will be over the moon." He looked over at the steaming cup of tonic sitting on his bedside cabinet and pulled a face. It looked like muddy, wet soup.

"You had a visitor," Hyperion said gravely. Galibrath lifted his eyebrows. "Your brother."

"Tantalus! What did he want?" The frail wizard took a deep rasping breath and coughed. "Had to gloat over my sickness, I suppose."

"No, he seemed sort of sad." Felicity hesitated. "He told me - years ago that he loved you."

Galibrath lowered his head and stared down at his hands - they were trembling slightly. He sighed and tucked them under his bed sheets. "You were here, with him, in this room?"

"I..."

"Felicity thought he might harm you so she followed him up here," interrupted Hyperion gently.

"I thought, if he saw how sick you were, he might - but, he just seemed - upset."

The sound of running footsteps made them turn to the door. Galibrath's nurse ran in, a large ladle clutched menacingly in her hand, followed by a gasping Al. "What's going on?!" she shouted. "Where's that toad Tantalus? Al tells me..." She stopped, her mouth dropping open. "Hyperion! I - I had no idea," she stammered. "I would never have come barging in..."

Felicity had a feeling Hyperion was a very important wizard.

"My dear Dorothy, calm yourself," Hyperion soothed her. "Felicity has already sent Tantalus packing."

"Felicity!" she cried, still brandishing the ladle.

"I went to get help," Al squeaked meekly.

"I didn't do anything. Really." Everybody was looking at her and she felt her face go beetroot-red. "I only spoke to him - for a second or two. There was no hand to hand combat or anything."

"RUBBISH!" bellowed the kilted wizard. He patted Felicity on the back. "I don't know many WANDD agents who would stand up to Tantalus, never mind a young girl."

"You were very brave," said Galibrath softly.

"I went to get help," squeaked Al for a second time.

Hyperion knelt down and put his hand tenderly on Galibrath's shoulder. Felicity noticed his eyes lingered on the glass key to Articulus's cabinet. "You must be tired. I will let you sleep, but I will see you soon, old chum."

"Not too soon, I hope," croaked Galibrath gravely. The two wizards looked sadly at each other and Hyperion ponderously nodded his head.

"Sleep well," he whispered. He stood up and walked slowly out of the room. The others turned to go too.

"Felicity, stay and chat to me," Galibrath murmured. Dorothy pursed up her lips but held her tongue. She ushered Al out of the room and gently shut the door. "Now tell me, have we had many customers?"

Perching on the bed, Felicity felt for the wizard's hand. "A fairy popped in, and a school trip of impsters with 'Get Well Soon' cards for you. But they were so badly behaved; they kept pulling the curls on Al's big toe and flicking conkers at the 'Witch Spotter's' book. Oh, and a gargoyle turned up too. He told me to tell you, if there's anything he can do to help, just ask."

"A gargoyle, you say!" Galibrath coughed. "Folk can be very kind." He sat back wearily in the bed, resting his head on the pillow. They sat in silence for a moment and somewhere a clock ticked loudly; a ponderous sound which seemed to slow down the seconds.

"Tell me more about the shop," whispered Galibrath. "Tell me about the books. Have they been misbehaving?" He sat up and looked at

Felicity earnestly. "Articulus, is he safe? Is he still in his cabinet?"

"Yes, yes, really, don't worry." Wondering why Galibrath kept calling the book a 'He', Felicity put her hands firmly on the wizard's shoulders and he lay back down with hardly a whimper. "All the books say 'hi'; they have been very good. They even offered to dust each other and to stay in order."

"Wow!" Galibrath smiled weakly. "I must be ill." He closed his eyes. "You probably think I'm a very lazy shopkeeper; all the dust and cobwebs, but many years ago when I lost," he swallowed, "the girl I loved, I seemed to lose interest in the smaller tasks in life. No excuse, I know."

Felicity nodded. The girl in the picture, she wondered. Pickle Pumpkin? She spotted it now hung proudly over his bed.

She looked back at the wizard and shuffled her feet.

"Is there something you wish to ask me, Felicity?"

"No, well - yes, I..."

"Felicity?"

"It's just that..."

"Yes?"

"Tantalus told me that if anything happened to you, The Wishing Shelf would be his." She did not want to ask. She was too scared of the answer. But she had to do it. She had to know.

Galibrath chewed thoughtfully on his lip. "Tantalus is not - evil, you know. He's just - jumbled up."

"But he's so, so - slimy," said Felicity with feeling.

The old wizard chuckled. "Do not worry, the bookshop is safe." Slowly, Galibrath stretched out his hand, resting it on the cabinet next to the bed. Felicity spotted the top drawer was slightly open. "In here you will find my will. I have left the bookshop in the hands of a person I love very much, who I think - hope, will remember the customs of my family.

"But Felicity, I must ask for your help. My imp, Al, will need to be looked after if I - well, you know. He is not very strong. He will need a big sister. Can you be that for him?"

"I promise," mumbled Felicity, smudging away a tear. She took his hand tightly in her own. "But you'll be better soon. I just know you will."

He smiled at her and for a moment his eyes sparkled. "Exciting adventures lay in front of you, Felicity Brady," he murmured. "You will face great perils and often you will have to walk the most dangerous paths, but walk them you will." He took another shallow breath. "Remember, at the end of every difficult journey is the most wonderful treasure. Not a chest of gold or a string of pearls." He looked closely at Felicity. "Do you know what the treasure is?" Felicity shook her head and wiped a tear from her eye. "That you complete the journey, child."

"Have you completed your journey, Galibrath?"

"The Wishing Shelf, tell me more about The Wishing Shelf."

So she did. She described how warm it was now that the fire was lit and how the cactus in the window had begun to blossom pink flowers. She told him of the magic folk who had been in and the books she and Al had sold to them. She joked about a bow-legged dwarf and the giant who had almost flooded the shop with his tears.

Galibrath lay silently and listened.

She described Al's new t-shirt, 'Make Tea, Not War' and his experiments in the kitchen. He had just invented a tea brewed from a tadpole and a bag of liquorice. It tasted vile. Occasionally, the old wizard would open his eyes and look fondly at her. Then the heads of the daffodils on the cabinet bowed, the petals turned brown, and he did not open them anymore.

Chapter 11

A Unicorn in the Woods

Host of the greatest procession seen,
Bathed in sunshine and carpeted green,
Wrapped in a cloak of brilliant blue,
And lightly covered in a sprinkling of dew,
Like dandelion clocks blown astray,
The clouds up above scuttled away.

A time for reflection for all who knew,
The precious cargo hidden from view,
Shrouded by the breath of six white horses,
A magic carpet drawn by magical forces,
Making their way to the top of the hill,
Passing the sails of the old windmill.

A modest man to a humble grave,
Amongst snapdragons and Bethlehem sage,
Like bees to bright petals the crowds were drawn,
From all over Eternus they came to mourn,
Feelings ebbed from their crumpled faces,
Remembering times and forgotten places.

Great wizards and witches led the parade,
Flying above them on carpets they'd made,
A funeral march, a thousand strong,
Chanting the words of a timeless song,
And it swayed to the beat of the gentle breeze,
The rhythm tapped out by the leaves on the trees.

Formed with the world, the wondrous sprite,
And fairies who guide the lost traveller at night,
Impossible pranksters, the mischievous imps,
And bow-legged giants with lop-sided limps,
Goblins with dorfmorons on tether,
Blue jacket, red cap and grey owl's feather.

A sprinkling of glitter lit up the sky,
As a cloud of fairies fluttered by,
And some playful chaps, those dinky elves,
To the troupe teleported themselves,
Wrapped up warm for they detest the cold,
And in their hands hired wands they hold.

Escaping their caverns, their hidden homes,
Seldom in public the reclusive gnomes,
A highly inquisitive, curious clan,
Taller than elves but shorter than man,
White hair on top of their bearded faces,
Consumed by the crowd in the smallest of places.

Caught in the sunlight the lectern glistened,
And beneath Hyperion they tearfully listened,
He addressed each of the sorrowful throng,
His voice compassionate, yet powerful and strong,
The laughter suggested some jokes were told,
He would have liked that, our friend of old.

Here rests, the epitaph begins,
A worthy wizard, a man of few sins,
He loved ice cream, he also says,
And chocolate sauce on strawberry sundaes,
A man of clear vision who could always see,
A loving man. Hyperion looked at me.

Each of their footsteps rocking the land,
In the shadow of a giant's hand,
I spy a young girl, a tear cleans her cheek,
She listens intently for the comfort she seeks,
She stands to attention so as not to betray,
But her lower lip trembles and gives her away.

He turned to the carpet and raising his arm,
Began to recite the ascension charm:
We bid farewell to our wizard friend,
His earthly career is at an end,
Gather up your soul magician most high,
And surrender your spirit to the forgiving sky.

It rained a cascade of magical dust,
An old brass bell was gently hushed,
A gust of wind wrapped his body up tight,
Releasing his spirit to begin its flight,
A chilling stillness crept through the air,
Where the body had lain the carpet was bare.

Like snow in spring, the mourners melt away,
So I sneak up to where my once-love now stays,
I tell him, I didn't mean to lose sight,
I didn't mean to quarrel and I didn't mean to fight,
We missed out on so many years,
I should have been stronger, faced my fears.

I tell him, I saw a unicorn in the woods today,
In solitude roam, a flowing white mane,
With horn of gold and eye of blue,
This is the magic pure and true,
To be with me and see, I pray,
The unicorn I saw in the woods today.

Chapter 12

A Toothbrush With Only One Bristle

For the first time in her life, Felicity wished the school bell had not rung. She trudged down the steps, children spilling past her, bags swinging, dashing to get the bus. What would they be doing tonight - chomping spaghetti, playing on the computer? Maybe even doing homework? A week ago she would have felt sorry for them, but not now. Now Galibrath was dead and she had to face working in The Wishing Shelf with only Al to help her.

Walking slowly out of the gate, she wondered who the wizard had left the shop to in his will. The night he had died, he had told her The Wishing Shelf was safe, that somebody very close to him would be taking over. But who was that somebody? Hyperion maybe, or the girl in the picture, or some witch or wizard Felicity had never even met. And would they still want her to stay and work there?

She stopped at a pelican crossing but the man was red so she pushed the button. The funeral had been horrible. She had never lost anybody before, except for her dog, Ketchup. But he had been really old. Even her grandpa was still tottering about, although he occasionally forgot where he lived and when he came for Sunday dinner, it was not always on a Sunday.

The green man flashed and beeped at her. With her eyes glued to the street, she plodded on, past a coffee shop, stools that were too wet to sit on littering the pavement. Then, by the library, she turned left.

She felt so bad. Bad, because at Galibrath's funeral she had been thrilled to be in Eternus at last - to see the unicorns, the troops of imps and the goblins in their green jackets and red caps. But now, maybe, she would not be able to go back.

Her feet dragged on the cobbles as she at last walked over the bridge and down the stone steps to the bookshop. Under her breath, she whispered "Gummy Bears and Liquorice Allsorts." She pushed on the door. Wallop! "Ouch!" she yelped and she stepped back, rubbing her aching shoulder. "Gummy Bears and Liquorice Allsorts," she repeated, a little louder this time. But the door stayed doggedly shut. "Al!" she hollered, giving the door an angry kick.

She moved to the window and, cupping her hands over her eyes, peered into the shop. To her surprise, she could see imps - lots of them, in grey t-shirts and baseball caps. They were scurrying around the shop carrying books and piling them up in a muddled heap on the sofa. Felicity jumped and she felt the hairs on the back of her neck prickle up.

Hunkered on the floor by the sofa was what looked like a huge, bushy dog; the sort you'd expect the devil to own, not the sort you'd see in a film star's handbag. Covered in a thick matted pelt, it had a long scabby nose and slanty eyes. A tooth, like a scythe, jutted out from chunky grey lips and silvery whiskers twitched on the chin.

A shadow fell over her, making her jump.

Somebody or something was walking past the window and was about to leave the shop. She pulled back from the glass and bolted to the door. It opened. "Doctor Dement!" she yelled. She could almost have hugged him.

"Why, Felicity," he exclaimed, smiling down at her. "But, it's Fireman Dement, if you don't mind." He squashed a yellow helmet onto his head.

"Oh, sorry." She caught the door with her hand to stop it from closing. "You didn't buy a book today?"

"They cost too much now. Crazy! CRAZY!" He tutted. "Anyway, I need old magic, Galibrath's magic - not this, this - trickery. Anyway, must be off. Cats in trees and all that."

He darted up the steps but at the very top, he stopped. "Galibrath was a wonderful fellow," he called down to her. "Everybody loved him."

Then his moment of lucidity ended and he yelled, "Felicity, never play with matches."

And, with that off his chest, he trotted off.

Puzzled, Felicity walked slowly into the shop, letting the door swing shut behind her. The imps were still piling books up on the sofa and the 'thing' was still crouched by it. Maybe it was asleep, she thought, but then it mustered a soft growl and a slanty eye snapped open. With a startled cry she stumbled back, knocking over a stool and grazing her knee. But it just watched her silently, like a hawk watching a field mouse.

An imp pushed past her dropping a book. She picked it up. "Felicity," it whimpered, flapping a brittle page at her. "Help me! I'm gonna be tossed in a box and thrown in the junkroom."

"Who? Who's taking you to the junkroom?"

"Felicity Brady," hissed a voice she knew all too well. "How do you like my new desk?"

Felicity looked up. Sitting in Galibrath's chair, behind Galibrath's desk was Tantalus and he was grinning from ear to ear.

"But..."

"I know, I know. Bit of a surprise. Actually, I was a little shocked myself." He swung his legs up onto the desk. "So, Brady, you'll be working for me, after all."

"But, Galibrath told me - his will. Galibrath's will."

"Well, I looked everywhere, didn't I, Mr Banks?"

The goblin stepped out of the shadows. "Everywhere," he agreed, with a sly smile. "But we just could not find it - anywhere."

"So, under wizardry law, The Wishing Shelf is now mine, and so, of course is Articulus." He reached for a gold chain hanging around his neck. From it hung a key. The key to the glass case.

"Galibrath would never have wanted you to have The Wishing Shelf; he didn't trust you. I don't trust you!"

"Stroppy," said Tantalus.

"Very," said Banks.

The wizard turned to the goblin. "You know, I don't think I like the name Wishing Shelf. It's so annoyingly sweet. I was thinking Hedes Spine Shop Number 13. Now, that's catchy."

"Why you, you..." but Felicity couldn't think of what to say. So she ran from the room and up to Galibrath's old bedroom. This couldn't be happening, she thought. This just couldn't be happening.

She knelt down in front of the cabinet and yanked out the drawer. Tipping it over, she spilled the contents onto the bed - quills with inky tips, a copy of 'Wizards from Mars, Hags from Venus', Galibrath's old half-moon specs and a mothball. But no will!

"Are we in trouble?" squealed a voice from the doorway. Felicity looked up - it was Al. He was wearing the same grey t-shirt and baseball cap the other imps had been wearing.

Slumping onto the bed, Felicity put her face in her hands. "Yes," she murmured. "Big trouble."

The next two weeks were a nightmare for Felicity, the shop becoming a circus of trolls (the thing crouching by the sofa had been a troll - Al had told her), knobbly-nosed wizards and hooded hags. All the while, Tantalus's army of imps were boxing up Galibrath's old books and flinging them in the junkroom.

Felicity listened in horror as Tantalus ordered the old fireplace to be bricked up and Galibrath's great, great, great grandmother's curtains were torn down. Next, the rugs on the floor were rolled up and stuffed in a big yellow skip along with all the wobbly stools and desks.

But worst of all was Al's suffering as, by order of Tantalus, all tea breaks were banned. He was made to work all day and night, scrubbing the wooden floor with a toothbrush with only one bristle. It was because of the imp that Felicity returned every day. She had promised Galibrath she would look after him and, right now, he needed a lot of looking after.

"I can't go on," whined Al, dropping the toothbrush and sucking on his red raw fingers. "You have to help me."

Felicity shrugged. "But my toothbrush's at home."

"Not to scrub the floor! You have to talk to Tantalus - I mean, Mr Falafel." He looked about nervously. "I have no skin left on my fingers or my knees."

Felicity patted the tearful imp on the head and rubbed one of his pointy ears. "I'll try," she promised. "Tantalus just laughs at me - but I'll try."

She left the imp sitting on the floor in the

corridor and went to find her new boss, but she knew it was no good. She had no clue why Tantalus didn't just sack her. Maybe, he just enjoyed watching her suffer as The Wishing Shelf was torn apart and Galibrath's dreams were destroyed. But she would not give up. She could not. Al was counting on her.

"Hold him, you fool!" Tantalus's voice boomed down the corridor. There was a howl and a growl, then Tantalus's voice even louder. "Trip it up! Jump on it! JUMP ON IT!"

As Felicity darted up the corridor she could see Tantalus with his back to her, next to the stairs. He seemed very excited, jumping up and down and flapping his arms as if he was trying to take off. She edged closer. The door to the cupboard was open and Cruncher was sitting on what looked like a large mop-head.

"Brady!" exclaimed the wizard, turning to beam at her in a demented sort of way. "Look what I just found in my cupboard - a very small monster."

The mop-head snarled and opened a surprisingly big mouth, biting down on Cruncher's bum. The puffdolt's eyes bulged and he began to clamber to his feet.

"Hold it!" Tantalus ordered sharply, jabbing at the puffdolt with a spindly finger. Cruncher tutted, grunted and flopped back down, squashing the mop-head even flatter. But it still kept hold of his bum. "Now then Brady, what do you think I should do with my new pet? I thought he would make a rather cosy jumper."

Felicity glared at him. "Let him go," she blurted out hotly. "He never hurt you. The cupboard is his home."

"No, no, Brady. The cupboard *was* his home. Now he will have a new home - on a shelf in my wardrobe." Tantalus sniggered. He crouched down and grasped a handful of the monster's shaggy locks. "He's a bit scrawny. Maybe, there won't be enough wool for a jumper." He scratched his brow with his other hand. "I suppose I could turn him into socks. You know, I have an awful time with my feet."

"Galibrath would never have..."

"Galibrath, Galibrath, Galibrath - I'm sure he would have fed it chocolate and wrapped it in woolly blankets. But he's dead - d-e-a-d and I'm not, so socks it is." He stood up and stalked off down the corridor and into the bookshop, Felicity hot on his heels.

"Tantalus, I mean, Mr Falafel, I want to talk to you about Al." But Tantalus ignored her. Kicking imps out of his way, he strode over to his desk and punched a key on a shiny new cash till. The drawer pinged open. Grabbing up a handful of flupoons he stuffed them in a black cloth purse hanging from a string in the folds of his cloak. "Mr Falafel, about Al."

"Al who?"

"Galibrath's Al."

"You mean my Al?"

"Galibrath's Al."

"You mean, MY AL!"

Felicity uttered something under her breath, which sounded a lot like 'Galibrath's Al'.

"What?"

"Why are you being so cruel to him?"

"Me? Cruel?" He feigned a look of shock. "My slaves love me." He grabbed a rosy-cheeked imp by her t-shirt and yanked her off her feet. "You love me, don't you?"

"Yes," squeaked back the imp.

"See. Told you." He tossed the imp over his

shoulder.

"Al's not used to hard work, well, any work really."

Behind the wizard the imp swayed to her feet, stuck out her tongue and toppled over onto her back.

The wizard rubbed his eyes. "He's just an imp. And anyway, why do you care? You're a teenager - you shouldn't care about anything." He chewed on a fingernail. "You must have a few pals you can hang out with or a spot to squeeze."

Felicity's face turned red. "I hate you!" she hissed. "You're a monster and - you smell of erm - rotten cabbage, and your breath, that stinks too of - brussel sprouts and..." but she couldn't think of any more vegetables.

"Making friends, Tantalus?" gushed Banks, sidling up. He winked at Felicity but she just ignored him. He had the sort of eyes that looked out at you, but didn't let you look in. The goblin gave her the creeps and made her feel sick. So now she called him Barf - but not to his face.

"You took your time," grunted Tantalus.

Banks stared at him blankly. "It took me four

days to track them down. You don't find warlords in the phone book under W."

Tantalus glared at Banks and the goblin snapped his mouth shut. They turned to Felicity.

"Why don't you go and help that imp of *yours*," suggested Tantalus. "You can borrow my toothbrush if you want."

"You have a toothbrush?" mumbled Felicity. Banks sniggered, but before Tantalus could think of a cutting reply, Felicity spun on her heels and stomped off. She yanked open the door leading to the corridor and shut it after her - well, almost - she left a small gap, not big enough to see through, but just big enough to hear through.

She dropped down on her knees and put her ear to the crack. She could hear the two of them, just, but the words were muffled and many of them were drowned out by the chatter of imps and the flapping of a book being forced into a box.

Then she caught the word 'Articulus'. Banks had mumbled it and Tantalus had quickly hushed him. Then she heard another word and she drew back in horror. But this was terrible, she thought. He had to be stopped. But how and who could she turn to? She stood up and gently pulled the door shut. Then she helter-skeltered down the corridor.

She found the imp still on his hands and knees, scrubbing feebly at the floor. "Al," she whispered, making him jump and drop the toothbrush. "We have to talk."

He tossed her a dirty look. "I can't. I'm too busy." He picked the toothbrush back up. "And don't sneak up on me. You scared me half to death though I'm halfway to death anyway, so I don't suppose it really matters."

"But it's about Tantalus."

"You spoke to him?" The imp looked up at her with wide eyes. "About me? This job? This SLAVERY!?" He spat out the word. "I need a cup of tea. Four days, now. FOUR DAYS! I'm parched."

"Well, I did try, but..."

The imp's face crumbled and he gave a theatrical sob. "When will it end?" he howled, throwing his hands in the air. The toothbrush clattered to the floor, snapping in two. "No! My brush! MY BRISTLE! MY ONLY PAL!"

A troll lumbered up to them, a path of muddy paw prints blotting the freshly scrubbed wood. Al glared angrily at the beast. "IT'S CALLED A DOORMAT!" he yelled. The troll growled softly and looked down at the imp, baring his teeth.

"Al," hissed Felicity. "Don't annoy him; he's a little bigger than you." She smiled weakly at the troll. "Just ignore the imp," she told the drooling beast. "He's having a bad day."

Growling, the troll twisted his head and glared at Felicity. A furry hand grasped her by the neck and slammed her up to the wall. He stepped up to her, his curved tooth grazing her cheek. "You smell of chicken," it snarled, sniffing her. "I like chicken."

Then Al did something very heroic. He stole between the troll's legs, clasped hold of Felicity's ankle and snapped his fingers. The troll's malevolent eyes vanished, the corridor vanished, and Felicity found herself standing in pitch black. With a whimper, she staggered back, sitting down heavily on what felt like a cardboard box.

"Felicity," came a voice. "It's OK. We're in the junkroom."

"W, w - where?" stammered back Felicity.

"The junkroom. The Never Ending Junkroom."

She heard Al snap his fingers for the second time and a small glowing ball bathed them in light.

It *was* the junkroom and she *was* sitting on a cardboard box - one of many piled all the way up to the cobwebbed ceiling. She turned to Al who was sitting next to her. "Thanks," she muttered, rubbing her aching neck.

The imp smiled. "So, what's the big news?"

Felicity looked at him blankly.

"You know, before you and 'SNUGGLES!' ruined my day. You told me we had to talk."

"Oh yes." Felicity scowled. "You know Tantalus's goblin, Barf?" The imp nodded and chuckled. "He just got back from - well, I don't know where - but he's been tracking down warlords."

"Warlords?" echoed Al.

"Yeah, and that's not all." Felicity was picking up steam now. "He's asked them to some sort of auction, here at The Wishing Shelf."

"What's he going to sell? Galibrath's books?" There was a muffled sob from the box they were sitting on.

"Worse."

"Worse?!"

"Articulus! He's going to sell Articulus."

"But, but he can't," spluttered the imp. "No, no he can't." He shook his head. "Can he?"

Felicity sighed and scratched her chin. "The Wishing Shelf belongs to Tantalus, so I guess so does Articulus. He can do whatever he wants."

"But, can't we tell a WANDD agent?"

"Do you know any WANDD agents?"

"Yes, I do and so do you. Many years ago, I worked for Hyperion. He's the top dog. If we can show him..."

"We need proof," pronounced Felicity boldly, clapping her hands together. "We need Galibrath's will. If we could show Hyperion that Galibrath did not give the shop to his brother, he couldn't sell anything." Then her face fell. "But he's probably burnt it. He's evil but he's not stupid."

"No, no," cried Al, jumping down from the box and turning to her, his eyes sparkling. "You can't burn a wizard's will - or a magic book for that matter. You can't melt it in acid; you can't even cut it up. It's protected by the most powerful of magic."

"Then all we have to do is find the will," said Felicity excitedly.

"Yeah," agreed Al.

"But it could be anywhere."

"Yeah," agreed Al for a second time, but a little more lamely.

"So."

"So."

"So, what is that doing here?" Felicity had just seen the picture, the one she had given Galibrath for Christmas, lying on its back near the door. She pointed at it. "I thought Galibrath hung it over his bed."

The imp spun his head and looked. "He did, but Tantalus took it down." He shrugged. "I guess he didn't like seeing Galibrath happy, or the girl, so he stuffed it in here with the books."

Felicity jumped down off the box and scrambled over a bunch of broken stools to the door. She crouched down, dragged the golf clubs away from the wall and gently rested the picture there.

"What was her name?" she asked, looking more closely at the girl. She really was beautiful with olive skin and long brown hair. Her eyes were full of fun and her smile made Felicity want to smile too.

"Kitta." The imp scrambled over the stools as well. "That's what Galibrath used to call her. I think it was short for Omoikitta."

"What a strange name."

"Yeah, Japanese, I think. Most charm makers seem to be."

Felicity looked thoughtfully at the girl in Galibrath's arms. "Kitta was a charm maker?"

"Still is, I think."

"So, she's a witch," mused Felicity, her face lighting up. "She can do magic."

"Sort of. But Felicity, Kitta isn't here to help us, so..."

"We have to find her. Al, don't you see. Galibrath loved this girl. He trusted her. She can help us find the will. She can stop the Warlords' Auction."

The imp shook his head and frowned. "Felicity, Kitta left Galibrath well over a hundred years ago when he was just a wizard teenager."

"But you told me she was a witch. They live as long as wizards, don't they?"

"Yeah, even longer, but she could be anywhere. Eternus is a big land, you know. That's why they call it Eternus."

Felicity's face fell and she looked back at the picture. They looked so happy, she thought, and so young. Gently, she touched the wizard's face. What would you do, she wondered. How would you find her? And why did you have to die and leave me in this mess? A tear trickled down her cheek and angrily, she brushed it away with the back of her hand. Crying was not going to help, she thought, looking back to the imp. "So, what do you think we should do?"

"Might I be of service?" echoed a shrill voice from inside the box they had been sitting on, making them jump.

The box wobbled and the cardboard lid bulged right in the middle. It bulged a little more and a little more and there was a lot of grunting. Then, with a sort of pinging sound, the top sprang off and a book popped up.

"Phew!" the book wheezed. "It was hot in there and I was right at the bottom."

Felicity clambered back over the broken stools, smiling. It was the 'Witch Spotter's' book - she could tell by the crackly voice. It sounded a lot like her granny.

"Hello," said Felicity.

"Hello," panted the book, lying down on top of another book and fanning her pages. "Oh, that's better. A bit of air, it gets so stuffy, you know?"

"Hmm." Felicity allowed the book a minute to catch her breath. She watched a furry black spider squeeze out from under the box. It seemed to be looking at her. She shuddered - she hated spiders, then, "You can help us find Kitta?"

"Oh no, deary," the book slammed shut and sat up with a creak, "but I know a book who can."

The 'Witch Spotter's' book stood up, leant back on her spine and opened her covers wide. Taking a deep breath, she hollered "WHO'S

GOT THE SEEKING BOOK? COME ON, WHERE Y' HIDING?"

"Not in 'ere," shouted a book from one of the boxes.

"No, can't see him," yelled another.

"He's in 'ere but he's sleeping."

"WELL, PROD HIM!"

Al scrambled back over the stools and whispered "She's off her rocker," in Felicity's ear. She threw him a stern look.

"'Ere he comes, bless him," cried the book in a motherly sort of way, flapping her covers. "He's a good sort but a little shy. I'd better do all the talking."

Felicity nodded and smiled. She had no idea what she would have said anyway. She elbowed the chuckling imp standing next to her and told him to "Shush," and to "Stop it!"

Pushing up the lid of a box marked 'JUNK', a very thin book popped up and peered out at them as if it had no clue what to do next.

"Come on, then," urged the 'Witch Spotter's' book and with a small whoop of joy, the book clambered out of the box and, like a mountain goat, leapt to the floor. It scuttled over to join them.

As Felicity bent down to pick it up she saw that it was rather scruffy - the corners were bent over and the leather was dry and cracked. She blew off some of the dust and attempted to read the faded words on the spine.

"'Seeking a Witch in a Cave, Cavern or Small Castle'," volunteered the small book, helpfully and in a very squeaky voice.

"Oh, that's a cool name," said Felicity.

Al snorted. "What if Kitta lives in a bungalow or a block of flats or..." But everybody ignored him.

"Now, Felicity, hold him in both hands," the other book ordered her. "That's it. Now, say the name of the witch you're seeking."

"Kitta. Oh, no - I mean. Al, what was her name?"

The imp told her.

"OK. Omoikitta."

The book shook in her hands sending tremors down her arms and making her teeth chatter. But she held on. Then, something that felt like a bolt of lightning shot through her body and her hair stood on end. With a yell, she dropped the book on the floor, where it fell open.

"Felicity! Are you OK?" asked Al.

"I - I think so." She reached up and patted down her spiky locks.

Crouching down, Felicity looked curiously at the book lying open at her feet. There only seemed to be one page and on it was some sort of map, but not like any map she had seen before. There was The Wishing Shelf, or a tiny picture of it and above it, a flashing red sign that read - *You're here.*

On the other side of the page there was a drawing of a cottage. It was so detailed, Felicity could see moss growing in the gutters, and there was ivy clinging to the walls. Over the cottage was a second neon sign, but it was flashing green and read - *Omoikitta, charm maker.*

The rest of the map was covered in clumps of forest, snaking rivers and a Wellington-boot shaped lake. There were towering mountains too and a big city. Felicity squinted and peered closer - *Cauldron City,* she read.

"Glad it's not me," muttered Al, looking over Felicity's shoulder. "But, you'll be OK. Anyway, you have a flying carpet."

"What do you mean?" exploded Felicity, twisting her head and glaring at the imp. "I'm not going. You can go. It's your land. You know magic."

"Felicity, if I go Tantalus will guess I'm up to something. But if you go, he'll just think you hated working for him so much that you stayed at home."

"But..."

"He just thinks you're a silly girl."

"Well, he's right," stormed Felicity. "I mean, I wouldn't stand a chance. What if I bump into a dorfmoron-thingy?"

"Nah, doubt it," piped in the 'Witch Spotter's' book. "They live mostly in the mountains. Probably bump into a krakor thunder serpent, or one of Tantalus's trolls."

"Oh, that's all right, then." She dropped down on the floor, wrapping her arms around her knees. She watched a spider scuttle down the wall and under the door. Blimey, they were everywhere.

"If you don't go, Tantalus will probably sell Articulus to a warlord." Al dropped down next to her. "A book that powerful in the hands of a blood-thirsty, power-crazy ..."

"OK, OK, no pressure." She looked back at the map of Eternus.

The imp was still talking to her but she was no longer listening. She was thinking about what Galibrath had told her the night he had died - that she would face great perils, that she would walk the most dangerous paths. Is this what he meant, she wondered. Is this the path?

"Al, please stop nattering in my ear. I have to study this map or I'll never find her."

Slowly, bit by bit, the bookshop door opened, a frosty wind whistling through the gap. So, the Brady-girl had showed up, thought Tantalus. He took a step back, melting into the shadow of Articulus's cabinet. His eight-legged spy had been correct. But, then, his spiders always were which is why he did not stamp on them.

He watched Felicity tiptoe in, a rolled up carpet hanging limply over her shoulder. She stopped. Did she sense him? The fury radiating from his black eyes? No! She possessed the magical powers of a wet nappy. But she was smart, he had to admit that. But much too much of a goody goody. Not the Brady-girl he had known so many years ago.

He watched her creep over to The Clock by the Door and whisper, "Eternus, please."

The wizard's fingers curled. He was tempted to grab her now, toss her in his dungeon with a cup of pond scum and a troll or two for company. He swallowed, trying to stop the fury climbing up his throat, but now it just sat festering in his stomach.

But still he wavered. Why not let her go? She was only a silly girl, not a skilled witch. There was no risk in it.

Then...

...he could enjoy the chase!

I'm going to enjoy hunting you down, Felicity Brady. Your dimply chin and your freckly cheeks will look simply perfect on my wall. In fact - the wizard chuckled - your eyes will match my wallpaper.

Chapter 13

Kids Today!

'Seeking a Witch in a Cave, Cavern or Small Castle' had told her to follow the River Cruor to a range of mountains called the Trimmels and then to fly over a city to the valley where Kitta's cottage was hidden. But the sun was still in bed and, peering over the lip of her carpet, Felicity saw that the river was lost in a gloomy mist.

She had seen on the map in the book that this city - Cauldron City it was called - lay to the east of Twice Brewed. So, with the river hidden, she had ordered the carpet to fly towards the rising sun.

Felicity was so excited to be back in Eternus; she even had goose bumps and not just from the cold. At Galibrath's funeral, she had only glimpsed the rolling hills and forests and the bustling town of Twice Brewed. But now, she had a chance to fly over where the wizard lay in his tomb and see how different this Twice Brewed was to her own town.

Over Christmas she had watched 'A Christmas Carol' on TV and Twice Brewed reminded her of the old London town. There were lanterns hanging over the cobbled streets (they were hanging in mid air!) but they helped her to see all the lopsided chimneys on the red-slated roofs and the cosy-looking ramshackle shops. The town looked surprisingly busy for 4 o'clock in the morning. Wizards on flying carpets nipped to and fro; there was even a gigantic carpet piled up with parcels, the postman perhaps? She spotted cows clip-clopping over the streets dragging wagons stuffed with hay, and on the corners there were pyramids of rocks. Felicity wondered what they were for.

All her life, her parents had dragged her from house to house, changing schools, trying to fit in, trying to escape the fists of a new bully. But The Wishing Shelf and this land felt safe, well, not safe, there were too many trolls, but here she did not need to worry that her dad was going to pop in and tell her to pack.

Felicity had now left the town in her wake, the sun clambering up over the hill tops, flooding the valley and stabbing mercilessly at her eyes. She lay on her stomach, mesmerised by the gigantic rainbow-washed forests. Here and there she glimpsed wisps of smoke, perhaps hinting of a goblin hut or a wizard's village. There was the river, just where it should be, like a hose pipe snaking its way to the tap. The 'Seeking' book had been spot on. She must remember to polish it when she got back.

Speeding up, she flew up and over a grassy hill and a castle perched on the very top. Skinny windows gazed up at her from grey stone walls and the towers were iced with lanterns. She guessed this must be Lupercus Castle, where the gargoyle, Geoffrey, lived.

Felicity waved.

She spotted lots and lots of trolls up on the towers. They were howling and jabbing swords at her. A whistling arrow arched over the wall, bouncing off the bottom of her carpet. Felicity rolled up in a ball. "Charming," she mumbled to her sleeve. "Not gonna borrow a cup of sugar off them."

The sun was climbing faster and faster into the sky now, much faster than in England. Birds were chirruping a good morning and Felicity just had time to see a gnome, his hands full of logs, staggering up a path to a thatched cottage.

WHOOSH!

Felicity yelped and bolted up. "What the..." She looked over her shoulder shading her eyes with her hand. Had she almost collided with a dragon? But all she saw was a tiny black dot hovering over the cottage. She looked to the front and spotted a second dot, but this was yellow and it was not so tiny. In fact, it was getting bigger and bigger and bigger. A flying carpet!

Felicity scampered on her knees to the front of the carpet and grabbed for the dancing tassels. With her left hand she tugged and slowly the rug turned. She glanced up. "Oh no," the words dripping pathetically off her lips. The other carpet had turned too! With a whimper, she yanked back with her other hand, but the pilot of the looming carpet was mirroring her. It reminded her of trying to squeeze by a fat kid in the school corridor but in the corridor she was not flying faster than a jet plane.

"Oh, crumbs," she whined. So Felicity did the only prudent thing: she hid her eyes in her fingers and trying not to pee her pants, screeched, "Ahhhhhhhhhhhhh!"

With only three feet to go and a horrifying crash imminent, the oncoming carpet dipped under Felicity's and shot off. "Sorry," mumbled Felicity, dropping her hands.

"SKY HOG!" yelled the shrinking wizard, frantically shaking his yellow cap at her.

"Oops," she muttered.

She raced over a Wellington-boot shaped lake. She remembered it from the map. It was called the Brewing Lake and now she knew why. It was bubbling and fizzing like a mouthful of sherbet and gigantic clouds of bubblegum-pink gas were erupting from the water making Felicity cough and splutter.

Thankfully, she soon got past it and she dropped lower, following the River Cruor. She could clearly see the Trimmels on the horizon; a line of craggy tops with helmets of snow. Not long now, she thought, and so far, no dragons!

Flying over the river, she spotted the water was now glowing orange. How odd. She dropped even lower for a closer look, but the carpet was flying so fast, water kept spraying up in her eyes, almost blinding her. She patted the rug. "Slow up!" she shouted over the rushing wind, and to her surprise, it did. So she stroked it and murmured, "Good boy."

Looking to the river, she discovered to her astonishment that it was not the water that was orange, but the wacky-looking fish who swam in it. They looked a lot like small barrels of rum but with crusty yellow lips, sunken eyes and a shark's fin that was all scabby and bent.

She watched one of the fish swim up to her, keeping pace with the carpet. The fish's lips popped out of the water as if it wanted a kiss. "No way," murmured Felicity with a grin. "I'm saving my first kiss for Teddy Trewhitt." This seemed to slightly upset the carroty-red porker for it jumped out of the river, flew over Felicity and landed with a squelch on the rug.

Felicity spun on her bottom and stared at the fish in surprise. "Wow! You jump really well -

for a fatty."

But the chubby fish was not in a joking mood. It opened a very big mouth and began to snap at Felicity's feet.

She pulled her legs up to her chin, but the fish was faster. Sharp teeth bit down on her foot, skewering the boot. With a howl, she jabbed at it with her free foot but it refused to let go; as if it had not eaten in days.

Then, three equally angry fish hopped up on the rug and started to crawl over to her too.

Felicity pulled open a pocket in her coat and peered in at the sentinel. "I might need a little help!" she bawled. It snored back at her. "Wonderful," she grumbled, and she smacked the carpet and yelled, "Carpet! Go! Go! GO!" Like a speedboat, they sped over the river, spraying up water and a shower of angry fish.

Felicity kicked back out with her foot. "Get off me you slimy," WHACK! "fat," WHACK! "ugly frog," and with a final hefty kick, the fish ripped free, a chunk of Felicity's boot still clamped in the teeth. It splashed back into the water.

Scrambling to the front of the carpet, Felicity

grasped hold of the lip and yanked back. Like a rocket, it shot up into the sky, so steeply she had to cling to the tassels, her feet flapping, her eyes the size of dustbin lids. She risked a glance over her shoulder and to her joy, she watched the rest of the fish tumble off the carpet and drop back into the river.

The rug levelled off. "Phew," Felicity gasped. They were a bit grizzly - for fish!

In horror, she looked to her torn boot. Mum's gonna kill me, she thought. Then she chuckled.

Mum, I'm so sorry I ripped my new boot, but as I flew over a river in the magical land of Eternus, a big orange fish jumped out, landed on my flying carpet and bit off the end.

She wriggled her big toe which now stuck out of the mangled tip. It still seemed to work, even if it was glazed in slime.

Peering over the brim of her rug, she saw she was now in a long steep-sloped valley blanketed with bushy trees. Oddly, the land was pitted with craters and a few of the trees had toppled over. The river flowed under her, still twisting and turning splitting the valley in two, and a mile or so away, looming over her, was a grey wall of rock blocking the way. The Trimmels, she thought with a shudder. They looked very drab, very cold and very, very scary.

Slowly, the carpet started to climb and the wooded valleys were left in her wake. The land was soon a messy toddler's bedroom of jagged boulders and splintered rocks. Even the trees had scarpered, but for the odd daring musketeer who stayed to battle the icy winds.

It was so barren, how could anything live here, mused Felicity, but a second later she flew over a cluster of rocks, tiny chimneys poking out of them. A village! She spotted lots of goblins riding on haycarts and playing football in the streets. A goblin village!

A little way on, she spotted four giants, two Fiat-Uno big, two London-bus big. Ooh, a family. How sweet! They often squeezed in the The Wishing Shelf hunting for books on fishing and clubs (not the 'golf' kind, but the 'knocking people on the head' kind). Felicity flew a little lower and waved, but then one of the Fiat Unos picked up a boulder and hurled it at her. She ducked as the carpet swerved and darted back up.

"Charming!" she muttered as the second Fiat Uno yanked a sling shot from her pocket and pelted her with a barrow-full of rocks. "Kids today!"

Her rug was climbing even higher now - higher and higher. She shivered; it was so much colder and her jumper felt all damp and bulky. Felicity looked up, a wall of grey meeting her gaze. She scowled. She so did not want to fly into the clouds - maybe there were krakor thunder serpents in there! - but she had to get over the Trimmels to get to Cauldron City and the carpet seemed to think there was no other way.

If I must do it, then I must do it fast, she decided, jutting out her jaw. So she slapped the carpet and yelled, "Faster! FASTER!"

Hitting the clouds, Felicity shut her eyes tightly, screwing up her face. They were so thick-looking she was scared she might bounce off them but the grey mist swallowed her like a river swallowing a pebble.

Slowly, she opened her eyes and looked around. But she couldn't see a thing, only the odd funny shape in the clouds: ugly grinning hags with eyes missing and wobbly grins, a troll or was it a gargoyle crawling on his knees, a dragon's wing flapping by. WHAT! She snapped her eyes shut; there was no way she had imagined that.

Seconds later, Felicity timidly lifted her eyelids to find she was free of the clouds.

She yelped.

A six foot green dragon was perched on the corner of her carpet, his claws digging into the bristly wool. He was eyeing her menacingly, smoke gushing from his nostrils like a bubbling iron and a forked tongue flitting in and out of his toothy jaws.

She let out an 'opera singer' trill.

The dragon tutted. "Kids today," he sizzled. Stretching his scaly wings, he flew away.

"Wow," Felicity gasped. There seemed to be no better word.

Then, gazing at the Trimmels in wonder, Tantalus's carpet smashed into hers and she was bundled over, the rough wool grazing her cheek.

Chapter 14

Ten Gold Flupoons If You Squash Her Flat

Scrambling to her knees, Felicity shot an angry look at Tantalus. "GO AWAY," she yelled. "JUST LET ME BE, YOU TWONK!"

"FELICITY," the wizard shouted back over the roar of the wind. "That's not a very nice thing to say to your new boss." He snarled at her and his face became twisted and ugly. "TRAITOR!" he bawled and howling like a banshee he swung his carpet at her.

Grabbing for a tassel, Felicity yanked back hard with her left hand, turning away from him. All of a sudden, her carpet juddered as she crashed into - she twisted her head -

CRUNCHER! Flying on her left and grinning like a moron.

"Felicity, don't go!" howled Tantalus, a cruel grin on his pasty face. "We have so much to chat about."

"I have nothing to say to you," yelled back Felicity. To her horror, there was a mountain peak right in her path. But they had boxed her in. She could not turn.

"But we need to discuss flowers." The wizard laughed in a mad sort of way. "Do you want poppodils or daffodils at your funeral?"

"Y' a ruddy nutbar," screamed Felicity. "Bonkers!" She yanked on a tassel, trying to push him away.

"RED POPPODILS IT IS!" yelled the wizard, slamming his carpet for a second time into Felicity's. "Adds a little colour, don't you think?" He winked at her.

Felicity glared back. Right, she thought. She slapped her carpet hard. "Go carpet! GO!" Tearing ahead, she grabbed at the flapping rug and yanked back, hurtling over the top of the summit.

She glanced over her shoulder. They were

there, coming up fast. But what was that glinting in Tantalus's hand? A knife? A KNIFE! He was going to cut up her carpet. He was going to cut her up. She swerved around a second peak - and a third. Hot on her heels, Tantalus and Cruncher kept on coming and coming.

The wizard slashed at Felicity's carpet, tearing a long gash in the cloth.

"Stop it!" she yelled at him but the wizard just laughed and swiped at the flapping tassels. In horror, Felicity felt her old rug stagger, like a car running out of petrol.

"What's up with y' carpet?" howled Tantalus gleefully. "Gremlins?"

And now Cruncher was moving up on her left, crouching, preparing to jump.

She needed more speed. She had to get away before Tantalus sliced her in two or his puffdolt jumped on her and crushed her to a pulp. So Felicity did the only thing she could think of. She plunged to the ground.

Faster and faster she went, the wind tearing at her face making her eyes water. She glanced back. Tantalus and Cruncher, caught by surprise, were now hurtling down after her. But she was heading for the clouds. Maybe, just maybe, she could hide in them.

Almost there.

ALMOST...

A ball of fire, like a small meteor, blazed over her head. She watched in horror as it exploded on the side of the mountain in front of her. Then a second, so close, she could feel her hair sizzling in the heat.

HE WAS THROWING FIRE BALLS!

And what could she do?

She couldn't even pull a rabbit out of a hat.

She was almost there.

Then, like a mother's hug, the dark cloud smothered Felicity and hid her in her misty arms.

The carpet pulled up, giving Felicity a chance to rub the sweat off her face. Her feet and hands tingled and her heart was thumping in her chest as if it wanted to be let out. She felt like she had run the London Marathon.

The clouds were as thick as before and just as chilly. Felicity crossed her arms and hid her hands in her armpits. She could hardly see a thing. It was like riding a bike at night with no lights, so she whispered to her rug to slow down a bit.

She did not need to see Tantalus to know he was still up there. Over her head, she could hear the bangs as balls of fire crashed onto the side of the mountain. The wizard must be furious, she thought and she mustered a tiny smile.

She was floating very slowly now. Crouched at the front of the carpet, she peered into the swirling mist, looking for - "Stop," she whispered. A wall of snow blocked her path. She would stay here, she decided, next to the mountain. They would never find her in all this cloud.

So there she sat.

Arms wrapped around legs.

Chin on chest.

Eyes closed.

She was trying to ignore the crash of fireballs and the rumbling. She frowned and opened her eyes. Rumbling!?

Splat!

Something very cold and very wet landed on Felicity's head. Gasping, she combed a hand through her hair. It was snow and some of it was now running down the back of her neck. She looked up and grimaced. "Not funny," she mumbled. At that moment, a second snowball smacked her on the tip of her nose.

Now there seemed to be snow everywhere, and the rumbling was getting louder and louder. "Avalanche," Felicity whispered. She slapped the carpet as hard as she could and screamed, "AVALANCHE! Step on it!"

She shot out of the clouds and raced down the mountain, a wave of tumbling snow crashing after her. "Come on carpet," she yelled. "Faster! FASTER!" She stole a quick look over her shoulder. The snow was hot on her heels, snapping trees and growling like a bear.

She could pull up and away from the ground but she knew Tantalus was up there, him and his puffdolt, ready to pounce. What can I do, she thought, what can I do? But the back of her carpet was already lost in a swirl of flying snow.

It was then, as the snow was about to bury her for a hundred years, that she spotted the cave. She spotted it because it was glowing orange and it was difficult to miss. So, with balls of snow and ice pelting her in the back, she swerved and shot into the gaping hole.

But just behind her, roaring like a mad bull, flew Cruncher.

Felicity looked back and groaned. "Not you!" The puffdolt leered at her and jabbed at her with his club. Felicity yelped and quickly crawled to the very front of her rug, as far away from the puffdolt as she could get. But now he was speeding up, moving up next to her. She would have to do something and do it quick.

She looked about. The tunnel was vast, so vast she could not even see the roof.

The walls were glowing, giving off an orange light, which was good as she didn't fancy flying in the dark. She peered over the lip of the carpet. She could see the ground, but it was too far to jump. Fat boulders sat like lost footballs on the cavern floor and everywhere pillars of rock sprouted out from the ground like branchless trees. Stalagmites! They were called stalagmites. She remembered them from geography class and they gave her an idea.

She pushed on the front of the carpet and it dipped down. Cruncher, who had had one foot on Felicity's carpet, now found he had one foot on nothing. He pulled back in fright and sat down with a grunt. "She's as slippery as a bangeroo worm,' he mumbled.

The floor of the cave rushed up to meet her but she did not pull up. Like a meteor, she tumbled to earth, then, at the last second, she yanked back. The rug staggered, pulled up out of the dive and shot over the rocky ground. Things suddenly got very difficult for poor Felicity as she yanked the carpet this way and that, dodging giant boulders and razor-sharp stalagmites.

Follow me now, you fat oaf, she thought wickedly, but she was too busy to look up and check.

A rock, shaped a little like a mushroom but sadly a lot bigger, loomed up in front of her. She tore around it only to find a second rock, this one shaped, well - like a very big rock, right in her path. She swung around that one too. It was like riding on dodgems but the things you had to dodge were a lot bigger and a lot harder.

She glanced up. Yes, Cruncher was there, peering down at her over the lip of his carpet, watching for her to smash her bones on a rock or to give up and fly into the open. Thankfully, he was too much of a chicken to come down here and smack her on the head with that club of his.

"Arghh!" screamed Felicity as her carpet flipped on its side and shot between two ugly, grey boulders. There was no time to think as she dodged left and right, so close to the rocks she could almost reach out and touch them. She began to feel like a pinball and to be honest, a tiny bit carpet sick.

The tunnel seemed to be getting smaller, the jagged walls crowding in on her. The roof looked to be dropping down too. Looking up, Felicity could spot hundreds of stalactites, as sharp as swords, hanging from it. If the roof got any lower, she thought, she would have to dodge them too.

It did.

The only good thing about this was that Cruncher now had to dodge the rocks as well and he was not as good at it as Felicity. But he did have a club and he was swinging it at the smaller rocks, smashing them, trying to bulldozer his way through. He only has to squeeze by the big ones, pouted Felicity.

Just when she thought she was going to be pulverised to mush, the cave opened out and there were no more rocks to dodge. It was as if they had been carted away in a wheelbarrow. But that was just silly. Who could carry rocks that big? Apart from giants.

GIANTS!

She yanked back on the carpet, trying to pull up but the roof was still too low. She would have to try and fly through them but they were so big and there were so many, all sitting in a huge circle, as if they were in the middle of a town meeting.

Sadly, they did not seem too overjoyed about being bothered by a girl on a flying carpet.

A giant with hair sprouting out of his ears and a bald head shouted, "COME ON LADS! GET HER!" Which Felicity thought, didn't sound too hopeful.

A second one hollered, "TEN GOLD FLUPOONS IF YOU SQUASH HER FLAT." With a war cry, he lumbered after her, swinging a log wildly over his head.

Felicity ducked and dived, the giants swiping at her with clubs. Now she knew what it was like to be a fly and soon they'd hit her and that would be that. No more adventuring. No more trying to chat up Teddy Trewhitt in the lunch queue. AND NOW, THEY WERE LOBBING ROCKS!

In a flash, Felicity felt very angry. It had been a long day. Tantalus had thrown fireballs at her. She had almost been crushed in an avalanche. AND A FISH HAD EATEN HER BOOT! So, without really thinking about it, she hauled back on her rug and stopped.

"STOP THROWING THINGS!" she yelled at the giants and, to her surprise, they did.

"Sorry," mumbled one, dropping a rock.

"Yep, sorry," muttered a second. "We got a bit excited."

"OK, then." What else could she say? Then, an excellent idea popped into her head. "Look, there's a puffdolt."

"Where?"

"Over there," bawled a giant, pointing with his club. "Do we like puffdolts?"

"No, we hate 'em."

"TEN GOLD FLUPOONS IF YOU SQUASH HIM FLAT!" And off they

lumbered.

Felicity was too scared to stay and watch the giants attacking Cruncher. You never know, they could decide to have a spot of girl stew for supper, and not puffdolt soup. So she gently slapped the carpet and flew away. She had to find a way out of here and there was no way she was going back.

The jagged walls still glowed orange so Felicity had no problem seeing where she was going, and it did help not being chased by an angry puffdolt. She could fly a lot more slowly.

The tunnel wound on and on but it seemed to be going up, which Felicity thought must be a good thing.

CRASH!

"Miss me?" growled Cruncher.

Felicity gawked at the puffdolt in horror. He was bleeding from a gash in his cheek and his carpet was torn and had big rips in it. He looked very, very angry.

"I – I tried to stop them," Felicity mustered, lamely and she smiled in what she hoped was a cute sort of way. But the puffdolt just growled and spat blood at her.

This time, Felicity's carpet didn't need to be told as it pulled quickly away from Cruncher and shot down the tunnel. She glanced ahead. There was a sharp bend coming up. As she hit it, she dragged the carpet to the right and pulled away. She looked back over her shoulder. The puffdolt had made it too but only just. Coming out of the bend he had scraped his elbow on the wall and now, Felicity guessed, that was bleeding too.

But then, there was A STONE WALL! Felicity screwed up her eyes. It couldn't be a dead end, could it? I mean, a tunnel should lead to some place, shouldn't it? There must be a bend, a really sharp one that she couldn't see yet. But which way to turn? Left or right? The last one was right and the one before that was left, so this one must be left too.

She was almost on it.

But what if she was wrong. She would fly right into a stone wall and that would be that.

No more shopping channel.

Decide.

NO MORE SATURDAY MORNING TV!

DECIDE!

But Felicity was out of time, so with a scream, she swung the rug from right to left and - YES, the tunnel stretched out in front of her and YES - SHE WAS STILL ALIVE!

Glancing over her shoulder, she watched in horror as Cruncher bounced off the rock wall, falling back in a crumpled heap on the cave floor. He lay still, his carpet falling over him so only his shaggy feet stuck out of the side.

Felicity winced. I bet that hurt, she thought. Should she go back? Try to help him. But maybe he was just faking. He might grab her and mash her brains in with that giant club of his. No, she had to go on. She looked ahead, her eyes searching for a way out.

She had a job to do.

Chapter 15

Cat and Mouse in Cauldron City

Tantalus stared down at Cruncher's limp body and grunted. "One less gob to feed," he muttered sourly, kicking the puffdolt's shaggy foot.

Covering the corpse back up with the rug, Banks looked up at his boss and tutted. "You know, a caring wizard like you should be doing charity work, looking for lost kittens or..."

"He failed me," sneered Tantalus, "and I have no time for failures." He strode a little way up the tunnel. "Now, where's that girl?"

The goblin stood up, took off his cap and scratched his brow. "She's a good flyer. If she discovered the way out of the cave she's probably over Cauldron City by now."

"Then you have to stop her," announced Tantalus flatly, not looking the goblin in the face.

"You want me to kill her!?" Banks pretended to sound shocked but he had seen this coming. He had been perched on a cloud watching the wizard and the puffdolt try to catch her. Tantalus was not used to his prey putting up a fight. Well, he would make the coward squirm if he wanted him to do his dirty work. "But I thought you loved the - now, what was it you told me - the thrill of the hunt? Was it hunt? No, the thrill of the fight."

"Chase," growled Tantalus, through gritted teeth. "The thrill of the chase."

"Yes, that's right. I remember now. I'd hate to take that away from you..."

The wizard spun back around, his eyes flashing. "YOU CALLING ME A COWARD?" he roared, the angry words bouncing off the tunnel walls.

"Me?! No!" The goblin smiled and chuckled, only the chuckle sounded a lot like the cluck of a chicken.

Tantalus glared, his face turning as black as a

thunder cloud. "Find the girl and sort her," he spat, "and if she gets to Kitta before you can grab her..." The wizard's left eye twitched.

"Sort her too?" piped up the goblin.

Closing his eyes, Tantalus slowly nodded. "Sort her too," he whispered.

"Sorry? Didn't catch that."

"Kill her," growled the wizard, opening his eyes and glaring at the smirking goblin.

"Oh, OK." Banks rubbed at his nose with the back of his hand. "And what about Cruncher?"

"He's food for the giants now." Tantalus leapt up on his carpet and grinned. "Who says I'm not a caring wizard?"

The goblin watched his boss fly away. "Turnip head," he muttered after him. Reluctantly, he jammed his cap on, jumped on his own carpet and took off after Felicity.

He was pretty confident Brady had flown on. If she had turned around they would have spotted her, and anyway, she probably thought the way back was blocked by the avalanche. She couldn't know Tantalus had blasted his way through it. But he had a feeling she was not the kind of girl to turn and run home to mummy.

She was going to take a bit of catching, he mused.

But he did have a very important advantage over her: he could fly much faster. He had grown up playing in these tunnels, hiding from the packs of giants that roamed them. The goblin elders in his village had told him to stay away from here. "Too dangerous," they had lectured him and they had been right.

But he had not stayed away.

Banks chuckled to himself. He had never done as he was told, even as a yoblin (a baby goblin). Maybe, this was why he had always had to play on his own. The other yoblins had been scared of him, of what he might do. Maybe that was really why he had been banished from his village.

A nasty corner was coming up but he didn't bother to slow down. He dragged the carpet around the sharp bend and then he pushed down, flying under a jagged rock that he knew jutted out from the roof just there.

The goblin grunted and wrapped his Louis Vuitton scarf twice more around his neck. Why was he going over the past? Then was then and now was now. And right now he had to stop Brady from meeting with this charm maker.

Tantalus was scared of her. He could see it in his eyes and the last thing the goblin wanted was for some old flame of Galibrath's meddling in Tantalus's plan. She might mess up his own plans and that would not do at all.

He zoomed up the tunnel, hurtling past giants and dodging the rocks they threw at him. He could see the way out now, but there was still no sign of the Brady-girl. She must be flying fast, he thought grimly. He slapped his carpet hard. "Come on! A potato sack can fly faster than you." The rug sped up, soaring out of the cave and right into...

...a traffic jam!

The carpets were parked nose to tail, like a long winding snake all the way to Cauldron City. They were hooting at each other and there were shouts of, "SHIFT IT, YOU OLD HAG!" and "GET THAT MOULDY RUG OUT OF MY WAY!"

Rush hour, thought Banks glumly. He had not got time for this so he yanked back on his carpet, soaring up and over the jam. It was risky and if he was spotted by a carpet-cop he'd be in all sorts of trouble and not only for dangerous flying. He had a feeling the cops had a long list of crimes they would like to talk to him about. A long, long list. The goblin smirked. But what else could he do? If the girl was stuck in the jam he could swoop down and grab her before she even got a whiff of his Hugo aftershave.

Flying above the other carpets and ignoring the angry shouts of the drivers, the goblin peered down. There were carpet-cabs and a carpet-truck piled up with cartons of Monster Hotdogs. There was even the odd carpet-bus crowded with impsters and yoblins on their way home from school. But still no sign of Felicity Brady.

Hold on!

The goblin braked and stared down at a girl kneeling on a carpet. He couldn't see her face but she had short sandy curls just like Brady's and the rug was torn at the back, where Tantalus must have slashed it. It was her. He knew it.

Very slowly, he dropped down behind her. He tapped the carpet softly. Closer and closer, he crept.

A little further.

Just a little further and...

"Hey you! Where do you think y' going? Trying to push in, hey."

The goblin spun around and blinked. A hag in a pink ballerina dress was sitting on the rug just behind Felicity's. She was shaking her fists at him and honking her horn.

"Get out of it," she yelled at Banks, baring gappy black teeth, "or I'll turn y' into a pond of slug goo."

Too late, the goblin turned back, but Felicity had already spotted him. As she pulled out and away from the traffic jam, he slapped his own carpet and shot down after her.

The goblin pushed his rug hard and soon he was right on Felicity's tail. But she was like a kite, twisting and rolling, looping over and over in the sky. Soon poor Banks wished he had not popped in The Droopy Wand Café that morning for a bacon and dragon's egg fry up.

They shot over a wood, a tangle of black trees which hung about the city like a noose of thorns. He'd only been there once, years ago, when the fire had killed all the trees. The wood was called Cauldron Rim and as Banks looked down all he could think of was the smell. He pinched his nose. The trees stank. They stank of death.

They were over the city now and it was just as ugly as he remembered it. A black sprawl of crooked houses and poky shops crowding in on each other as if they were scared of being left alone. Black smoke leaked from hundreds of chimneys, staining windows with liquorice syrup.

They zoomed down the crooked streets, swerving around the black lanterns hovering over the doors of the old shops. The goblin's carpet was almost touching the back of Felicity's as they tore down an alleyway smelling of mouldy cabbage. If he could just get a grip on her carpet and drag her to the ground but she was flying so fast.

"Come on!" he screamed. "Come on!"

They shot over a wall topped with barbed wire curled around metal spikes. Reaching out a hand, the goblin grabbed for the back of Felicity's rug. He almost had her. But she swerved, diving under an old stone bridge.

Banks, with a growl, shot after her.

Flying neck and neck, they sped over the river, spraying up water like speeding boats. The goblin looked over at Felicity and snorted. She was smiling. Smiling, fumed the goblin. In a rage, he crashed into her, sending her carpet into a wobbly spin.

He looked over and sneered. Not smiling now are you, he thought wickedly.

"Banks! Pull over! NOW!" The goblin spun around. There was a carpet-cop right on his tail.

"Land or we start shooting," shouted the wizard. In his hand he clutched a glowing ball of fire.

The goblin frowned. We? So, where were the others? He glanced up and the frown turned to a scowl. Three more rugs flashing red, yellow, blue then green were circling above him like vultures. Local cops, he thought and he relaxed just a little. As long as they were not WANDD agents. They flew black carpets with red dragons on them and they never shouted a warning. They just blasted you out of the sky.

He looked ahead, just in time to see Felicity fly over the muddy bank of the river and slip down an alley. How did she get out of that spin!? He growled and spun his carpet about.

It was getting dark, a lazy mist hanging just over the cobbled street. Candles were now burning in the black lanterns but the flames were too feeble to light the darting shadows on the street below.

The goblin looked down from his speeding carpet and groaned. The town was waking up and that could only mean trouble. In Cauldron City, most things happened at night and most of those things were bad.

Banks ducked under a drooping washing line, scraping his elbow on a wall, ripping a hole in his jacket. He'd only bought it a week ago. He snarled and gave his carpet a wallop. There was no way he was going to give up - not now - not now he'd torn his jacket.

At that very moment, an old witch, her hair wrapped in orange curlers, tossed a bucket of scraps out of a window, soaking the goblin in stew and brown gravy. The goblin picked a bit of carrot out of his ear and scowled.

Right!

He had planned to do her in quick.

But now he was going to slowly drown her in a bowl of pea soup.

He scanned the street and spotted Felicity slipping down a small alley on the left. She was heading to Hags' Square! Was she mad, the goblin wondered, and he shuddered. It was the last place in Eternus any girl should want to go at night. It was the last place he wanted to go too.

A red ball of fire blazed past him and smashed into a lantern sending it crashing to the street. Followed by a second, so close he could feel his eyebrows sizzle. The goblin shrugged and slapped his rug.

It seemed there was no other way.

There is a place at the very heart of Cauldron City where all the cobbled alleys meet. There, every night, just as the shadows grow tall, there is a market. Grey tents with flaking patches and frayed ropes are put up and stood in line like troops in a beaten army. Crouched in the tents, hunched up over bubbling cauldrons you will find the Skanky Hags.

With bony hands they stir smoking brews and eyes peer out from deep craters and watch the flapping door.

They sit.

But not for long.

To the hags come the trolls, the demons and the dorfmorons. "Poison," they growl, handing over a clinking bag of gold.

"Purple or pink?" The hags always cackle at this for the venoms they sell are all the same. They all give death.

Then the monster will slip away, clutching a small bottle full of revenge and stoppered with a black cork.

The goblin shivered as he floated over the mist, flanked by the hags' grey tents. The head of a puffdolt drifted by, his body hidden in the fog and a dorfmoron's horns waddled past, sticking out like chocolate flakes in vanilla ice cream. There were one or two other carpets about now, the drivers huddled up under smelly mounds of rotting rags.

Banks floated to a stop and peered around the

corner of one of the tents. But there was no sign of Brady, only more hovering heads and a troll perched on a carpet made for a dwarf. Where was she? He looked up. There were the cops. Watching for him to try and sneak out of Hags' Square. But they knew if they dared to come any lower, they'd be crushed by a puffdolt's club. Cops were not welcome in Cauldron City at night.

He swung left; there was still no sign of her, then right, under the black claws of a dead tree. He could see a carpet up ahead, about fifty feet or so, but it was too gloomy to see who was sitting on it. But it could be her, thought the goblin, slapping his carpet.

But where was she going? They were almost at the end of the long line of tents and she did not seem to be slowing down. The goblin watched as the carpet shot out of Hags' Square and down another alley.

Then he noticed a sign and he smiled. For the first time in a long time things were looking up. It was an old word, in a language the Brady-girl would not understand. It meant DEAD END.

He had her at last.

The goblin leapt down from his carpet and landed like a cat on the cobbles. He stood very still, only his eyes moving, looking for danger. But it was dark, too dark to see far and the mist still clung to his eyes.

He crept down the alley, his rug rolled up and tucked under his arm. He glanced up. He had heard flapping. But it was only the cops.

Banks was so busy watching for flying carpets that he didn't see the trash can. SMASH! His knee hit it and the tin lid clattered to the floor.

The goblin froze.

Drip.

Drip.

Drip.

Water leaked from a rusting pipe.

"Oops," he muttered. He lifted up his hat and rubbed his damp brow. Killing this girl was going to get him killed.

He plodded on, by a dorfmoron snoozing on the littered ground, only he was not snoring. Green blood leaked from his bulbous lips and the two heads of a skinny bloodgrub rat guzzled on the dorfmoron's stubby big toe. The furry

225

heads popped up, four black eyes gazing at the goblin as if he would make a very tasty pudding. Banks gulped and shuffled on.

Almost at the end of the alley now, Banks looked around him. "Where are you?" he muttered, his eyes hunting in the shadows. But Felicity was not there, only a mound of skulls and twisted bones. The goblin scratched his head. The alley was blocked by a wall but if she had flown over it he would have spotted her. Or the cops would have grabbed her. No, she was down here, hiding.

Tripping over a rusty stove, the goblin stumbled, his elbow smacking a wall. But it felt a bit too smooth to be a wall. He stepped back and looked up. It was a door, and hanging over it was a very old, crooked sign. "Wizardry Gadgets," he read. "Hmm." Perhaps Brady had found a way out after all.

Banks stepped up and grasped the grimy handle. He twisted it and pulled the door open. Peering into the gloom he could just see winding steps. Was it a trap? A ball of fire hit the battered stove and it exploded, a spark singeing his jacket sleeve.

"Now, I'm annoyed," he mumbled sourly.

Chapter 16

Hags, Cowboys and a Pirate or Two

Her big toe was freezing. She stopped and perched on one of the grey stone steps and began to rub her icy foot. Her dad had told her that in the army the most important thing was to keep your feet warm and dry. But her dad had never had his foot chomped on by a slimy, orange fish.

Suddenly Felicity felt homesick. Cauldron City was so spooky and so black. It was very different to Twice Brewed and the rest of Eternus. Trolls, rotting monsters in alleys being fed on by rats, and the woods she had flown over. Every tree had looked burnt. A tear trickled down her cheek and dripped off her chin to the floor. She was having no fun at all and now this creepy goblin was trying to capture her.

Felicity rubbed at her swollen eyes and lifted her head. She could hear whispering, or maybe somebody was talking very loudly but a long way off. She stood up. It seemed to be coming from above her. But she couldn't go back, not with Banks on her heels.

So, up and up she crept. Thankfully, a candle had been placed on many of the steps but there were no windows and it was still very dark.

She stopped. What was that?

THUMP! THUMP! THUMP!

It sounded like - oh no! The goblin! He'd found the door and he was coming for her.

Two at a time, Felicity raced up the steps, dragging the flying carpet with her. But no matter how fast she ran the thud of goblin feet got closer and closer. He was like a nuclear-powered robot.

THUMP! THUMP! THUMP!

She was too scared to turn her head and look. Keep going, she ordered her legs, but they were crying out for her to stop. But not nearly as loudly as her lungs were.

He was going to grab her by the shoulder and drag her back down the steps. He was going to smash her over the head with a brick. No, no, a club, a really fat one. He was going to...

She had reached the top of the tower and there, right in front of her, was a door. Almost in tears, she grabbed at the handle and yanked it open. She dashed through, slamming it shut behind her.

The first thing Felicity saw were hundreds of imps, perched on purple stools. They were grabbing up hats off a conveyor belt and putting them in boxes. How odd, she thought.

As well as the imps there were about twenty or so hags, all wearing black cloaks with the hoods pulled up. They were crowded around the far end of the conveyor belt, listening to another hag. But she had on a silver cloak and the hood was pulled back. She was very ugly with a crooked nose, bubbly warts and a saggy chin. She looked, thought Felicity, very much like a hag ought to.

But where to hide? She could see no other doors and there was only one window, but it was covered by shutters. There were no desks to squeeze under and no cupboards to climb in. Only hat boxes, but there was no way she could get in one of those.

There was only one thing for it. She would have to mingle in with the hags and hope Banks did not spot her.

She crept over, not that she needed to, because the conveyor belt was cranking away like a rusty lawn mower. But the hags did not seem very interested in her. They were too busy watching the hag in the silver cloak. She had picked up a cowboy hat from off the conveyor belt and was trying to squash it over her greasy head.

Felicity gasped and cupped her hand over her mouth. The hag was changing. The warts on her chin vanished with a 'Plop! Plop! Plop!' and her crooked nose lost its crook with a sharp crack. Then, the wrinkles on her face melted away as if somebody was ironing over them. Her saggy chin lost its sag, the bags hanging under her eyes shrivelled up, and her long hair raced up her neck and hid under her hat. Then her cloak vanished and in its place she now wore faded jeans and a blue checked shirt with a gold star pinned to the pocket. Brown leather boots reached up to her knees and a gun on a belt hung from her hips.

The witch was now a cowboy and a very young cowboy at that.

"You see," croaked the witch (she still sounded like a witch). She slapped her knee making the spurs on her boots jangle. "The Cloaking Hat gives you more than just a costume. It can change everything, and I mean *everything* about you."

The witches whooped and hollered and one of them reached for a bobby's helmet.

"So, if you want to slip a drop of venom in y' mother-in-law's soup but for some reason, she don't trust you," the hags cackled loudly at this, "then you can masquerade as the cook." She held up a white, floppy hat. "She'll never know!"

As Felicity slipped into the crowd, the hags began grabbing for the hats. All of a sudden, she was surrounded by firemen, baseball players and pirates with swords and pistols on their hips. At the back of the room, the door crashed open and quickly Felicity grabbed for a hat too.

"Now, as you can see," crowed the cowboy, "you only look different to other people."

"Why?" shouted a policeman, handcuffs swinging from his belt. "I want to see what I look like."

"Remember, it's a Cloaking Hat and you are in the cloak. But if you look in a mirror..."

FLASH! The policeman conjured up a mirror. He began to prance about in front of it shouting, "LOOK AT ME! LOOK AT ME! EVENIN' ALL! EVENIN' ALL!"

The other hags laughed and shrieked and conjured up their own mirrors.

Felicity looked down. The cowboy was right. She still looked the same. She glanced at her reflection in one of the mirrors and she gave a startled cry.

White hair! Bent nose! WARTY CHIN!

Ooops! She had grabbed a witch's hat. Now she stood out even more.

Slowly, Felicity looked up. She felt the goblin's eyes on her. Yes, there he was, standing by the open door. He seemed to be looking right at her. But he wouldn't know it was her. How could he? She looked like an old hag. But, just in case, she jostled her way deeper into the crowd.

"These wonderful hats usually sell for twenty gold flupoons, but today and today only," the cowboy smiled, pulled out his pistol and spun it in his hand. "TEN GOLD FLUPOONS!" he yelled, firing his cap-gun.

"Hey, what's this mean?" shouted a hunched-over hag standing next to Felicity. She had just taken off her motorbike helmet and at once her black leathers had vanished. "Don't work on spindlysloths," she read from a white label on the side of the helmet.

The cowboy whipped off his hat and changed back to the crooked-nosed, saggy-chinned witch. "Ah - yes," she stammered. "You know how it is. Such clever fellows, spindlysloths. So the hat don't work too well on them."

Grumbling, the hags began to pull off the hats. "That's no good is it," shrieked one of them.

All the hags nodded and a second one shouted. "I was hoping to sneak up on one of 'em and squash him flat."

"Girls! Girls! There are so many other folk you can trick. Dorfmorons, trolls, gob - actually, no," the hag shook her head, "they don't work too well on goblins either."

Felicity felt like being sick. She felt like she had been kicked in the stomach. There was a growl and she felt the hairs on the back of her neck stand up. HE WAS BEHIND HER! Very slowly, she turned around.

"Hi," she mustered. "And, er - how are you?"

The goblin slowly shook his head. "My left ear is blocked up with beef stew and bits of carrot. Oh, and I tore my Yves St. Laurent jacket." He showed Felicity the hole. "And I singed the sleeve."

"Nasty," said Felicity, taking a small step back. "So, you're here to take me back to Tantalus."

"No." The goblin grinned. "I'm here to crush you into very small crumbs and to feed you to a dorfmoron."

"Oh." She took another, much bigger step back.

"Hey, I didn't see any goblin hats," bawled a witch, tottering up to Banks and grabbing his shoulder "Where did you get it? Go on, tell me."

Felicity span around and began to push her

way through the crowd. But the old hags were unwilling to move. "Shift! Shift!" she growled at them. Finally, she broke free. "Quick!" she whispered to the carpet. "We have to go."

In a flash, it shot out from under her arm and unrolled. Tossing the witch's hat on the floor, Felicity clambered on and yelled, "GO! GO! GO!"

They were heading for the only window in the room. She could see that it was blocked by shutters but she would just have to smash her way through. There was a blinding flash and exasperatingly, there was Banks, crouched in front of the window, blocking her escape.

"Come on!" screeched Felicity. "Faster. FASTER!" She was heading right for the goblin but he was just standing there. So, he wanted to play chicken. Fine by her and she slapped the rug hard.

For the second time that day, Felicity covered her eyes with her hands and screamed. THUMP! The carpet smashed into the goblin. But she was still moving. There was the sound of glass shattering and wood splintering and then - nothing. Slowly, Felicity parted her fingers and looked about.

She was out. And the goblin? Felicity looked back and chuckled. He was hanging by his finger tips from the window. And peering down at him and not looking too happy, were a lot of very upset hags.

Chapter 17

Brewing Tea and Plucking Chickens

Where am I now, wondered Felicity. But it was too dark to see and the moon was hidden by a cloud.

She felt the carpet nudging her. It had rolled up and now it wanted to park, so she tucked it under her arm. She sighed; it was like having a spoilt dog.

Looking around, she could just make out the shapes of trees and she could feel wet grass on her sticking-out toes. She squeezed the carpet, gently. "You think this is the place?" she whispered. The rug quivered and Felicity hoped that was a 'yes'.

The last part of her journey had been a nightmare. It had been so dark and she had had no idea where she was going. And now it seemed, the carpet had dropped her in the middle of a creepy forest.

"Probably full of demons," she muttered gloomily.

But there was a glow, like hundreds of tiny stars peeping out at her and silhouetting the trees.

Felicity blew out her cheeks. Maybe she was being a bit harsh on the poor carpet. She patted it kindly. Maybe it had found Kitta. So, picking up her feet, she set off through the wood.

Stumbling from tree to tree, branches whipped at her face and more than once she heard her jeans rip as she snagged them on thorns. But it was getting brighter, the lights in front of her now resembling glowing baubles.

She stopped.

There was a fence, a very old one. The paint was peeling and it was rotten in places. There was a gate too, just as old with a frayed rope for a hinge.

A scaly lizard with a long tail and red eyes shot out from under a bush, making Felicity jump back in fright. She watched it wriggle under the gate.

What to do now, she pondered. "Hmm."

She decided to follow the lizard. Had to be preferable to being in the spooky forest.

Pushing open the gate, she discovered a path. Very slowly, she crept up it. Paper lanterns hung on almost every tree and many seemed to hang on nothing at all. It was these that she had seen from the forest and now they lit up the winding path and the garden around her.

She was soon surrounded by trimmed grass, hushed ponds and bushes proudly showing off red-spotted jumpers. Baby trees grew everywhere and to Felicity they looked just like tiny sprigs of broccoli.

As she walked, her feet crunched on small grey pebbles. She could hear crickets singing in the grass and the drumming of water as it tumbled into the ponds. A marble dragon spewed water and not fire from his yawning jaw, and as she crept past, she had a strong feeling the head turned to follow her.

She shifted the carpet from under her left arm to under her right. I hope this path leads somewhere, she thought.

Thankfully, it did.

The house looked very old and was made of wood. Black tiles covered the roof but a lot of them were cracked and clumps of moss grew out of the gutters. There were no windows, not that Felicity could see anyway, but there was a door, shiny marble steps leading up to it.

She knocked.

But nobody shouted, "Come on in!"

She rested her rug on the porch floor and knocked a second time. She couldn't see a handle so she gave the door a gentle push. It wobbled but it didn't open. Then, feeling a little stupid, she slid the door to one side.

"Hello," she called in a whisper that nobody was going to hear. She munched on her lip. Should she go in? But it could be the wrong house. "Hello," a little louder this time but still no reply.

Peering into the room, Felicity could see a circle of candles burning in brass holders on a low square table, and in the middle, in a silver frame, sat a picture of Galibrath.

I guess this is the right place, she thought, and boldly, she stepped into the house.

The floor was covered in an old straw mat and scattered around the table there were four pillows. They were all squashed flat as if recently they had been sat on by very plump rhinos.

Nervously, she picked up the photograph. She spotted there was a sheet of paper hidden under it, on it, in black swirly writing, a poem. 'A Unicorn in the Woods' she read. It seemed to describe Galibrath's funeral. Had Kitta been there then?

Replacing the photograph, she crept over to another sliding door and gently drew it back. Now she was in the kitchen. A log stove sat in a corner, the door left open to warm the room and next to it a tap dripped into a stone sink. There was a table too and on it was a pile of black bowls, a poker, she guessed for stoking the stove, and a jug of limp daffodils.

Suddenly, Felicity felt very hungry. She hadn't eaten all day. Maybe - she walked over to a curtain which hung down just past the table and pulled it back.

The pantry! Great, thought Felicity and her tummy rumbled its thanks. Then her face fell. A wok teetered on the edge of a shelf and an onion sat pickling in a jar next to an old treacle tin. At the back, three very dead chickens dangled from metal hooks and on the floor lay an open bag of rice.

"I'd kill for a bag of crisps," she muttered.

"I don't think we have any," murmured a husky voice.

Felicity screamed and spun on her heel.

By the door stood a woman wearing a kimono and a sash just like in the picture Felicity had found in the junkroom. Her hair was pulled up in a bun and two what looked like chop sticks, were holding it in place. She looked about twenty but Felicity knew she was closer to a hundred and twenty.

"But I could make you a cup of tea."

"That, er - would be lovely - thank you," stumbled back Felicity.

The woman took a pan out of the sink and filled it with water and then she put it on the stove. Felicity watched her pick up the poker from the table and begin to stoke up the fire.

Curiously, the witch's skin looked to be paler than in the picture she had seen, and her eyes seemed much duller. Perhaps she was sick, or just tired.

"Do you plan on telling me who you are?" Kitta asked, standing up and turning to look at her. Felicity spotted that she still had the poker in her hand.

"Felicity," said Felicity. "I'm a - I mean, I was a friend of Galibrath's." Kitta grimaced. "He was a wizard, he..."

"I know who he was."

"Sorry."

"Is green tea OK?" She put the poker back on the table and walked over to the curtain. She pushed past Felicity. "I don't have anything else."

"Wonderful - thanks."

Felicity listened as she fumbled about in the pantry and returned holding the treacle tin with the lid already off.

"So, why are you here?" Kitta smiled a not too friendly smile. "Why did you break into my house?"

"I didn't break in," fired back Felicity indignantly. "I just - snuck in. I was looking for you. I need your help."

"Milk?"

"Yes, please."

"We don't have any. Sugar?"

"Do you have any?"

"No." She slipped back into the pantry. "You need my help, you say." Her words echoed back hollow from the tiny room.

"Yes. Tantalus, that's Galibrath's brother..."

"I know him too." Kitta popped her head out of the pantry. "I can't seem to find the cups."

Felicity pointed to the bowls on the table. "Will these do?" She picked one up. "No handles though."

"Er, yes." Kitta smiled for the first time. "Must be losing my marbles."

Felicity smiled back but she didn't dare to nod.

She took the cup from Felicity and another one from the pile and set them on the table. Then she poured some tea leaves from the treacle tin into her hand and sprinkled a little into the two cups.

"Tantalus stole The Wishing Shelf..."

"He stole a bookshop? Now, how did he get that in his pocket?"

"No, no, I mean he stole Galibrath's will." The water was boiling now. "So nobody knows who he left the shop to."

Feeling confused, Felicity watched Kitta roll up the sleeves of her kimono and pick up the bubbling pan. She didn't seem too bothered about the theft of the will. She didn't seem too bothered about anything.

"So now Tantalus has the shop and he's planning to auction the book off to a warlord."

She poured the water into the cups and handed Felicity her tea. "What book?"

"Articulus," Felicity took a sip. "He's going to sell Articulus."

With a grunt, Kitta jumped up and back, perching on the lip of the table and spilling a drop of tea on the sleeve of her kimono. She brushed at it with her other hand and then reached up and felt for the sticks in her hair.

"You should tell somebody."

"I am telling somebody." Felicity was beginning to feel a bit cranky now. "I'm telling you. I think you loved Galibrath once and he loved you. I know he did." She put her cup down on the table. "You have to help me. You have to help me find the will."

"Felicity," Kitta shook her head, "my life is here, not chasing wicked books. As for Galibrath, well, not seen the old goat in years. We just had a summer fling. I don't owe him anything."

"But you still have a picture of him..."

Kitta frowned.

"...on the table, in the other room; and I saw the poem."

Slurping back her tea, Kitta jumped off the table and walked over to the sink. "I'm sorry," she mumbled, twisting the tap and washing out her cup. "You're asking the wrong witch."

"Yes, you should be asking this witch."

A second woman walked in, her flip-flops clicking on the wooden floor. She looked exactly like Kitta but her skin was olive-brown and her eyes twinkled. She tossed a straw basket full of spiky purple cacti onto the table and smiled at Felicity. "Well, well, Felicity Brady."

"You know me?" mustered Felicity, startled and standing up.

"Why, yes - sort of. I spotted you at Galibrath's funeral. I was there too. But you," she turned to Kitta, "you I don't know - unless I'm looking in a mirror."

The cup fell into the sink and smashed.

The tap dripped.

Then Kitta span around and to Felicity's horror, she lashed out at the new woman with her fist. The woman ducked and backed away as Kitta grabbed for the poker on the table. She attacked her - stabbing at her and trying to slice off her head, but the woman in the flip-flops was too fast, dodging left and right like a boxer.

Then Kitta did something very odd - she dropped the poker on the floor and closed her eyes. Lifting her hands out in front of her, she spread out her fingers as if she was going to strangle somebody. The woman, standing with her back to the wall, began to make choking sounds and grabbed at her neck.

"Stop it!" screeched Felicity, and without thinking, she picked up the treacle tin and threw it at Kitta, smacking her in the eye.

Dropping her hands, Kitta turned and glared at Felicity. "I'll get to you next," she growled in a voice Felicity didn't know - or did she?

Turning back and with her head down just

like a bull, Kitta charged at the woman. But like a matador, she stepped to one side and Kitta missed and went hurtling past. She smashed through the wall in a shower of wooden splinters and there was a gigantic splash.

Felicity rushed over to the jagged hole and discovered Kitta up to her knees in slimy pond water. The drenched witch shook her body, spraying up water like a dog after a bath and the sticks in her hair flew out, landing in the pond.

And there, suddenly, as ugly as ever and with bits of soggy carrot still clogging his ears, crouched the goblin, Bartholomew Banks.

"Barf," yelled Felicity and the goblin scowled. He must have grabbed the sticks from the factory; from Wizardry Gadgets.

"Watch your back," he roared at her. "One day, very soon – I'm going to stick a knife in it. Oh, and DON'T CALL ME BARF!" He snapped his fingers and vanished.

Charming, thought Felicity and she turned back to the woman. They smiled uneasily at each other.

Then the woman spoke. "Hi," she said, and she bowed. "I'm Kitta."

Sitting in the kitchen on a low stool Kitta had got for her, Felicity looked down at the chicken carcass lying on her lap.

"Go on then," Kitta chided her. "It won't pluck itself."

Scrunching up her face, Felicity grasped the bird by the neck and with the other hand she took hold of a clump of brown feathers. She tugged.

Kitta tutted. "No, no. Not like that. Give them a good yank. She's not going to peck you."

Felicity smiled weakly. "A good yank. Right." So she did, the feathers tearing out from the skin.

She pulled a face – she didn't feel hungry anymore.

"So, Kitta," she said, trying to take her mind off her grisly job, "this is your home?"

"Yes. Sorry, bit of a mess, I know. But what with Galibrath's death and the funeral I, well..."

Felicity nodded.

Squatting by the hole Banks had made in her wall, Kitta picked up one of the many broken bits of wood that were scattered on the floor. She turned it over and over in her hands and then dropped it back down.

"I could help you fix it," offered Felicity ripping out a second handful of feathers. It had to be better than doing this job. "If you have a hammer and a box of nails."

Kitta shrugged and stood up. "I know a quicker way," and she chanted,

> "A gaping hole at the foot of the mound,
> A pile of wood litters the ground,
> Rubble and dust, panel and pane,
> Patch up and build the wall again."

The broken bits of wood sprang up and swirled round and around as if they were trapped in a tornado. Then one of the splinters tore loose, and Felicity watched it dash over to the hole and begin to try and slot back into place. First one corner and then another, turning over and over, trying to squeeze in. When it had found its old spot and had fitted snugly back, a second splinter raced out to look for a place in the jigsaw.

"Cool," whispered Felicity as the last bit found a home. "Much faster than hammering in nails."

"Much." Kitta walked over to the sink and picked out a knife. She handed it to Felicity. "When you finish plucking, you'll need to cut off the head and the legs. Oh, and then gut it."

Felicity put her hand to her mouth. "But..."

"I'll go and find you some clothes. They might be a bit big for you but they'll look better than ripped jeans." She looked down at Felicity's feet. "Maybe I can find you boots too."

Felicity thanked her and watched her walk over to the door. "You will help me - to find the will?"

The witch grinned. "First we'll feed you, then we'll clothe you and then we'll talk about Galibrath's will."

Chapter 18

That Is Not A Cloud

The carpet rose gently and hovered a few feet above the ground. It was trembling slightly, as if eager to be away. Felicity crawled to the front and grasped hold of some of the rug's tassels, winding them around her hands.

"Hold on!" she warned Kitta, who was crouched just next to her.

But the charm maker just laughed. "Hardly a sports model, is it?" she scoffed, looking down at the shabby rug and fingering one of the rips Tantalus had made.

Felicity shrugged her shoulders and chanted,

> "Twisting and turning, spinning around,
> To Twice Brewed this carpet is bound."

The carpet, somewhat upset by Kitta's rude remark, shot away a little faster than usual.

"Whoa!" the witch gasped, grabbing hold of Felicity's hand. "Where's the seat belt?"

Felicity chortled. "I think you offended it," she yelled over the roar of the wind.

Kitta just nodded.

They soared through the air -

Faster. Faster. FASTER!

Making tunnels in clouds and zooming past birds who squawked in dismay at being overtaken by a raggedy old mat. They raced between hills, skirted bridges and skipped over ponds, the wind tearing at their clothes, distorting their faces and filling their mouths.

Felicity still felt a bit jumpy after her last carpet ride. Scared of being ambushed, she kept glancing over her shoulder, but there were no evil wizards bearing down on them, only a blue-speckled bird with a crooked beak, flying just over their heads.

As they flew over a waterfall and traced the winding river, Felicity spotted the bald head of a giant. He was sitting on the bank, legs pulled up, his knees almost touching his face. In his hands he was grasping a small tree but the branches had all been torn off. A thick rope hung from the end and dangled into the water. He looked up at the carpet, and then with a shrug of his shoulders, he returned to the more important job of catching his breakfast.

Kitta did not seem to be in the mood to chatter, but Felicity did not mind; she had a lot to think about. In her head she kept returning to the night Galibrath had died and her promise to take care of Al. But now she had left him at the mercy of Tantalus. Anything could have happened to him. He could have been turned to stone or boiled and served up with mashed potato to a troll. Imp and mash! What a horrible thought.

They had been flying for what seemed like hours. They had flown over Cauldron City and the ring of black trees, and were now heading for the mountains. Felicity had been kneeling, squinting over the edge, and her legs had fallen to sleep, so she stretched them out in front of her and began to rub them vigorously.

She still had on her ripped jeans as the kimono the witch had found for her had been too long. But she had borrowed a woolly jumper and some boots.

"You OK?" murmured Kitta groggily. She was lying down next to Felicity, her eyes firmly shut.

"I thought you were asleep," said Felicity, through gritted teeth as pins and needles stabbed at her legs.

"No, I've been thinking."

The wind was deafening, so Felicity shuffled closer so she could hear her better.

"About what?"

"Hedes Spine." The witch sat up, leaning back on her hands. "When we chatted yesterday, we decided the will must be hidden there. But any shop of Tantalus's is going to be well guarded. If we try and break in, we will probably get nabbed."

"You have a different plan?" asked Felicity, prodding the speckled bird, who had landed on the end of the carpet and was now pecking at the flapping tassels.

Kitta grinned. "We're going to bluff our way in. Tell me, Felicity, do you enjoy acting?"

The carpet lurched and a thunderous rumble drowned out Felicity's reply. As the carpet staggered, the bird gave an angry screech and flew away. The girls clung to each other in fright. Suddenly, it was very dark, black clouds rolling towards them from every direction, spitting rain and hurling spears of jagged light.

"We have to go back," Felicity yelled. A cloud burst over them and she hid her face in her hands as the rain lashed at her cheeks.

"We can't. We seem to be trapped. This feels like magic - dark magic. Tantalus's magic."

"But how...?"

"Is not important. JUST HOLD ON!"

Like a steamroller, the swirl of black cloud rolled over the girls, drowning them in a wave of booming crashes and stinging rain. Felicity crouched as low as she could, her arms wrapped around her head, her nose hidden in the soaking carpet. She could feel Kitta huddled next to her. She was shaking and Felicity wondered if it was from fear or because of the cold.

A tongue of lightning split the sky, chased by a second growl of thunder. It burst through Felicity's head making her cry out in fright. It seemed so close, as if somebody had slammed shut a gigantic book just next to her ear.

She lifted her head, shielding her eyes with

her hand. The wind seemed to be getting stronger and stronger, driving into her, trying to throw her from the jumping carpet. It was like riding in a rodeo, on an out-of-control bull. They were being tossed all over the sky.

She watched in horror as a lightning bolt scorched the carpet just in front of her. There was now a frisbee-sized hole in it, smoking and sizzling as the rain soaked the blackened rim. The carpet staggered, as though in pain and plummeted like a brick towards the ground.

"PULL UP!" Felicity heard Kitta scream. "CARPET - UP!"

The witch dragged herself to the front of the carpet and took hold of a corner, pulling back on it with all of her might. "Help me!" she yelled. Felicity crawled forward too and tightened her wet hands around the other corner. Together they hauled back.

But they kept falling, faster and faster. "WE MUST PULL HARDER!" Kitta shouted. Felicity gritted her teeth and tugged, her arms almost being wrenched from their sockets.

"Don't crash, please don't crash," Felicity whimpered. She could see the ground now and it was rushing up to meet them. She stole a glance at the witch. She was staring ahead, her eyes fixed, her lips pursed and white. But she did not look frightened or defeated.

Slowly, they began to tilt back, pulling up from the dive. There was a forest below them and Felicity could see the trees bending in the wind. She yanked back even harder. The carpet seemed to give a little more, the rushing air catching under the lip, slowing them down. Then, with only a few feet to spare, they pulled up, skimming over the tops of the trees.

The girls collapsed in a crumpled heap. The rain was slowing now, the thunder muffled and much further away. Kitta reached out and grabbed Felicity's shoulder. "You OK?"

Felicity smiled weakly. "I - I think so," she stammered. "Is it - the storm, is it over?"

Kitta looked up at the sky and her face darkened. "No, Felicity, it's not." Fearfully, she followed Kitta's gaze. Far above them there was a grey cloud but it was acting rather strangely. It looked to be falling, as if the whole sky was caving in.

"That cloud, it's..."

"That," said Kitta, stonily, "is not a cloud." She began to look around frantically, as if searching for something.

Felicity was still looking up at the cloud that was not a cloud. "So, er - what is it then?" she asked, not really wanting to know the answer.

Kitta ignored her.

"It looks like a cloud, I mean it's sort of grey and it's in the sky. It seems very cloud-like."

"It's not a cloud." Kitta was looking to her left, shielding her eyes from the few drops of rain that still fell. "Maybe, yes - maybe."

"It's not very fluffy though and..."

"IT'S NOT A CLOUD!" Kitta reached forward, took hold of the carpet's left corner and tugged. "The mountains, carpet. Head for the mountains." Obediently, it veered to the left, quickly picking up speed. "It's hail. Giant hail."

"Giant hail," echoed Felicity slowly. "So, er, how giant is giant hail?"

"Faster, faster," Kitta urged the carpet on. "About the size of a football."

Felicity gulped. She should have kept her trap shut.

"If we can get to those mountains in time,

before the hail hits us, maybe we can find somewhere to shelter."

Felicity lowered her eyes and stared at the mountains. They seemed miles away, stretched out on the horizon. She felt so helpless. They were never going to make it, and even if they did, where would they hide? Then she remembered the cave – the one she had escaped into when Cruncher had been chasing her. If only she could find it.

They reached the mountains as the first hailstones tumbled past them. Like small meteorites they crashed into the ground, pitting the earth with craters. The carpet weaved from side to side trying to avoid the lethal balls of ice. But then, their luck ran out as a hailstone slammed into the carpet, just missing Felicity's feet. The carpet juddered and began to tip back, the girls grabbing for the front of the carpet where they hung on grimly.

"Over there," screamed Felicity, nodding her head at the glowing mouth of the cave. She let go of the carpet and pointed. "Carpet! The cave - go for the cave."

The hailstones were falling fast and furiously

now and as the carpet dipped and zigzagged, two more stones smashed into it making it wobble and shake. But they were so close and with a last burst of speed they shot into the glowing cavern.

They were slowing down and sinking. They looked ahead and nestled in the valley they could just make out Twice Brewed, a rainbow arching over the town, crashing into the clouds in a burst of yellows and reds.

Silently, they circled over the buildings. It was as if the carpet was lost and had no clue which way to go. But after a little twisting and turning it plunged to the ground, landing with a bump in a narrow alleyway.

Felicity scrambled off and gently put her feet down on the cobbled street - her legs always felt a little wobbly after riding magic carpets. She stared about. The alleyway felt small and cramped. Shops with dusty windows and crumbling bricks crowded in on her, making it feel dark and gloomy. They looked deserted, but for a shop called 'Curly Tongs, Monster Catcher', as if they had not been open for years. The plaster on the walls was shabby, peeling away like the skin of an orange and spiders crouched in all of the corners. What an odd place to find what Tantalus had called 'the best bookshop in Eternus', thought Felicity.

In a flash, the carpet rolled up and stood on one end. Felicity watched as it hopped over to a rusty drainpipe and squeezed up it, two of its tassels still sticking out of the hole at the bottom.

She turned to Kitta. "I don't understand," she muttered, looking puzzled. "Where's the bookshop? Where's Hedes Spine?"

Kitta pointed to a scruffy-looking warehouse at the far end of the alley. "There. The big one. The one with all the glass."

They crept a little closer, hiding in shadows and pausing in doorways.

"There's a lot of barbed wire," whispered Felicity uncertainly, "and the sign - 'Keep Out. Puffdolts on Guard'. Not too welcoming, is it?"

The witch grinned and patted her shoulder. "The shop's protected by a powerful charm.

Only wizards and other magical folk can see through it."

"But I'm not a wizard."

"Too true."

"So," seethed Felicity, getting a little annoyed now, "how am I supposed to break into a shop when I can't even see it?"

A blast of wind ruffled Felicity's hair as a black carpet rocketed by, landing just in front of the wire fence. A stooped-over hag, her face hidden in a black scarf, stumbled off it. "I'm not gonna to be long," she shrieked at the still flapping rug. "Be 'ere when I get back or I'll cut you up and sell you as door mats." She tottered up to the fence and much to Felicity's astonishment, vanished. There was not even a puff of smoke.

Felicity's mouth fell open and she rubbed her eyes and blinked. A wizard with a limp and spiky violet hair hobbled up to the fence and simply melted into it. Then two imps scuttled past and they vanished too.

"Shut your eyes."

"Why?" said Felicity, still gawping up at the fence. She watched as the witch's carpet limped over to a line of metal pipes, which hung on the barbed wire like the flumes of a church organ. Swiftly, it jumped up, coiled up tightly and slid into the third pipe on the left.

It seemed to be parking.

"Felicity - CLOSE YOUR EYES!"

"OK, OK."

Turning Felicity towards her, the witch chanted in her ear,

> *"Cleanse your eyes, illusions crumble,*
> *Castles in the sky begin to tumble."*

Felicity winced in pain as a flash of red light burst in her head, just over her left eye. She staggered back, leaning on a shop window. Kitta reached out to steady her.

Slowly, Felicity opened her eyes.

She gasped. The old warehouse with its crumbling bricks and rotten wooden shutters had vanished. But there was no gaping crater where it had once stood and no pile of rubble. Now, towering over her was the most magnificent shop she had ever seen. It dwarfed the others and they seemed to shy away as if scared of being struck.

It was huge! A glass monster with a great flight of marble steps leading up to a revolving glass door. Round and around it spun as a torrent of imps and hunched-over wizards rushed in and left carrying heaps of books. Over the door, held up by two stone pillars, was a moon-shaped balcony, a low wall running around it and a stone statue sat perched on the edge.

"Is that...?"

"Yes," mumbled Kitta brusquely.

"Oh." Felicity chuckled. "So, what now? How do we get in?" She looked warily at the puffdolt slumped on the top of the steps. It had on a crumpled grey uniform and a peaked-cap five or six sizes too small.

"Just before the storm hit, I told you we were going to bluff our way in. Do you remember?"

Felicity thought for a moment. "You asked if I was any good at acting."

"So, are you?" The witch smiled wickedly.

Chapter 19

Professor E. Gomorrha's Head Topples Off

Tantalus spied the imp cowering behind a wobbly tower of books. The wizard marched over, grasped the wriggling creature by a long, dangly ear and dragged it to the front of the shop. There, he thrust a bundle of loose papers he was carrying into the imp's shaking hands.

"Nail them to trees," he barked.

The frightened imp, his knees knocking, whimpered, "Every tree? But..."

Tantalus yanked his ear viciously and the imp yelped in agony.

"If you miss even a tiny shrub," Tantalus hissed, "I'll be nailing you to it. GOT IT!?"

The imp, his eyes wide open in fright, nodded

furiously. Then he scampered away, dropping posters all over the floor as he went.

"Torturing imps, Tantalus," Banks murmured softly, sidling up. "Really, you'll be in trouble with WANDD."

Tantalus sniggered spitefully. "That bunch of boy scouts. HA! About as much use as - as, YOU!" He glared down at the goblin. "You let Kitta and that Brady-girl slip through your claws and now I..."

"Fingers," murmured Banks, smiling slyly.

"WHAT?" rasped Tantalus, his eyes blazing.

"Fingers." He held up a hand for his boss to see. "Goblins have fingers, eight of them, not claws. Oh, by the way, I was told you conjured up a storm to try and stop them. Did it work?"

The fuming wizard clenched his fists and there were tears of fury in his eyes. "One day soon, you and I..." The threat hung in the air like the smell of a rotting dorfmoron. But the goblin just grinned, looked bored and began to make a clicking sound with his tongue.

The wizard's eyes bulged and with a snarl, he spun on his heel. He spotted an imp gingerly stacking books, one on top of the other, to form a pyramid. He swaggered over and gave the pile a mighty kick, sending the books tumbling to the floor. Leaving the imp fumbling on his hands and knees, he stormed out of the shop.

The goblin pretended to yawn, stretching his hands over his head. He did not want any of the wizards milling about the shop to think he was scared of Tantalus. But he did feel a bit jittery. There was so much fury raging in the wizard's eyes. Maybe he was pushing his boss too far.

With a sigh, he bent down and scooped up one of the posters the fleeing imp had dropped. Curiously, he read it.

WANTED
Felicity Brady.
For the cold-blooded murder of sweet, old Cruncher, who never hurt a Smogly fly.

REWARD
A book token.

By order of
Hedes Spine Inc.

It was signed at the bottom,

Tantalus Falafel

"What do you mean the professor is not in the visitors' book?" bawled a voice. "He must be. We travelled all the way from Cauldron City. Let me see."

The goblin looked up. Over by the front desk, a frazzled-looking imp was furiously thumbing the pages of a black book, as a spindlysloth bent over him, trying to wrench it from his hands. A few feet away, crouched over a knobbly stick, was a wizard. He was very old, his nose all swollen and crooked, his cheeks and chins hanging in small fleshy sacks.

"I spoke to Tantalus only last week and he promised he would be here to welcome the professor in person." The spindlysloth folded his arms and glared furiously at the imp. "I insist on seeing him."

"But, he's popped out."

"Out! Where?"

The imp scratched his head and looked down as his feet. "Well, I - I don't know." He shrugged his shoulders.

"You don't know," the spindlysloth rasped. "YOU DON'T KNOW!" A long spindly arm shot out, grasping the startled imp by his collar and yanking him half over the counter. "Do you know who this is?" The spindlysloth wagged a long finger at the old wizard. "This is Professor E. Gomorrha. His books are best-sellers in Eternus. There are more imps, goblins and giants in his fan club than hags at a Halloween party." He pushed the imp back over the desk. "Find Tantalus. We will be in his office."

"But...," whined the imp, rubbing his neck and looking horrified.

"The professor is not going to sit on a hard stool, choking on Hedes Spine stale muffins and being tormented by autograph-happy yoblins."

"But...."

"And," the spindlysloth smiled a victory smile, "the professor is a close pal of Tantalus's; has been for years. Now, if your boss finds out that you..."

"Follow me," the imp howled, scampering around the desk. He led them to the back of the shop.

Banks snatched up a book and hid his face in it, peering over the top as they walked by. The spindlysloth was very tall and gangly, for a man anyway, and had a very big head which to the goblin looked just like a pumpkin. His eyes were small and sat on top of a hooked nose with one very big, flared nostril. But the strangest things were his hands. The fingers seemed stretched as if they were made of sticky dough, and on every finger he had six knuckles.

Then came the professor. Banks watched him closely. His skin was so pale it was almost transparent, pitted by tiny red veins giving his face the appearance of a road map. But his eyes were bright and he hardly seemed to need his stick. The goblin dropped the book he was holding, spun on his heel and snatched up a copy of the popular 'Out of Your Body, Out of Your Mind' from a stack of books, making it wobble.

"NO!" bawled the imp, as the pile of books toppled over for a second time. He shrugged his shoulders in defeat, dropped to the floor and began to sob.

Banks flipped the book over in his hand and glared at the picture of the professor on the back cover. The face was the same, the wrinkled skin, the double chins, but the eyes were gloomy and grey, not at all like the eyes of the wizard he had just seen. The goblin scowled. How odd. Then a light bulb flashed on in his mind.

He yanked the still snivelling imp to his feet and roughly shook him. "Stop blubbering and open y' lugs. I want you to grab the fastest carpet you can find and fly to The Wishing Shelf. Find Tantalus and bring him here." The imp sniffed and rubbed his dripping nose on the sleeve of his jumper. "NOW, YOU FOOL!" The goblin shoved him away.

Banks snapped his fingers and vanished in a puff of cherry-pink smoke. A split second later he was crouched in a dark corridor, his ear glued to the door of Tantalus's office. But there were no muffled footsteps on the carpet and no sound of drawers being slid open or the rustle of secret papers being read. What were they doing in there?

Hang on! He had heard a muffled snivel. Could they be injured? Had Tantalus booby-trapped his office?

He could storm in now, he thought. Catch

them in the act and scare the ghouls out of them. He chuckled softly, but then a scowl traced his brow. Only yesterday, that witch had almost broken his neck. He rubbed his still throbbing ankle. Maybe he should be more wary. He rested his hand gently on the door handle and slowly twisted it. Then he nudged the door ajar and peered into Tantalus's office.

The room was a jumble of dark lumps and shadows, the only light coming from the oil-lamp sitting on the cabinet next to the door. He screwed up his eyes, and then opened them. Much better. He could dimly see the heads lined up on the wall, and there were two statues - STATUES! The only statue in Hedes Spine was of Tantalus, but that was on the balcony.

CRACK! The goblin jumped back in horror, the door swinging shut. Gulping, he pushed it back open. CRACK! A head wobbled, then it tumbled to the floor with a thud. It rolled over to the goblin but he was too shocked to move. Closer and closer. WHACK! It hit the edge of the door and a grey face glared up at him. Professor E. Gomorrha!

Cold beads of sweat dribbled down the

goblin's neck, drenching his Armani shirt, gluing it to his body. In shock, he stared at the wizard's gnarled face and his thin lips frozen back in a snarl. He looked up. Now the other head was rocking from side to side – it was the spindlysloth. It toppled off too, bouncing on the floor and splintering.

Hands shot out of the severed neck searching for a hold. They found the collar bone. The knuckles turned white as Kitta hauled herself out and sat on the spindlysloth's shoulders, her legs still dangling down into the body. Then, a crack sliced down the spindlysloth's chest, racing down his left leg, all the way to his boots. Then a second, ripping down an arm and shattering the hand. The statue began to crumble and Kitta fell from her perch, spilling onto the floor.

She looked up and screeched, jumping back as the professor's headless body split in two, and crashed over. There, where the statue had stood, curled up in a ball, crouched Felicity. Slowly, she lifted her head and smiled feebly at the witch. "Now I know what a mummy feels like," she mumbled, climbing shakily to her feet.

Kitta jumped to her feet too and grinned at her. "It was a bit of a tight squeeze," she admitted.

"A tight squeeze! You were in a, a..."

"Spindlysloth," suggested Kitta, helpfully.

"Yeah, a spindlysloth. You could get three of you in there." Felicity rubbed her back and grimaced. "I was stuck in a shrivelled, old wizard - and he smelled."

"The Masking Charm had to fool a lot of Tantalus's imps," retorted the witch loftily. "So you had to smell the part too."

Felicity looked at her sourly. "Easy for you to say," she mumbled. She stared around the office and sighed. "Where do we begin?"

So they had used the Masking Charm, observed Banks, still crouched in the doorway. Tricky bit of magic that - old magic and dangerous. The sort Tantalus was most scared of. Tantalus had called Kitta a fool; feeble and needy, he had told him. But no, she was strong. He would have to watch his step.

The blubbering was getting louder. He looked slowly around the room but there were so many hidden corners, it was hard to see. Hold on!

Under the window there was a wriggling lump. It was the imp. The one they had tricked into showing them up to Tantalus's office. He was bound up in rope, the sort that you use to tie back curtains, and a sock had been wedged in his mouth. *Tantalus is gonna fatten you up and feed you to a dorfmoron*, thought Banks.

Now, where were they? Oh, yes. There they were, two shadows hovering over the wizard's desk. What were they looking for? Secret files? Or a will, perhaps? They must have broken the lock on the drawer. Now, that would not do at all. If anybody was going to discover Tantalus's secrets it would be him. Quietly, so they could not hear him, he whispered,

> *"I need a rope of the strongest kind,*
> *Two robbers before me, they must bind."*

There was a flash and two ropes, knotted at the ends, wriggled out of the snout of the goblin's head on the wall. Wriggling and squirming like freshly-caught eels, they dived down and coiled around the struggling girls. Felicity, her arms pinned to her sides, fell in a heap next to Kitta. Fearfully, she looked up as a dark shadow passed over them. "Oh no," she groaned, dropping her head, "not you."

"Did you miss me?" asked Banks mockingly. He knelt down and clasped Felicity's chin in his hand. "I did enjoy our little chat. It was a shame..."

"Keep your slimy hands off her," yelled Kitta, struggling even harder.

Like lightning, Banks was on his feet. He kicked the witch viciously in the stomach. "You tore my shirt, AND," he thundered, "I LOST A CUFF LINK!" He sighed and lowered his voice. "If you find it, I'd love to have it back."

Chapter 20

Fight!? They Only Teach Us Netball!

The dark wizard stormed into his office and stared in shock at the girls wrapped up in rope on the floor. "Omoikitta?" he murmured. He took a shaky step towards her. Kneeling down, he gently brushed a curl away from her face. "It has been so long."

She pulled away. "Not long enough," she seethed, glaring up at him. "Now, undo this rope."

But Tantalus shook his head and slowly stood back up. He turned to the goblin who was perched cheekily on the corner of the wizard's desk. "You captured them? Single-handed?"

Banks grinned slyly and nodded.

Grunting, the wizard strode over to the

279

curtains, yanking them open and bathing the murky room in sunshine. He gazed out of the window. He could see clear across Twice Brewed to the old windmill and Lupercus Castle perched on the hill and a small brook glistening in the winter sun. As a child, he had fished in it. Back then, the tiny men in the town had told him that the fattest trout in all the land swam in it. He sighed. He was always suspicious now of old gnomes and their fishing tales.

He turned back from the window. The goblin had sprung off the desk and was prodding Kitta cruelly with his foot. "They were hunting through your papers. Probably looking for your brother's will." He smiled mockingly at her. "No luck though, eh?"

"Don't touch her," warned Tantalus, a dangerous look clouding his face.

But the goblin ignored him. He grabbed Kitta roughly by her ponytail and yanked her head back. "Look at me when I'm insulting you," he hissed, poking her in the ribs.

The goblin yelped as a flying book slapped him in the face. He rubbed his smarting cheek and glared angrily at Tantalus. But on a shelf, under the window, a second book was trying to wriggle loose. Quickly, Banks let go of the witch's hair and backed away. "OK, OK," he whined.

Tantalus ignored the goblin and looked at Kitta, but he stayed by the window as if he was scared of being too close to her. "You journeyed all the way to Twice Brewed just to stop me from keeping The Wishing Shelf." He smiled soberly. "You must really despise me."

"This is not about you or The Wishing Shelf. Galibrath chose that dusty old bookshop over me."

The wizard stared at her in surprise. "Then - why?"

"Because it's the only way to stop you from selling Articulus and killing us all."

Killing us all! Poppycock!" He waved his hand at her mockingly.

"If you sell the book to a warlord, he will destroy this land, and you. It will not matter how many gold flupoons you have. Don't you understand? Can you be so blinded by greed?"

"It is you who is blinded," Tantalus snarled. He turned and gazed back out of the window.

"In a few short hours I will be the richest wizard in the land."

Over in the corner, Banks shuffled his feet. "We need to go," he mumbled sulkily. "The warlords will be showing up soon."

"Yes, yes," snapped the wizard. He smoothed back a greasy black curl and hooked his cloak more tightly around his neck. "How many of the blighters will be there?"

"Two."

"TWO!?"

The goblin shrugged. "The night demon told all the other warlords he'd stab 'em if they showed up. So there's only IT and Jumble Mud left."

"Hmm. I suppose Jumble Mud's too stupid to worry." The wizard looked to the girls. "I hate to be rude but I have a book to sell, but we can carry on chatting very soon." He marched over to the door. "Oh, and Brady," he called back, stopping. "I have not forgotten you and your irksome meddling. I will interrogate you by sunset. OK?"

Felicity's eyes opened wide in fright.

"She knows nothing," fumed Kitta, struggling

with her binds. "Let her be - she's only a child."

"Oh, I know she knows nothing, but I'm going to interrogate her anyway because, well - I think it will be fun." He chuckled and swept out of the room.

Banks shuffled after his master but as he passed by Felicity, he bent over and whispered in her ear. Then he left the room as well.

The girls lay in silence, listening to the sobs of the imp who was still trussed up under the window. Felicity heaved at her ropes but it was as if they were alive. Every time she got an arm free, or a leg, the end of a rope would strike out like an angry python and coil around the escaping limb.

"What did the goblin say to you?" panted Kitta, as she too struggled with her binds.

"I think," gasped Felicity breathlessly. "I think - he was teasing me. YES!" she yelped, as her left arm slipped free. "No," she sighed, as a rope shot out and grabbed it.

"What did he say, Felicity?"

"Who?"

"The goblin! What did he whisper to you?"

"Barf? Well, it sounded like a song - or a

chant. I - I don't know." She growled. "This rope is driving me crazy."

"Felicity!" yelled Kitta

"Kitta!" Felicity yelled back. They lay there in silence.

"Tangled - no, no, tangling ropes, no - rope, listen to you - to me, I mean, er - ."

"Felicity," warned Kitta.

"I'm trying! I'm trying! Tangled - rope - listen - to - me - er," then in a sudden rush of words – "slacken your knots and set me free. YES!" Then she looked down at the rope still wrapped snugly around her body. "Oh," she muttered dejectedly. "You see, he was just teasing me. I so detest that goblin."

But the witch just grinned and echoed her words, her binds falling away and slithering to the floor. She stood up and stretched her hands over her head. "Much better," she mumbled smugly.

Felicity gawped up at her, her mouth open catching flies. "But - why...?"

"Magic is not that simple," she lectured. "You have to mean the words or they won't work."

"Oh, OK. Right. Mean the words." So she

had a second go, but this time she spoke each word much more slowly. But it still didn't work.

"Help me," she wailed, but the witch ignored her. She was too busy. Slowly, she was feeling along the walls with her hands and tapping on the dark wood with her knuckles.

"Fine! I'll just sit here then, shall I - like a trussed-up turkey." Felicity shook her head sulkily and returned to the charm. She whispered it - no luck, so she had a go at shouting it - nothing, though she made Kitta jump, so that was good. She sang it - ten times, to the tune of ten different ABBA songs. Then, in frustration, she did all of the above, but with her eyes shut.

In disgust, she looked over at Kitta who was now crawling on the floor, her nose glued to the carpet. "Pretending to be a dog is not going to help," she remarked crossly.

The witch did not even bother to look up. "I'm hunting for a trap door or a hidden lever. Maybe Tantalus hid Galibrath's will in a secret room." She sighed. "But I'm just guessing. I knew a wizard called Jasper Pottywalrus who hid his jewels in a Wellington boot on top of the cistern in the loo."

Felicity lifted her eyes and looked around the office. It was much brighter now Tantalus had let in a bit of sun, but apart from the door they had come in by she couldn't see a second door - hidden or not. "Shall I check the loo then?" she asked. "Or, I suppose you could ask them," she suggested, nodding at the grotesque heads resting in a line on the wall.

"Who?"

"The heads. I bet they saw where Tantalus hid the will."

"Felicity!"

"Sorry, just joking. Keep your..."

"No, no. That's a fantastic idea!" Kitta jumped up and dashed over to Tantalus's desk. Hastily, she fumbled through his papers, scattering many of them on the floor. "Here we go," she announced triumphantly, picking up a gold letter-opener. She crouched down next to Felicity and began to saw through the rope.

Felicity looked at her sorely. "You could have thought of this a little sooner. I've lost all the feeling in my legs, you know. I do hate that goblin." She frowned. "I wonder why Barf even bothered to help us? Y' know, whispering the charm to me."

But Kitta just grunted. The rope was thick and difficult to cut. "Yes!" she gasped, as the rope tore apart and fell wriggling to the floor, squealing like a wounded pig. "OK, we have to find a book. Come on." She threw the letter-opener back on the desk and rushed over to the wizard's bookshelf.

Felicity struggled to her feet but then had to lean on the desk for a long moment. Her legs felt all wobbly and her head was spinning. She had gotten up too quickly.

"Felicity! Come on!" shouted Kitta. She was peering at the books, her ear resting on her shoulder.

"OK, OK." Felicity staggered over and began to help, though she had no clue what she was looking for. "Any particular book?" she asked wearily.

"We need a charm to wake up the dead."

"Oh, right. Of course. Silly me." She pulled a book off the shelf and began to staunchly flick through the pages. "Wow! Here's a charm to bring a teddy to life. I can try it on Biggleswick;

he's my teddy. And here's a long fiddly-looking spell to kill spiders. There's a big black hairy thing sitting on my netball skirt and Miss Quinn says it's not a proper excuse to skip PE."

Crouching down, the witch yanked out a brown book. She opened it gently and began to study it. "I think this is it," she murmured, flicking through it. She looked up and grinned. "Yes, this will do. I just have to change the odd word to fit our - dilemma."

She stood back up and marched over to the wall where the heads hung. Felicity followed her, looking up at the dead animals and wishing they did not have such big teeth. There were six in all: a giant, three gnomes, an imp, and a goblin. The gnomes and the imp looked shocked, as if somebody had just shouted 'Boo!'. But the giant and the goblin looked angry, their eyes awash with hate.

She watched nervously as Kitta lifted the book up and began to chant,

"Nameless faces on a scoundrel's wall,
Sinister trophies from one-sided brawls,
Hateful secrets you've had to keep,

In a deeply troubled and ill-fated sleep.

Bewildered, confused, awaken your mind,
Dimmed eyes flicker, no longer blind,
Gulp in fresh air, revenge can be yours,
A chance to get even, settle old scores."

Felicity peered up at the wrinkled faces expectantly, ready to jump back if they so much as wiggled a whisker. She glanced over to the witch but she just tossed her one of her pet 'just relax' looks. She edged a little closer to the goblin. His eyes were open, but they were dull and empty, staring back at her like glass marbles which, she thought, is what they probably were. Cheekily, she reached up and prodded his cheek with her finger.

"Felicity," warned Kitta. "Don't get too close. They could wake up any second."

Felicity turned her head and shot the witch her pet 'yeah, right' look, rolling her eyes. Then, casually, she looked back to the goblin and his now gaping mouth.

"Ahhh!" she screamed, staggering back. Her legs seemed to turn to jelly. They buckled and she fell to her knees.

The goblin glared down at her, drool dripping from his mouth. "WHERE IS HE?" he bawled. "WHERE'S THAT DAMNED WIZARD?!"

"W, w - what w, w - wizard?" stammered back Felicity.

"I'LL WRING THAT COWARD'S NECK!" boomed the giant, who had also woken up and seemed to be in just as foul a temper as the goblin. "CREPT UP BEHIND ME, HE DID. SHOT ME IN THE BACK."

"Shhh," whispered Kitta, urgently. "They'll hear you."

But the giant just laughed loudly. "I'VE BEEN DEAD FOR TEN YEARS AND NOW YOU WANT ME TO SHUSH. HA!"

"Are we dead, then?" asked a gnome. "I mean, how can that be? We were just out having a picnic and then, well, it all went black." The other gnomes nodded sadly.

"IT WAS THAT DARK WIZARD," shouted the goblin. "KILLED US ALL." He bared his teeth and growled. "I'LL RIP HIM TO BITS!"

"He murdered me because I spilt a drop of ink

on his best cloak," the imp murmured, sighing sadly. "His cloak's black, so there was not even a mark."

The other imp, still trussed up on the floor, sobbed pitifully.

"HE'S AN EVIL MONSTER!" bellowed the giant's head.

"A MADMAN!" yelled the goblin's head.

"And he's not very nice," murmured a gnome.

"Shhh," urged Kitta, for a second time, but too late. The pad, pad, pad of running feet could be heard coming from the other side of the door. The closed, but not locked door, thought Felicity. Wildly, she ran and grabbed up a stool. Holding it in front of her, she rushed to the door. Already, she could see the handle was turning and the door was being slowly pushed open. Felicity crashed into it with her shoulder, slamming it shut. Fumbling a little, she jammed the top of the stool under the handle.

Kitta stared at Felicity in surprise. Then, grudgingly, she smiled. "Good thinking," she said. Felicity smiled awkwardly back.

"BANG!" The door shook violently. Kitta

span back around and glared up at the heads. "Listen," she ordered them, "Tantalus, the wizard who killed you, has stolen a scroll from us and we want it back. Can you help?"

"I don't see how," the goblin mumbled gruffly. The other heads slowly shook on the wall.

"But there must be a safe or a secret room, you know, where he can hide - things."

"Things?" quizzed the giant, looking puzzled. Felicity had a feeling if he still had hands he would have scratched his head.

"Yes, things - you know. Gold. Secret papers."

"Oh yes," nodded the giant. The witch's face lit up. "No clue." Her face dropped back down.

The door creaked loudly as the imps' small fists bashed at it. Leaning her back on the wood, Felicity dug her heels into the carpet. "Kitta," she called, "they really do want to come in."

"But, you must have seen him. Maybe - I don't know. Maybe, he pulls a hidden lever and a secret door opens. Maybe..."

"But we're dead," growled the goblin bitterly.

"Yes, but..."

"Dead," the goblin spelt out the word. "So we don't see very much."

"But, I thought that..."

"No," the imp butted in. "The last thing I saw was Tantalus's pasty face, just before he jinxed me."

"Kitta!" yelled Felicity, as a sliver of wood splintered from the door. "They're almost through."

With her hands on her hips, Kitta turned to face Felicity. Her face looked calm but her eyes flashed angrily. "Step away from the door. Let them in."

Felicity stared at her, stunned. "You must be crazy. There must be hundreds of angry imps out there. They'll rip us to shreds."

The door shook even harder.

"We are going to have to fight our way out of here. Better to face them now, before more of them show up."

"But - I don't know how to fight. I mean, it's not something they teach us at school. THEY TEACH US NETBALL!"

"Felicity, we fight or we're captured. And if we're captured we face Tantalus's torture chambers."

"HE HAS TORTURE CHAMBERS!?"

Like a gunshot, the legs of the stool shattered, sending it crashing to the floor. Slowly, the door began to open. With a startled yell, Felicity thrust her shoulder into the door, but grasping hands with sharp claws were already poking through the gap, clawing at her jumper. She pushed even harder, the imps squealing in agony as tiny fingers got trapped.

"In the corner, under the carpet," squeaked the imp's head. "I used to work for Mr Falafel remember, before he murdered me. He can be a bit odd. Keeps his stuff hidden under the floor."

"Which corner?" asked Kitta, slowly turning back around. She could not understand why a wizard as powerful as Tantalus would hide the will in such a ridiculous place.

"Over there." The imp nodded his head at the desk. "In the corner. Just lift up the carpet. Most wizards have a secret room protected by evil charms and nasty booby traps. But not Mr Falafel. I mean, who would think of looking under the floorboards?"

But Kitta was no longer listening. There was

no time. She ran to the corner of the room, sliding over the top of the desk, and quickly knelt down. Clawing at the carpet with her fingernails, she managed to get a grip on the edge and she yanked it up. There! A crack in the wood, about the size of a penny. She slipped a curved finger into the hole and pulled. The floorboard popped up and there, looking all innocent, was a yellow scroll of parchment. Galibrath's will!

"Got it!" she yelled, but just then the door crashed open, sending Felicity sprawling to the floor. Howling in anger, a sea of imps poured in, brandishing tiny wooden spears. Kitta stuffed the scroll safely in her kimono. Then she stood up and rolled up her sleeves.

Chapter 21

Spitting Out Trolls

Most of the imps ran at Kitta, ignoring Felicity. But two of them stopped, dropped their spears and grabbed hold of her feet. She yelped and kicked out but they hung on and began to drag her from the room. "Help!" she yelled, but Kitta was too busy dodging spears to hear her.

Droning like an angry bee, the sentinel leapt out of her pocket and dived on the imps, smacking the tallest of them on the top of the head. Seeing stars, the dazed imp staggered back, slamming into the cabinet and knocking the lamp to the floor. It smashed, spilling flaming oil over the carpet. The other imp dropped Felicity's foot and grabbed for his spear, stabbing at the spinning ball. But he missed and as tongues of flame began to crawl up the side of the cabinet, he dropped his spear, flung his woozy pal over his shoulder, and limped out of the room.

Clambering to her feet, Felicity grabbed up the fallen spear and ran to help Kitta. But she did not need any help. A pile of hands and feet - too many imps to count - lay in a tangled heap on Tantalus's desk. Three more imps were prodding at the witch with spears but they seemed to be too scared to attack her. They had seen what would happen if they did. Suddenly Kitta's hands shot out and grabbed hold of a spear. Before the imp could even think of letting go, he was being spun round and around. Then, SPLAT! He landed on the top of the pile and lay there, whimpering like a baby.

The last two imps gulped in unison, wet their shorts and with frightened squeals, scampered out of the door.

Kitta eyed the swelling fire in alarm. The cabinet was engulfed in jumping flames and black smoke was filling the room. "We have to get out of here," she howled. They ran to the door, but there they froze, for charging up the corridor was a tidal wave of trolls.

Dashing back in, they almost tripped over three more imps who were trying to get out. They let them go, then Felicity slammed the door shut. It swung back open. The lock had been smashed. They needed to jam it shut, but everything seemed to be on fire. She felt a hand grabbing at her jumper. She was being pulled away. Sparks flew as the cabinet crumpled to the floor, blocking the door with splinters of flaming wood.

"Quick!" yelled Kitta. "The balcony! It's our only chance." Grasping a burning stool by the legs she spun it around, once, twice and then flung it at the window. Like a fiery meteor, it soared through the smoky room and crashed through the glass.

They ran to the window but it was set too high up in the wall. Kitta quickly clambered onto the bookcase nestled below it, then she reached down to grasp Felicity's hand to help her up too. But Felicity was busy. She was trying to untangle the imp they had captured but she was struggling with the knot.

"Felicity!" Kitta shouted down. "Come on! There's no time."

"But he'll burn to death," yelled back Felicity. She looked up. "I need the letter-opener. Where did you throw it?"

The witch shook her head. "On Tantalus's desk. I left it there." But the desk was hidden by a curtain of flames.

Felicity tore at the knots but the smoke was making her eyes water and it was hard to see what she was doing. She crouched lower, below the swirling smoke and bit down on the stubborn knot, tearing at it with her teeth. It loosened a little. With her fingers, she worked it loose and quickly she tugged the rope off the blubbering imp.

"Up to you, now," she muttered, standing up. She turned back to the bookcase, coughing as sour smoke filled her nose and mouth. The curtains were now on fire too, black smoke billowing from them, making Felicity's eyes sting. But she could still see Kitta, perched up on the top shelf.

"I hope I'm not hurrying you," shouted the witch, as they clasped hands.

Felicity grinned back at her. "I couldn't let an imp cook," she bellowed, above the crackling of the flames. "Al'd string me up."

Slowly, Kitta dragged Felicity up, but it was hard work. The choking smoke was filling their lungs and the fire seemed to be sapping what little strength they had left. But she was almost to the top now. Then, the blazing curtains bellowed out, caught by a gust of wind, and they drove into Kitta's face. Howling, she toppled back out of the window and Felicity found herself clutching smoke. She landed with a thud and a grunt back on the carpet.

"Kitta," she yelled, but there was no answer. With a cry of panic, Felicity leapt to her feet and made back for the window. She reached up, grabbed at the lip of the top shelf and began to haul herself back up. But hands were clawing at her feet, pulling at her and dragging her back down.

Felicity screamed and kicked out, but whoever it was hung on grimly and wouldn't let go. She felt her grip on the shelf weaken and she kicked back out but the hands seemed to be stuck to her like glue. "Let me go!" she yelled, peering down into the smoke. It was the imp she had just rescued. "Hey, I just saved your life."

"If I capture you," the imp howled back, "Tantalus will reward me, not cook me."

"Charming," she murmured. "Listen, if we don't get out of here now, we'll burn to death. NOW, LET ME GO!"

To her horror, there were now trolls in the room, dodging the fires and creeping ever closer. Wonderful, she thought. Where was the witch? I mean, a little magic might be helpful about now. She gritted her teeth, her fingers screaming at her to let go. Just hold on, she thought. Kitta would be back any second and she would zap this pesky imp.

Like a black hole, a gaping jaw leered down at her off the wall, and in her shock she almost lost her grip. But the giant's head did not touch her. She watched as he clamped his teeth down on the imp and tore it from her leg. The giant pulled an ugly face and in disgust, spat the squealing imp clear out of the door.

"Ruddy good shot," growled the goblin.

"Cheers. It's been so long, I forgot how bad imps taste."

The goblin head glanced down at Felicity who was still hanging from the shelf. "Climb up. My old pal here cannot hold them off for long."

Scrambling with her feet, Felicity gritted her teeth and hauled herself up. Soon she was lying on the top shelf. She looked down at the trolls who were trying to climb up after her. But the giant's head was keeping them at bay, stretching his long neck, plucking them up off the floor. Like a bowling ball, he spat them across the room, knocking over the other trolls like skittles.

"I think you got seven that time," chortled one of the gnomes. The other heads cheered excitedly.

The giant looked very proud. "All in the twist of the neck, you know." He grasped another wriggling troll in his jaws.

Felicity sat up and looked anxiously at the goblin. "What about you? You'll all burn if you stay here."

The goblin shook his head and managed a wry smile. "We don't have the legs to run away anymore. But you must go."

"But..."

"Don't worry about us. The charm your

witch put on us will soon fade. In fact, I'm starting to feel a bit drowsy already."

Felicity smiled sadly. "Thanks for your help. I won't forget you." She swallowed and jumped out of the window.

It was a big balcony, made of scrubbed stone and shaped in a half moon. A low wall ran around the edge held up by small curvy pillars and perched on the top, looking snootily down on Twice Brewed as if he owned it, was the statue of Tantalus.

There was no sign of Kitta. Felicity ran to the wall and peered over. Maybe she had discovered a way to climb down. Or maybe she had fallen. But there was nobody clinging to the pillars and there was no sign of a broken body lying twisted on the ground.

She stood and watched a stream of wizards and hags scurry out from the shop below her. They were all looking up and waving. But not at her. They were waving at the black smoke billowing from the smashed window just over her shoulder.

CRASH! The balcony shook. A growl - Felicity felt the hairs on the back of her neck stand up. There was a monster behind her. A monster who smelt like a sewer. She knew that foul smell - Cruncher had smelled just as disgusting and he was (she span around) A PUFFDOLT!

The monster leered at her, a glob of greenish drool oozing from his crooked lips. It trickled slowly down to a bulbous chin and hung there like a gigantic pussy zit. Felicity shuddered. He was the puffdolt she had seen before, sitting on the steps to the shop. She remembered the crumpled overalls and the baseball cap which was still perched precariously on his bullet-shaped head.

Felicity shrieked as the puffdolt lunged at her. "Help!" she yelled, waving her arms madly at the people below. But they simply ignored her, but for a witch who beamed and waved back.

She ducked as the puffdolt's hands thumped together, just where her head had been. Now on her hands and knees, she scrambled to her left, grabbed up the blackened stool - the one Kitta had used to smash the window - and slung it over her shoulder. It smacked the puffdolt in the face, but to the huge monster, it was like being hit by a bumble bee.

Her back scuffed the balcony wall. As the puffdolt bore down on her she knew there was nowhere left to run. Even her sentinel had deserted her. And where the heck was Kitta!? Feeling angry now, she glared up at the puffdolt and shook her fist. "Squash me, then," she yelled. But the puffdolt had stopped. "Hey, dung beetle! Wakey, wakey! Did you know you are the most gormless..." Felicity stopped too. What was he looking at? She looked up and saw the statue of Tantalus. Was he scared of breaking it?

Quickly, she clambered to her feet and jumped up on the low wall. As the puffdolt shuffled closer, she wrapped her hands around the statue's neck, linked her fingers, and swung her legs out over the edge of the balcony.

There she hung, the puffdolt, roaring and gnashing his teeth, trying to get to her. But he could not reach and he seemed to be too scared of Tantalus's wrath to risk toppling the statue to the ground. She was safe, for now anyway.

Felicity hung on grimly to the statue, staring up at Tantalus's pompous face. If only she had worked harder in gym, she thought miserably. Already, her arms were throbbing and her fingers felt like they were about to drop off. She glanced over at the puffdolt. He had quit trying to get to her and was now sitting on the balcony wall, staring at her grumpily.

Then, the statue began to move and Felicity screamed.

A crack sliced down the statue's chest, racing down the left leg, all the way to the boot. A second ripped down the arm, shattering the hand. The statue began to crumble and Felicity, still clutching the head, fell to earth.

Shakily, Kitta got to her feet and gazed up at the smashed window she has just fallen out of. She rubbed her stinging back and grunted. It had been a long drop and the balcony was made of stone.

"Felicity," she called, reaching up to grasp the window ledge. But it was too high. She winced as daggers seemed to stab in her spine.

She dragged the still smoking stool under the ledge and stood on it. But there was no way she could reach and she had forgotten the Finger-Stretching Charm. She called for Felicity a second time. Where could she be, she wondered crossly. She only had to climb up on the shelf and jump out of the window.

Gingerly, she stepped down from the stool and fearing Felicity might land on it, she pulled it away from the window. Then she moved slowly to the balcony wall and peered over. She would have to climb down and get the flying carpet. But how? She could just see the stone pillars holding up the balcony. She could climb down them, she supposed. But how to get to them?

She turned back and sat on the wall. Looking up at the window, she fearfully watched the black smoke pouring from it. Where was Felicity? Had she been overcome by the smoke or was she trapped by the fire? Or, even worse, had she been devoured by a troll? Ignoring the pain in her back, she stumbled over to the window, calling Felicity's name loudly.

But there was still no reply.

Then she spotted a marble ledge. It seemed to sprout out from the balcony and trail along the side of the glass building. About twenty feet along, on the left side, there was a pipe running all the way down to the ground. If she jumped up on the ledge perhaps she could reach the pipe and slide down it. Trying to hurry, she stumbled over to the corner of the balcony.

She stepped up onto the wall and looked at the ledge. It was very narrow, maybe only a foot wide and there was nothing to hold on to, just smooth glass. She would just have to hug the glass and shuffle along as best she could. So she stretched out a foot and placed it on the ledge.

Kitta kept her face almost glued to the glass as she shuffled along, her arms pinned to her side. The wind tore at her kimono, trying to drag her off the shelf. But she kept going. Almost there now, she thought. Almost there. She reached out her foot...

BANG!

The glass trembled as a troll bashed at it with

bushy fists. Kitta gave a startled cry and pushed back from the quivering window. Too late, she clawed at the smooth glass. She was toppling back; she was going to fall. But, just before her feet slipped from the ledge, she jumped to her left, grabbing for the pipe.

Gasping, she hung there, not daring to look down - not daring to do anything. She had forgotten about the pain in her back. Her mind was only full of plunging screams and shattering bones. She nestled her face on the wall and kept her eyes tightly shut.

Just above her, a window burst open. It slammed into the wall and shattered, raining droplets of glass down onto her, slicing at her hands and face. Looking up, Kitta watched in horror as a troll scrambled out of the window and reached for the pipe above her. It was coming after her. It was going to - MAKE HER FALL! Forgetting her fear, she began to clamber down, hand over hand like a monkey, gripping with her feet. The pipe shook as the troll chased after her.

Finally, her feet were on the ground and a loud cheer went up.

"You were so brave," bawled a grinning witch, showing Kitta her crooked teeth.

A wizard with very furry ears clapped her on the back. "A daring escape," he snorted. "Thrilling stuff. Better than Coronation Street." He began to fiddle with the hairs sprouting out of his left ear hole.

They thought that she had only escaped from the fire and not from Tantalus. Feeling her shoulders relax, she pushed her way through the crowd. Running down the steps, she dashed down the alleyway. Looking back, she spotted the troll and, to her horror, saw that it was almost to the ground too.

Where was that rug? She whistled sharply. The guttering hanging down the wall of an old bakery began to jerk and rattle. In a shower of dust and scraps of plaster, the carpet squeezed out of the end of the pipe, coughing and spluttering.

"If you would choose the oldest pipe," she scolded it, as it reared up and sneezed.

She heard the thump, thump, thump of paws on cobbles. The troll! "Oy!" she shouted to the carpet. "Get over here." In a snap, the carpet unrolled.

It shot down the alley as Kitta sprung up and landed on her feet in the middle. Howling in rage, the troll leapt for the carpet too, but it was flying too fast and he missed. Yelling and cursing, the troll tumbled to the ground, crashing into a dustbin. He lay there whimpering, covered in banana peel and mouldy muffins.

"Faster, carpet. Faster!" Kitta urged it as they soared over the heads of the gasping crowd and headed back to the balcony. She could still see smoke spilling from the window and the once sparkling glass walls of Hedes Spine were now black with soot. But where was Felicity? Then she spotted the puffdolt sitting on the balcony wall. Her chin dropped to her chest, for next to him, hanging off the statue of Tantalus, was Felicity.

"There she is," Kitta gasped. She tugged at the carpet's tassels. "You have to fly faster," she implored it. So, it did. "Just hold on," she murmured, "a little bit longer." Then, the worst thing happened. The statue started to break apart and Felicity, her legs kicking wildly, tumbled towards the ground.

The carpet plunged after her, Kitta, tears streaming from her eyes, clinging on as best she could. Faster and faster, the earth rushing up to meet her. Abruptly, the rug pulled up sharply, slipping under Felicity and the head still clutched in her hands and they shot back up into the sky.

"You OK," yelled Kitta, crawling over to her. She took Tantalus's head from Felicity's shaking hands, glanced at it, smirked, and tossed it over the side.

"I - I think so." Felicity looked at the witch and smiled, quietly hoping the lump of stone did not land on anybody. "Thanks."

The witch smiled back. "You should be thanking the carpet, not me." Felicity nodded and gave the flapping rug a pat.

Then her sentinel flew up and slipped back into her pocket. It sat there trembling as if it knew it was in trouble. "Where have you been?" Felicity cursed it. "I needed you to sort out a puffdolt." But she was glad to see it anyway. She looked over at Kitta. "Where we off to now? To show the will to Hyperion?"

"No. You remember what Banks told Tantalus? That the warlords will be showing up soon. If we don't go there now, we may be too late." The witch reached into her kimono and pulled out the scroll of parchment, a red ribbon wrapped around it, dancing in the wind. "Now, we fly to The Wishing Shelf."

Chapter 22

Really Gross Over-Sweet Toffee Popcorn Balls

Across the river from The Wishing Shelf, Felicity crouched in the shade of a big yellow skip. It was packed full of stools and old desks Tantalus had tossed out of the shop. But this was not her major concern. For there was a troll guarding the door to the shop. The same troll who had slammed Felicity up to the corridor wall but now he had on armour and a studded collar around his neck.

"How we gonna get by Tantalus's rottweiler?" Felicity murmured, shaking her head. "He's as big as a bus."

"No problem," whispered back Kitta. "I know a sneaky way in." She waved a finger at the river.

Felicity screwed up her eyes and peered into the gathering gloom. "I can't see a thing."

"Trust me. There's a tunnel. It leads to the cellars. But to get to it we have to jump in the water."

"But what about Tantalus? He'll know about it. He lived here, right?"

The charm maker chuckled. "Only Galibrath and I have ever used it. To sneak in and out of the shop so we could meet in secret. So, fingers crossed, there should not be any guards. I hope," she added.

"Me too." Felicity looked back at the river. A floating tree shot by, hitting the bank and splintering in two. She scowled. The dark water looked icy cold. She enjoyed swimming in a pool with a shallow end but this was a different kettle of fish.

Kitta took her hand in hers and squeezed it. "Come on," she urged her. "In and out. Only be in there for a minute or two."

Wishing she was at home in her warm bed, Felicity followed the witch upriver till they were safe from the troll's prying eyes. He was now resting his bulky shoulder on the shop window, digging mud from under his nails with a knotted twig. Felicity screwed up her face. Disgusting!

Gently, so as not to splash, they dropped down into the rushing water. Felicity clenched her teeth as tiny needles seemed to stab at her legs. Then, she was up to her neck in freezing water, clinging to the grassy bank to stop herself from being swept away.

"Ready?"

"Yes, I - I think so." But she did not feel ready. She could not feel her hands and her soaked jumper felt like a brick, trying to drag her under the swirling water. "M - maybe, this is not such a w - wonderful plan."

But Kitta had swam off.

Scared of being left on her own, Felicity pushed away from the bank and began to swim as hard as she could for the other side. But for every foot she swam, the current dragged her five feet downriver. Foul-tasting water splashed in her face and seeped between her pursed lips. Coughing and spluttering, she battled on. But already she was nearly level with the shop and she was only half way over.

Trying not to panic, Felicity struggled out of

her jumper and kicked off her boots. She struck back out for the bank, but the river would not let her go. Like a giant's hand it clasped her tightly, yanking her under the choppy waves. She was being dragged away from the shop and under the bridge.

She was going to drown.

Felicity desperately wanted to shout for help, but she was scared the troll would hear her. She would be putting Kitta in greater danger. All of a sudden, a hand grasped her by the wrist and pulled her, splashing, to the shore.

"OK?" a voice whispered in the dark.

"Y - yes, I - I think so." Her teeth were chattering, making it difficult to speak. "Th - thanks for..."

"Shush! What's that?"

Fearfully, they looked up. THUMP! THUMP! THUMP! Coming closer and closer.

"The troll!" whispered Felicity urgently, her face stricken. They took a deep breath and ducked under the water.

Felicity clung to the bank and kept her eyes tightly closed. Seconds dragged. She forced her eyes open and looked up, craning her neck to see if it was still there. It was. Stay calm. Stay calm. But her lungs felt as if they were about to burst. She looked back up. A huge shadow seemed to hover over the water. Lingering. Searching. But Kitta was with her and if the troll spotted them they would fight it together. Suddenly, she felt a hand tugging at her t-shirt, dragging her back to the surface.

The water broke over her head and she opened her eyes to find it was Kitta holding her tightly by the arm. The troll had vanished.

"Where's the tunnel?" Felicity gasped, gulping in air as quietly as she could.

"I don't know. It should be here." Felicity's shoulders sagged as she watched Kitta feel along the muddy bank with her hands. Tantalus must have found out about the tunnel and blocked it off. Now what? If they couldn't get into The Wishing Shelf, how could they stop the Warlords' Auction?

"Hold on," whispered Kitta. Felicity watched as she dived under the water.

A few seconds later she was back. "I've found it," she spluttered. "About three feet below the surface, just under us. We can swim down to it."

"But why...?"

"The water must have risen, that's all. But we can still get through. Take three deep breaths and hold the last one. OK?"

"OK."

"Just follow me. Stay close. It's dark down there."

They sucked in as much oxygen as they could and sank down into the murky water. The river was not so powerful this close to the bank but Felicity stayed right on Kitta's flapping feet, just in case. It only took a couple of seconds for the witch to find the tunnel for a second time and she ducked into it.

Felicity dragged herself through the small opening too, scraping her back painfully on the jagged rocks. It was much smaller than she had hoped, the walls pressing in on her, trying to squeeze the breath from her body. She kicked her feet as hard as she could and felt along the rocky walls with her hands. She knew that they must be bleeding but she did not care. Her only thought was of reaching the end of this watery nightmare and filling her bursting lungs.

A light! She could see a light. Her hand

grasped hold of a rock and she pulled as hard as she could, propelling herself up. Suddenly, she could breathe and she drank back the oxygen in big, greedy gulps.

She was floating in a pool in a large cavern. The walls glowed red and glistened with damp and from the roof huge droplets fell, landing with a splash in the water. Away from the pool, fat boulders sat on the ground and pillars of rock stretched up into the darkness.

"Hey! There's no time to have a bath."

Felicity swung around in the water and spotted Kitta huddled over a glowing red boulder. It was this that was lighting up the cavern. She swam to the edge of the pool and pulled herself up onto a ledge. She sat there for a moment, rubbing her sore eyes.

"Come and get warm," the charm maker shouted. Felicity scrambled to her feet and sprinted over to where the witch was sitting. "Sit close. You'll soon dry out."

The rock was red hot and Felicity sat as close as she dared. It was a wonderful feeling as the heat surged through her and after only a few seconds her t-shirt and jeans were dry and she had managed to stop shivering.

Kitta looked at her curiously. "What happened to my jumper?"

"I couldn't swim in it. It was too heavy. I kept getting my arms all tangled up." She rested on her palms and lifted up one of her feet. "I had to drop your boots too."

The witch looked at Felicity's muddy sock and laughed. "You didn't drown, anyway."

"I almost did," mumbled Felicity sorrowfully. "I think I drank most of the river - tasted like Al's daffodil and slug tea."

"But you feel better now?"

"Yeah. Loads." She rubbed her hands together and held them over the rock. "How did you...?"

"Just a charm. A simple one, but rather handy. Not too good on people, though. Tends to cook the guts."

"Oh, nasty." They sat quietly for a moment then Felicity spoke. "I was so scared in the river. I thought I was going to be swept away. Then, in the tunnel, I thought I was going to drown. I just wanted to go home."

"But you didn't."

"No, but..."

"Felicity, the right path is often the most risky one and you stay on it because it is the right thing to do. It's not important that you want to get off. What is important is that you don't."

"Galibrath told me, the night he - left us, that I would have many adventures and face many dangers. He said that I would face up to them; that I wouldn't turn away." She looked over at the water. "Maybe, this is what he meant."

"Maybe."

"He also told me, at the end of every difficult journey there is a prize, but not a trophy or a shiny medal."

"I think the prize is the knowledge you stayed on the path."

Felicity puffed up her cheeks. "Oh, I was sort of hoping for a new bike."

Chuckling, the witch pulled her to her feet.

They stumbled through the cavern, trying not to trip over any of the sharp rocks. Kitta conjured up a small ball of light, which hovered just over her, helping them to see. But it was hard work anyway; the cave was huge and soon Felicity began to sweat. Small pebbles kept digging into her bootless feet, so she had to stop every couple of seconds to dig them out.

At last, the cave narrowed and the ground became smoother and less painful to walk on. They were starting to climb now, very gently, and Felicity was sure she could smell muffins.

"Is it much further?" she panted, picking another stone from her foot. With a cry, she stumbled and fell to the ground. Her scream echoed through the cavern, bouncing from wall to wall. Then, silence. Gingerly, Felicity sat up, pricking up her ears. There was a sound, a rush of wind, squeals growing louder and louder, a black mass heading her way.

"On the ground!" screamed Kitta.

"I'm already on the ground," huffed back Felicity, rubbing a grazed knee. She frowned as the witch dropped to her tummy.

"Get down. NOW!"

A swirl of bats screeched over Felicity. She dived to the cave floor but a bat was already tangled up in her hair, trying to escape the tightening strands. She reached up, grasped hold of the struggling bat and yanked it hard. The bat tore loose. She dropped it and clasped her hands over her head, her nose squashed hard to the cold rock.

The whirlwind of beating wings streamed over her. It was deafening, like a train when you stand too close on the platform. Then, as suddenly as the bats had appeared, they were gone. Slowly, Felicity lifted her head. "Sorry," she mumbled to Kitta.

The witch stood up and brushed the dirt from her kimono. She tossed Felicity a sour look. "Just keep going," she muttered coldly.

They stumbled on. The path was getting steeper, winding its way into the darkness. Felicity was tired now but she plodded on. She kept her eyes glued to the cave floor, careful not to trip over any more loose rocks. Every minute or so she patted her jeans pocket just to check the sentinel was still there. It was and it made her feel safer. At last, they reached some very old stone steps, so worn that they sank down in the middle, as if they had been scooped out by a JCB. They rested at the bottom, hands pressed to the cold walls.

"These steps lead to a secret door hidden at the back of the pantry," panted Kitta. "Try not to make too much of a racket. If there's anybody in there, they could hear us."

"OK."

Then they were off, charging up the steps, two at a time. They stopped in front of a stone wall.

"Where's the door?" howled Felicity urgently, forgetting to keep her voice low.

"Shush!" Gingerly, the witch put her ear up to the wall. A second later she pulled back and grinned. "I think we may be in luck," she announced. "If I can only recall the secret saying. I think there was the word 'toffee' in it..."

"Now there's a surprise," murmured Felicity, remembering Galibrath's dessert-themed passwords for The Wishing Shelf door.

"Oh, I got it now. Really gross over-sweet toffee popcorn balls." Felicity watched mesmerized as the wall in front of them crumbled away.

The weary imp hauled the old sofa out of the shop and along the hall to the junkroom. The metal legs dragged on the floor, crafting tracks in the shiny wood. But Al was past caring. Grumbling, he pushed it in and slammed the door shut.

"Phew," the imp muttered, rubbing his aching shoulders. Crouching down, he rested his back on the wall.

He was feeling so miserable. Felicity had deserted him, run off, left him here to a life of slavery. No kettle, no new t-shirts, no Hobnobs and no hope. He had been forced to pack up every book in the shop, block up the fireplace and lug all the old desks and the sofa to the junkroom. He yawned. He felt so sleepy and his hands were covered in blisters. They hurt too, and one had just popped.

"Hey, you!" barked a cruel voice. "What you doing?"

"Nothing," yelped the imp, jumping to his feet.

It was Banks. Nasty goblin. Always shouting orders. He stomped up to Al and looked at him in disgust.

"Get in the kitchen and brew Mr Falafel a cuppa." He cuffed the imp around the chin. "Be sharp about it."

"O - OK," Al spluttered.

The goblin sneered and pushed the imp roughly to the floor. "Go on, then, and remember, Hedes Spine tea only. Mr Falafel told me you brewed him a pot of slug and salami yesterday. He was not a happy wizard."

The imp scuttled off to the kitchen rubbing his battered chin. He had to escape before they hurt him badly. There was no sign of Felicity. She must have been captured. Probably in Tantalus's dungeon by now. But how to get by the wizard and his nasty goblin? Never mind all the blooming trolls?

He knew the tea was kept in the very back of the pantry, on the top shelf. Hmm, maybe he could hide in there for a bit. He could pile the sacks of tea up around him and have a nap.

He slipped quietly into the kitchen, stepped over a tin of Monster Hotdogs, and sidled along the back wall to the pantry. Nobody had spotted him; the other imps were too busy baking muffins for the warlords. He opened the pantry door and crept in. A rope hung from the roof just next to the door. The imp yanked it and a bulb flickered on.

"JEEPERS!" His jaw slackened as he stared, goggle-eyed at the hole in the back wall. Scratching his brow, he edged a little closer. This could easily be a trap. Tantalus's doing, or that evil goblin of his. They wanted to see if he would try and escape and then they would pounce on him and clobber him on the head. No chance. He would go back to the kitchen. Then, before he could yell, a hand snaked around his head, covered his face and yanked him off his feet.

"Al, it's OK, stop kicking. It's me. Felicity." She let go of his mouth.

"Felicity!" Jumping up, he spun around and hugged her, almost weeping for joy. "I looked for you every night."

"But I only left yesterday, silly." She beamed down at the gleeful imp and patted him on the back. "I found help too."

"You found her?" yelled the imp, letting Felicity go. "You found the girl in the picture?"

"Keep it down," whispered Kitta, stepping out

from the shadow of a pile of flour sacks. "They can hear you in Cauldron City."

"Charming," squeaked Al, looking pained. "Never met me and not even a 'Hello' or a 'How are you?'"

Kitta sighed. "Hello. How are you?"

The imp showed them his very best 'martyr' look. "Just terrible. They tossed all my t-shirts in a skip. Every day, I have to put on this, this - monstrosity. Feel how tight it is around the neck too. I'm being slowly strangled, you know. I'm forced to work as a slave day and night," his face crumbled, "and they stopped all my tea breaks." He opened his mouth wide and howled.

Felicity shushed him, but too late. The door to the pantry hit the wall and they froze.

"Gross over-sweet toffee popcorn balls," Kitta whispered urgently. A hundred or so bricks jumped up off the floor and like a jigsaw puzzle, built up the wall all the way up to the top, hiding the tunnel.

Dragging the still blubbering imp, they hid by a crumpled Monster Hotdog box and a sack of Jasper Pottywalrus's spuds. Felicity covered Al's lips with her hand, stifling his howls.

Two imps in chef's hats crept into the pantry. "I think there's a banshee in here," one of them mumbled.

"Stop being so soft," mumbled the other.

"But all the howling and crying?"

"No, y' dimwit. Too cutesy to be a banshee."

"Maybe it was a baby banshee."

"IT WAS NOT A BANSHEE!"

"SHHH! You'll wake the banshee."

"THERE IS NO..."

"OK! OK! Keep y' nappy on. Maybe it was just a ghost."

"A ghost? In the pantry?"

"Well, I dunno, do I. Maybe it gobbled up a dodgy Monster Hotdog and it killed it, so now it haunts the pantry."

"You see them chickens over there, hanging by the necks?"

"Nasty."

"Yep, very nasty and if you don't stick a sock in it, I'm gonna hang you up next to 'em."

"Ooh, charming!" They crept further in. "I remember I had a dodgy Monster Hotdog once.

"THAT'S IT!"

"OH NO!"

"Oh no - what?"

"A witch!"

"Where?"

"Over by the spuds. No! Don't look!"

"What's she doing?"

"No clue, but she looks a bit nasty. I got a plan. Let's grab her and take her to Mr Falafel. Get a reward."

"OK. Good plan."

"Hang on! She just shut her eyes. Maybe she's gonna chant a charm. Quick, let's get her."

"No! Let's scarper!"

"Oh, OK."

"Run!"

"What, now?"

"JUST RUN!"

"Call to this pantry a chilly breeze,
Imps in chef's hats, body freeze."

"My legs!"

"I know!"

"I can't move 'em!"

"I KNOW!"

"I bet she's a banshee."

"I'm gonna kill you."

"But..."

"I'M GONNA KILL YOU!"

"But I really, really, really don't want to go," Al blubbered. He crossed his arms and legs in a huff. "You go. I can stay here and guard the two imps. Anyway, Hyperion and I don't get on too well."

Felicity sighed. "But only you know how to find him. You worked for him, remember?"

The imp grunted. "I'm trying to forget. In fact, it's all a bit fuzzy."

"Listen, Al." Kitta knelt down and grasped the trembling imp gently by his shoulders. "We need Hyperion to stop Tantalus selling the book. You know what will happen if a warlord gets his hands on it. Hyperion is the only wizard who can stop him."

"But..."

"He has to see Galibrath's will," butted in Felicity, "to prove the shop belongs to Kitta, not to Tantalus."

"If he left it to me."

Felicity rolled her eyes at her. "Of course he did. Who else?"

The witch shrugged. She had not yet opened the will, as if by doing so she'd be hammering the final nail in Galibrath's coffin.

"As soon as Tantalus is locked up," Felicity continued, turning back to the imp, "you can go back to brewing tea."

"You can wear any shirt you want," added Kitta.

Al yanked at his collar. "I can put my old t-shirts back on?"

"Yep." Felicity rubbed his head. "We can go shopping, buy you a wardrobe full."

"But how do I get out?"

Kitta jerked her thumb over her shoulder. "The same way we got in."

The imp looked very nervous, chewing on his top lip and scratching his tummy and neck. "So, if I risk my neck clambering on my knees in a dark tunnel, what will you two be doing?"

Felicity opened her mouth but then snapped it shut. She decided not to tell Al the bit about swimming the river.

Kitta winked at Felicity. "We shall be busy delaying the Warlords' Auction till you storm in with the cavalry."

Once they had hidden the two frozen imps under a pile of flour sacks, the two girls slipped out of the pantry. There was nobody in the kitchen, so they crept over to the door and peeked out. But a gang of trolls were marching up the corridor so they had to quickly duck back in again.

Felicity gulped down her fright and pressed her body to the wall. Annoyingly, her tummy decided, as they were in a kitchen, this was the perfect moment to growl and let her know how hungry it was. But the trolls were too busy stomping to hear it.

Tiptoeing down the corridor, they passed the old junkroom and stopped at the closed door to the shop. Gingerly, Kitta twisted the handle and edged the door ajar. She peered through the gap and gasped. Her face froze and her body went rigid.

"Can you see anything?" Felicity quizzed her in an urgent whisper.

But the witch did not reply. Felicity watched her step back, crouch on her heels and rest her chin on her fists.

Silence.

"Kitta?"

The witch looked up and waved Felicity over to the door. Hesitantly, her legs like jelly, she crept over, put her eye to the crack and peered into the shop. Her eyes almost popped out of her head as she reeled back, her face a mask of horror.

"He's a dorfmoron," mumbled Kitta, before she had a chance to ask.

She peeked back through the crack. He was a nasty-looking monster, as big as a grizzly bear and covered from snout to paws in a straggly, brown pelt. Jagged teeth erupted out of his gooey jaws and from the top of his scalp sprang two horns, sharpened to ice picks.

"He's not very - cuddly, is he," whispered Felicity, trying to sound nonchalant.

"The dorfmoron's not the problem. Check in the corner, over by the desk."

She did as she was told. The dorfmoron was grunting and growling, stomping about the shop. He knocked into a bookcase piled high with books. Snarling, he swept them onto the floor, thrusting the bookcase roughly onto its back.

"Relax, Jumble Mud." The silky words froze Felicity's blood. They had originated from the front of the shop, by the window, but it was difficult to see; the gap was too small and she was scared to open the door any further. Hold on! "Holy cow!" she mumbled. She had just spotted a - a SKELETAL MONSTER! But it kept melting away, fading in and out like a torch low on battery power. For a second she saw a flowing robe and the wisps of a veil, then it vanished in a hazy mist.

"What is it?"

"That," murmured Kitta, rubbing her eyes, "is a night demon. A very tricky customer."

"I don't think he's a customer," Felicity murmured. Hypnotised, she watched the spectre float across the room. It stopped, hovering in front of the dorfmoron.

"Grab a stool." The demon spoke softly, the innocent words laced in malice. But the dorfmoron was too brave or too stupid to worry. "SIT DOWN, SCUM, OR I'LL RIP OFF YOUR LEGS AND FEED 'EM TO YOU!" the night demon howled. The dorfmoron looked like he had been slapped very hard in the face. He scrambled over to a stool and almost fell onto it. He sat there shaking.

"Now, now, boys. Tempers!" joked Tantalus, marching into the room.

Behind him scampered Banks carrying Articulus. He placed it gently on the desk next to the wizard and then crept back into the shadows.

"Now I understand dorfmorons despise demons," Tantalus began, "and I know for a fact demons rarely get invited to a dorfmoron's birthday party, so let's skip the Hobnobs, NOT pop the kettle on and forget the cosy chat." He rested his elbows on the desk and grinned wickedly. "Who would like to make the opening bid?"

Perched cross-legged on a boulder in the cave, Al took a long, lingering slurp from his mug. "Hmm, yummy," he murmured. Next to him there was a thermos, a rosy-red apple and a slug and salami roll wrapped in plastic.

No rush, he thought. If I drink up, I can just squeeze in a fifth cup.

Chapter 23

A Spider the Size of a Fiat Uno

The dorfmoron jumped to his feet, sending the stool clattering to the floor. "Me! I wanna go first," he boomed. He glanced warily at the night demon but the veiled spectre seemed to be much calmer now and waved him on with a flick of a skeletal hand.

The dorfmoron sniggered and waddled over to a stained and rather shabby wooden chest nestled under the window. A bronze handle jutted out from the side and fixed to the lid was a hinge and a bulky-looking metal padlock. He grasped hold of the handle and hauled it into the middle of the room.

"What do we have here?" oozed Tantalus, rubbing his hands in glee. He had begun to sweat, the greed seeping out of his skin. "Silver goblets? Strings of pearls?"

But the dorfmoron was still fumbling with a hefty bunch of keys hanging on his belt; his fingers were like bananas and the keys were too small. Finally, he worked one loose and forced it in to the lock. He twisted the key, tore off the bolt and wrenched open the lid.

The chest was filled with thousands of gold flupoons, spilling over the edge like a plunging waterfall. They bounced and scuttled across the floor, hitting stool legs and falling over to form tiny glittering pools. Tantalus shot up from the desk he was sitting on and with a whoop of joy, thrust his hands into the hill of gold. He grasped a handful of the nuggets, then let them seep through his fingers and rain back into the chest.

"Impressive. Very impressive," marvelled Tantalus gleefully.

"This 'ere chest is nothin'," grunted the dorfmoron, casting a sly glance at the demon. "I got me eleven of 'em, all burstin' to the brim."

"A remarkable bid, Jumble Mud." On tiptoe, Tantalus rested his hand on the dorfmoron's beefy shoulder. "Go on then, tell me everything.

How did y' do it?"

"Nicked from the richest buggers in all of Twice Brewed." His chest swelled with pride. "I plundered most of it myself, with a little help from the lads."

"Is this a joke?" spat the night demon, drifting by. "Chests of gold for Articulus? The most powerful book in the land - in all the lands!"

"BULL!" growled Jumble Mud, glowering at the spectre. "This 'ere gold is a good trade for that old book..."

"SHUT IT, MUD!" The night demon had shot back over to the dorfmoron and was now hovering eye to eye with him. "Or I will slip back in time, visit your sweet mother, decapitate her and then you will not even be born. Mr Falafel has listened to your pitiful bid and now it is my turn."

For a moment, it seemed as if Jumble Mud was going to argue, but then he thought better of it and skulked off to a shadowy corner of the shop.

The demon twirled and faced Tantalus.

"I know what you want, what has always

slipped through your fingers. What has evaded you and kept your eyes open in the dark." The demon floated a little closer to the wizard and whispered in his ear. "You want power."

Tantalus nodded slowly.

"Do you know what stops you? What holds you back? Regrets. Get rid of them, you can do, you can be anything you want to. You can crush your enemy or your best buddy and feel nothing. Just the joy of power."

The wizard frowned. "So, what's your bid? What are you offering me?"

"I am offering, Mr. Falafel, to destroy that irritating part of you that holds you back - the part which stops you being the wizard you can be - your soul."

The wizard shook a gangly finger at the demon and tutted. "Maybe, my dark skeletal pal, I need to clarify how this 'Sale' works. You see, buying a thing tends to imply - giving, not taking."

"You fool," rasped the spectre. "Don't you get it? Why, even this idiot dorfmoron gets it."

Jumble Mud grunted. "Not a clue."

The night demon threw up his hands in

disgust.

Scratching his head, Tantalus eyed the spectre suspiciously. "But how...?"

"How is not important. What is important is that you can stamp on your granny's false teeth, shear her fluffy cat, even chop off her legs and not loose a wink of sleep."

The wizard's eyes widened and he chuckled. "Yes, yes. I see now. A tempting offer. Very tempting." He picked up a gold flupoon off the floor and put it between his teeth. He bit down on it. "Hmm," he mumbled, flipping it over and over in his hand, studying it. He tossed it back in the chest. "Difficult. Very difficult."

"We don't got all day," grumbled Jumble Mud, from the back of the room. "I got folk to chop up and a stone church to burn - not easy."

"Yes, yes, of course." The wizard blotted his hands on the front of his cloak. "Gentlemen, thank you for your bids. They were - inspiring. But, I always wanted a yacht, so Articulus shall go to..."

"TANTALUS! NO!" yelled Kitta, bursting in the door.

The wizard's jaw dropped to his weedy chest.

"But - but, how did you escape?"

"Interesting story, actually, but not important." The witch smirked, slipped her hand in the pocket of her kimono and pulled out a scroll of parchment. "But this is. Galibrath's will. Articulus is not yours to sell."

"How interesting," murmured the demon silkily.

"Is the books yours, then?" bawled Jumble Mud, trooping over. "Can I interest y' in eleven chests of gold?"

"STOP!" Tantalus hammered his fist on the desk. "The Wishing Shelf belongs to me, so Articulus belongs to me." In the corner of the bookshop a spider suddenly grew to the size of a Fiat Uno. "Any problems, talk to my old chum, Roth, here."

Dropping the scroll, Kitta backpedalled to the wall. "Tantalus, I do not want to fight you."

"Then go."

"I can't.

"Then..." The wizard shut his eyes and slowly the monster spider advanced on the witch.

But she did not run. Calmly, she shut her

eyes too and, like Tantalus, bowed her head.

WHAM! Suddenly, the floor in front of Roth exploded, wooden splinters flying up, a huge fist punching through the floor. Slowly, it uncurled to reveal razor-sharp claws. A huge werewolf clambered up, stretched open his jaws and howled.

Growling like a rabid dog, the werewolf rushed over to the spider, his hands curling and uncurling. With a boxer's punch, he hit the spider hard, bulldozing him over onto his back. Then the snarling werewolf jumped up on flailing spider and clawed at the soft underbelly. Tantalus fell to his knees with a whimper as deep cuts ravished his own chest, mirroring the wounds to his monster.

With a high-pitched cry, Roth wrapped his long legs around the werewolf, pinning the struggling animal to his chest. He squeezed.

The werewolf was wheezing now and a few feet away, Kitta gasped and clutched at her neck. But the witch's monster had not given up. Opening his jaws, he bit the spider's leg, his mammoth incisors cutting to the bone. The spider screeched, grasped hold of the werewolf and flung him away. Colliding with a bookshelf, it lay on the floor gasping. With a sinking-ship creak, the shelf collapsed, spilling hundreds of books on the werewolf's back.

The spider struggled to his eight feet, blood seeping from the cuts to his swollen body and leg. Drunkenly, he swayed over to Kitta and swung back his front pincher. But over in the corner, the jumbled hill of books began to move.

The spider thrust out his snapping pincer, but staggered back as the werewolf jumped on his back, digging sharp claws into the monster's bushy flesh. Like a rodeo bull, Roth lurched and bucked, but the werewolf clung on. In whimpering agony, the spider drove back into a wall, crushing the poor werewolf. A bone cracked sharply and he slithered to the floor, defeated. He crumbled to dust and the witch, a few feet away, collapsed on her side.

The spider picked up a fallen bookcase in his pincers and, on his hind legs, swayed over to where Kitta had fallen.

"STOP!" yelled Felicity, dashing into the room and kneeling down next to the fallen witch. She brushed a curl from Kitta's eyes; they were shut but they fluttered gently, as if she wanted to open them but could not.

"You have been in the wars," she whispered softly. "Jumping in, not thinking. Just like me, I suppose."

"Get out of my way," Tantalus ordered her, snapping open his eyes, "or I will crush you too."

"Destroy her! Grind every bone in her body," cackled the demon. In a frenzy, it glided around the room, knocking over books and sending the lamps on the desks crashing to the floor. "Remember, no regrets. JUST POWER!"

Felicity ignored the demon and glared up at Tantalus. "How could you hurt her? You loved her once."

"Once, but not now!" yelled Tantalus, his voice cracking ever so slightly. "She chose my darling brother, remember? But he's not here to help her now. Or you."

She looked up into the eyes of the power-hungry wizard and remembered how different he had been the day he had stood over Galibrath's bed. The sadness she had seen in his face. Perhaps, just perhaps there was still a chance, she thought.

"That day, in Galibrath's room, the agony in your eyes."

Tantalus snorted "Poppycock! I just had a spot of wind."

"But I saw you, remember? You told me that you loved him once. That you wished things had been different."

"La de da de da," the wizard sang in her face.

"Ignore her," screeched the night demon. "Rip out her tongue."

"Punch her in the chops," yelled Jumble Mud, jumping up and down, making all the books judder.

Tantalus closed his eyes for a second time. Oh no, Felicity thought, he's going to do it. They were going to be crushed. Urgently, her words brimming with fear, she stumbled, "The regrets you felt that day. If you let that thing steal them away from you, you'll just be an empty shell."

His eyes were still closed.

"You'll be a monster, just like it is."

STILL CLOSED!

"And you will love nobody and nobody will

ever love you. And I feel sorry for you."

Slowly, Tantalus blinked open his eyes and looked curiously at Felicity. A deep hush fell on the room, accentuated by the ticking of the clock. "Kids and idiots always tell the truth," he finally murmured. Then he looked to the witch, her kimono torn, her body a road map of cuts and welts. He swallowed and his jaw softened.

"Falafel, you coward," blazed the demon. "Must I do all the killing!?"

"NO!" yelled the wizard, throwing up his hands to protect her. But in the blink of a cyclops' eye, he was thrown over the desk, bouncing off the wall and falling in a crumpled heap on a growling rug.

The spider instantly shrunk, scampering away, and the bookcase it had been holding crashed to the floor, just missing the witch's feet.

Nobody moved. Even the demon looked shocked. Then the goblin emerged from the shadows, whistling softly.

"Mr Banks," croaked the spectre, gliding over to him. "Turning on your master; shooting him in the back. That's my kind of hero."

"Cut the drivel!" Banks undid the top button of his shirt and smiled slyly. "You want Articulus, then you shall have it." He stared stonily at the demon. "But you will be paying me."

Chapter 24

The Cavalry Storms In

The dorfmoron wrenched up Tantalus's head by the roots and put an axe to his throat. "He's not a gonna yet," he sniggered. "Shall I chop 'im up a bit?"

"No," rasped Kitta. She battled to open her eyes. "Let him go - YOU CREEP!" Her face was all puffed up and blood was oozing from her lips and a gash on her cheek.

"You must stay still," whispered Felicity. "There's so much blood."

"I'm fine," Kitta croaked, trying to sit up. But then she slumped back, crying out in agony.

"Told you," mumbled Felicity, trying to smile. She stroked the witch's cheek.

"How touching," sneered Banks. He clutched at his mouth. "Anybody got a paper bag?"

The night demon thought this was very

funny and cackled, dodging around the room like an out-of-control bumper car. It seemed to be having a ball.

"Oy, demon-thingy," yelled the goblin. "Do you want to buy a book, or what?" He bent over the desk and patted Articulus.

The spectre dropped down and floated in front of him. "So, Articulus is mine," it hissed. "In return I can destroy your soul, every regret will be lost..."

"Hey!" Banks waggled a finger in the demon's skeletal face. "I got no soul, so no problem in the Regrets Department. Remember, sinning is my life. No, what I want from you is..."

"Gold!" bellowed Jumble Mud, lumbering up. "Eleven chests jammed full of it."

"Magic! I want the power to kill in the blink of a cyclops' eye." Banks jabbed a bony finger at the night demon. "Offer me that or Articulus can sit on a shelf and rot."

"Perhaps," wheezed the creature slyly, drifting over to Tantalus's shattered body and leering down at him.

The goblin grunted. "Perhaps!? I'm not

interested in 'perhaps'." He sat down on the dorfmoron's chest of gold. "If you don't want Articulus, I bet Jumble Mud here..."

"Falafel here is a witness. Slay him and the two girls and let me watch you." It quivered at the thought. "Then, we will see."

"Wonderful!" Banks smirked. "No problem." It was as if he had just been asked to pass the salt pot. "Chuck me your axe, Jumble Mud."

With a sulky grunt, the dorfmoron tossed the hatchet to the goblin. He caught it niftily by the handle, marched over to where Felicity was still crouched on the floor and lifted it over his head.

"But - you saved us," stammered Felicity, "in Tantalus's office; you helped us to untangle the rope."

"Yes, I did. Y' see, I knew my old boss over there had a soft spot for the witch, and I knew if she got to The Wishing Shelf, she'd distract Tantalus, giving me the opportunity to..."

"Mutiny," finished Felicity.

"Exactly."

"But..."

"Brady, forget all that," he mimicked her, "you must be a good goblin really - drivel. I'm cruel, my mum never hugged me and chopping up silly girls is fun. So zip it and say your prayers."

Like a firework, the sentinel sprung out of Felicity's pocket and dived on the goblin. But Banks simply stepped back and lashed out with the axe, slicing the ball in two.

"Amateurs," he muttered, stamping on the fallen fragments. But Felicity was already on her feet, scrambling past him, reaching for the desk - for Articulus.

"BRADY!" yelled Banks, and as her hands curled around the book, she turned back to look at him. "CATCH!" He flung the axe at her head.

Looking down, she ripped open the book and quickly thumbed a page. Then she sneaked a look up. The axe hung in the air, the blade tickling the tiny hairs on the end of her nose.

She jumped back.

They had frozen; all three of them. Banks looked angry, the night demon looked shocked and Jumble Mud - well, he just looked ugly.

She watched as the axe slowly - very slowly - twisted in the air, finally spearing the door. The night demon was drifting closer to her but it moved like a snail and Felicity easily circled around it. It took ten seconds for the demon to turn back around.

She crept up to Banks and smiled. She felt so powerful. "You know, I think Barf is a nice name. Barf, Barf, Barf," she sang. The goblin's face grew slowly blacker and blacker.

With a deafening crash, the shop door burst open hitting the wall, the hatchet clattering to the floor. Standing there was Hyperion, kilt and all. The cavalry, thought Felicity, as the wizard stomped into the shop, swinging his umbrella. Hanging on his leg, like a frightened child, was Al.

Then six more wizards rushed in, sheriff badges pinned on dragon-crested cloaks. "Spread out," ordered Hyperion. They did as they were told, taking up posts on each side of the three villains.

"Felicity Brady!" The tall wizard beamed at her. "You have been a busy girl."

Felicity looked up at him, confused. "But, the book - why has it no effect on you?"

"Because," Hyperion winked at her, "I'm not

your enemy." The imp ran up and hugged her leg. "You can shut Articulus now. We can handle this lot." He nodded to the other WANDD agents. "Ready?" he bellowed.

"Ready," they chorused back.

But Felicity was not. The book was shaking in her hands and in her mind it was howling.

No! No! I will protect you. I am your destiny.

"Why don't you grab them now?" she asked, still slowly thumbing the book. "You will be so much faster than them."

"True..." Hyperion lifted a bushy eyebrow. "But it's vital you shut the book now. Not later, Felicity. Now. Did Galibrath not tell you how dangerous Articulus can be? Soon, it will start to control you, and remember, you're just a young girl; easy prey for so powerful a book."

Oooh! He wants me too!

"But..."

"Felicity." The wizard looked at her sternly. "Close - the - book."

Felicity pulled a face. She had felt so powerful, so...

"OK," she muttered and slowly, fighting the

words swimming in her mind, she shut Articulus. Slipping it under her arm, she grabbed for the imp's hand and dived on top of Kitta.

The room seemed to explode. There were thumps and hisses, yelling and crying, shouts of, "GET 'IM OFF ME!" and "MY LEG! HE'S BITING MY LEG!"

A loud bang bounced off the walls and Felicity smothered her ears with her hands, dropping Articulus to the floor. But she was so scared, and anyway, she was past caring.

CRASH! A bookshelf hit the floor, spilling books everywhere.

SMASH! The window shattered and Felicity felt shards of glass slicing at her bare hands and feet.

Stools toppled over, doors slammed and...

A hand gripped Felicity's shoulder. "You OK?" a friendly voice asked. She looked up to see Hyperion.

"I, er think so." She looked over at the imp, who had rolled up in a ball on the floor next to her. He seemed OK too. But Kitta! "Tantalus hurt Kitta, he..."

The wizard knelt down and put his fist gently on the charm maker's head. Then he uncurled his hand and sprinkled what looked like glittering dust over her face. Like sand in an egg timer, the glow poured back into her cheeks.

"She'll be fine now," said Hyperion gently. "But I'll call for Dorothy. Just to be safe."

"Thanks," muttered Felicity. She sat up and looked about. The Wishing Shelf now resembled the junkroom. Flayed books with bent spines and torn pages littered the floor and the old desk had flipped over and lay like a dying turtle. Most of the bookcases had toppled over too and now rested amongst buckled reading lamps and legless stools.

Jumble Mud and the night demon had vanished.

But hanging from the roof...

Snared in a net...

Wriggling...

And shouting...

Was Bartholomew Banks!

"Soon Brady, I will escape," he seethed, "and then I shall find you, and when I do, no sword will be too sharp, no hammer too blunt..."

"Felicity." Hyperion stood over her. "Where's Articulus?"

"It's here. It's right - oh," Felicity leapt to her feet - maybe she was sitting on it. "I - I dropped it. I..."

The wizard's eyes sparkled in fury. Or was it terror? As if his mask had been lifted up for just a tiny second to show the true wizard lurking under it. Had she also spotted greed burning in his eyes?

Hyperion turned his back on poor Felicity. "One of the rascals has snatched Articulus," he shouted to his fellow wizards. "You, Cuthbert," he turned to a pimply-faced wizard with blond spiky hair, "follow that demon. He's probably skipped back fifty years. The rest of you, find the dorfmoron."

The WANDD agents dashed out of the door and Felicity watched Cuthbert twist on the spot like a spinning top, faster and faster, and then vanish in a puff of daffodil-yellow smoke.

"I'm sorry," she mumbled to Hyperion, but the wizard ignored her and marched out of the shop.

Felicity's legs were trembling so much she

knelt down. She felt so miserable, so - so, useless. With a soft moan, Kitta rolled over onto her back and a small voice squeaked, "Is it safe now?" It was Al.

"I think so," mumbled back Felicity. She spotted the scroll lying on the floor. The will! Kitta must have fallen on it after her fight with Tantalus.

She picked it up and looked at it. It was still bound in the ribbon and sealed with a blob of red wax. Nobody had read it, not even Tantalus. She ballooned her cheeks and sighed. The Wishing Shelf was safe anyway and with shaky hands she pulled off the ribbon and split open the seal.

I, Galibrath Falafel, hereby hand over The Wishing Shelf to my brother, Tantalus Falafel, in the hope that he will remember our family customs. And into the safe hands of Felicity Brady, I give Articulus.

Galibrath Falafel

But she'd dropped it.
SHE'D DROPPED IT! And The Wishing

Shelf was Tantalus's after all.

The scroll slipped from Felicity's hand and curled back up on the floor and a very unhappy girl knelt in a bookshop and started to cry.

Chapter 25

Another Cup of Tea

A drop of rain rolled down Felicity's nose and hung off the tip. She wiped it away with her thumb and knelt down. In her hands she clutched a bunch of yellow and white daffodils, which she placed on the wet grass next to a small rock. She sat there watching the rain bounce off the grey marble.

"There are no words," she mumbled. She stood back up and turned to look at Hyperion. "Why?"

The wizard smiled at her wearily, black smudges hanging like dirty washing under his eyes. "You were the last person Galibrath spoke to, so you must choose the words."

Felicity frowned and rubbed her eyes. They felt sore and gritty.

"It is our custom," he added with a wise

smile. "The custom of wizards."

"But, I'm not a - I mean, I wouldn't know where to begin." She shrugged her shoulders.

She felt a hand on her arm. "Years ago," said Kitta, moving up to stand next to her, "when Galibrath and I were young, he was always helping his dad in The Wishing Shelf."

"Or riding off on some mission or other for WANDD," murmured Hyperion wistfully. He smiled sadly at the cobwebbed memory.

The witch nodded. She still had a nasty cut on her cheek from the fight with Tantalus and she looked as pale and tired as Hyperion did.

They stood in silence for a long time, the blustery wind dragging at Felicity's scarf and her mittens on strings. On the very top of the hill, a small cluster of trees battled the gale, complaining bitterly and somewhere a braying donkey started to 'Eee Orr' for his supper.

Just below them stood a fort, Lupercus Castle she'd been told, and next to it a tumbled-down windmill rested its crumbling body on the side of the hill. Felicity turned and watched the torn sails lumber around in the stormy winds. They'd turned one time too many, she thought.

She shivered and tugged at the zip on her coat, pulling it up as far as it would go. Then she stuck her hands deep into her pockets.

"He can rest now," she said softly.

With a wave of Hyperion's umbrella and a wiggle of his fingers, chips of marble flew from the rock. It was as if an invisible chisel was cutting into it and when the wizard lowered his hand Felicity read the words -

Galibrath Falafel of 173 Years. Rest After Toil.

"So young," murmured Hyperion, "for a wizard." Felicity couldn't help but smile.

She moved away from the grave and stared down the hill at Twice Brewed, but she couldn't see much of the town. Angry clouds were driving through the valley whipped along by the blustery wind, hiding it in a swirl of black mist. The foul weather seemed to match her foul mood. She kicked at a rock, stubbing her toe.

It had been a torturous week, waiting for news of Articulus, but nobody seemed in a hurry to tell Felicity anything. In fact, she had heard nothing - all week. And now she was angry. Angry at Hyperion for not telling her what was happening and angry at herself, for letting the book slip from her hands. And now it was in the skeletal claws of a demon or the furry paws of a dorfmoron.

If only she had grasped the book more tightly. If only...

She sighed and kicked the rock even harder.

The last few days had been very busy in the shop, magic folk spilling in, keen to listen to Felicity's tale of killer puffdolts and demonic dorfmorons. But she had stayed hidden in the back of the shop. She felt too guilty about losing the book to talk to anybody.

"What happens now?" She heard Kitta quiz Hyperion. "About Articulus, I mean."

The wizard shrugged. "No luck finding it yet. But we will. I have my best agents tracking down Jumble Mud. He'll be holed up in a cave, probably up in the Trimmel Mountains. But I shall catch the rascal."

Felicity frowned. "But what about the night demon?" she asked, walking over to them. She had a feeling it was not the dorfmoron who had snatched the book. He had been too far away, skulking at the back of the shop.

"Yes, well, a little tricky them night demons. You see, first we have to find out where it is and then we have to find out when it is." He sighed and combed a hand through his red hair. "They jump time you see. Such fiddly blighters and a nightmare to catch."

He stabbed the air with his umbrella. "You know, I once trapped a night demon in a castle dungeon but the sly beggar kept vanishing through the walls..."

Felicity had stopped listening.

"...I managed to keep up with it but then it skipped a hundred years into the future. Why, the castle had been turned into a fancy hotel by then..."

She was thinking about Galibrath's last words, the night he had passed away. *At the end of every difficult journey there is the greatest of treasure*, he had told her. *Not a chest of gold or a string of pearls. Do you know what the treasure is?* She hadn't known the answer. He had told her but she hadn't really understood. But now - now she understood.

"...and the dungeons, they were now the

restaurant. We knocked over a few soup bowls that day, I can tell you." The wizard chuckled, a little too loudly.

"I could help," she burst out. "I mean, I saw the night demon so I know what it looks like. I could help you to track it down."

Kitta frowned.

Hyperion forced a smile.

And Al, who had been sheltering under Kitta's coat, popped his head out and murmured dryly, "A witch short of a coven, that girl," and he ducked back in.

"Felicity," said Kitta sternly, "chasing after warlords isn't a game. It's very dangerous, even for a WANDD agent."

"But I want to help. I want to," Felicity sighed and rubbed her eyes, "I don't know. Do something."

"Felicity, you are doing something. You're helping me to run The Wishing Shelf. That's what Galibrath would have wanted."

"No, it isn't." Felicity stared crossly up at Kitta and the witch stared crossly back. "He told me to look after Articulus. That I would walk on dangerous paths, that I would face..."

"Going after a night demon is not a dangerous path, it's a suicidal one."

Felicity pondered this, then she lowered her eyes and mumbled, "Not if…"

"Not if what?" asked Kitta suspiciously.

Felicity looked up. "Not if you help me. Show me how to do magic."

"Help you!" cried Kitta, throwing her hands in the air. "Help you to do what? Kill yourself?"

There was a stony silence, the girls staring angrily at each other.

Finally, Hyperion cleared his throat. "Must be off," he announced. He stretched his arms and yawned. "Lots to do. No easy task tracking down warlords, I can tell you."

He mustered a shrill whistle and a carpet emblazoned with fire-breathing dragons sprang from behind a tree and dashed over. An old gnome with a black cap on his head was already sitting on the carpet. His legs were crossed and he was gazing ahead in a very stern sort of way.

"Listen to me, Felicity," said Hyperion bracingly, "you must not blame yourself for losing Articulus." He looked at her kindly but to Felicity his words still held a hint of annoyance.

"Without you and Kitta," there was a sniff from under the witch's coat, "and Al, of course, we wouldn't have known about Tantalus's plans. We wouldn't have even known the book had been lost."

"But I want to help."

"You will. But not now. Not today. Do not worry. Remember, a Brady-girl will always be needed in the end."

Felicity scowled. "I'm sorry?" Why was it she felt as if everybody was keeping a big secret from her.

But the wizard just smiled and, like a king mounting his horse, he stepped grandly onto the carpet and sat down behind his small chauffeur. He lay his umbrella down next to him and then he turned back to Felicity. "Now, no more talk of chasing after warlords," he scolded her. "My agents can do that."

"And Tantalus. Is he OK?" Felicity asked, quickly changing the subject. She didn't want Hyperion to order her not to help.

"He's still in Funny Bone Surgery recovering from his wounds. He was hurt rather badly, so I hear." A roguish grin enveloped Hyperion's face.

"Will he go to jail for nabbing Galibrath's will?" asked Kitta.

"And trying to kill me," Felicity murmured.

"I doubt it. Too many old pals in high up jobs. But we shall see. Oh, and Banks has been sent back to his tribe for punishment for a loooooooooong list of misdeeds. Could be a bit nasty. Trial by fire. You know the sort of thing. They pour red hot coals over you and if you burn, you did it."

Felicity shuddered.

"And that's the best bit. If they find you guilty, they cut off your ears and nose and then they hang you by your feet for a week."

"But that sounds terrible."

"Yes, well, a little primitive, I admit, but the rascal has it coming. I've been after him for some time. Used to be one of my agents, you know. One of my best, till he turned on me."

Felicity watched the wizard tap the gnome on the arm with his umbrella. She wondered why he even bothered to carry one; it was still drizzling but his hair and kilt were dry anyway.

The carpet gently rose up and Hyperion flew

away.

"Ow!" yelped Kitta, grabbing at her leg.

"Sorry," came a small voice. Al slipped out from under her coat. "Hot flask," he explained with a grin. "Cup of tea, anybody?"

The imp snapped his fingers and a cup with an orange elephant ear for a handle leapt out of his pocket. He caught it niftily in one hand.

"What flavour is it?" asked Felicity suspiciously, watching him pour some steaming tea from a silver flask.

"Well, actually it's, er - Darjeeling," Al mumbled, a little sourly.

"Darjeeling!" gasped Felicity, in grateful surprise. "How very - ordinary."

The imp ignored her. "Grown on the Indian slopes of the Himalayas. It's light, quite delicate, with a touch of..."

"You travelled all the way to India to buy tea," Kitta mocked him.

"No. They sell it at Slurp A Cuppa Inc. A factory in the town." He shrugged. "I've been busy," he explained huffily.

They passed the cup around and drank in silence. It had stopped raining and the warm tea made them feel much better.

This time, Al tried to snuggle under Felicity's coat, but she pushed him away. "Why did you not put on a jumper?" she scolded the shivering imp.

He smirked and spun around. On the back of his t-shirt were the words,

SMALL BUT DANGEROUS

Felicity giggled and then, when the words magically changed to,

I KICKED TANTALUS'S BUTT!

she burst out laughing.

"We should get back to The Wishing Shelf," announced Kitta, looking sternly at Felicity. "We have a bookshop to run. Well, we do till Tantalus gets better and throws us out."

"You still need to fix the hole in the floor," peeped up Al, "and the sofa too."

The charm maker nodded. "I know the ideal charm."

"And I had better hit the books," declared

Felicity, a cheeky grin on her face. "I'm free on Sundays. I could have my first lesson then. Maybe, we could begin with charms or, well, it's up to you; but if I'm going to catch a warlord and find Articulus I will need a bit of magic up my sleeve."

Kitta gaped at her. She rolled her eyes, grunted angrily and stormed off down the hill. "You're not a witch and you never will be,' she called over her shoulder.

"I don't want to be the weakest anymore," Felicity yelled back after her, but she didn't stop and she didn't turn around.

"I think you upset her," Al chuckled, screwing the lid back on the flask. He gulped down his tea and then threw the cup in the air. It vanished in a burst of silvery dust. "Forget it. She's just trying to be all big sisterly."

Felicity shrugged and nodded. "I suppose."

The imp shivered and rubbed his goose-pimpled arms. "Come on. I'm freezing."

They began to jog back down the hill and at the bottom they clambered over an old wooden stile. But a rusty nail snagged Al's shirt, pulling him back. He yanked it free, ripping a hole in it and he toppled to the ground.

"You OK?" asked Felicity running back. But the imp didn't answer. He was staring open-mouthed at a chair which sat in a field of long grass under a huge oak tree.

"I don't remember seeing that on the way up," he mumbled wryly, waving a finger.

"No, nor do I," observed Felicity, turning to look. "How very odd." But then they were in Eternus. "KITTA!" she yelled, but her friend had walked too far ahead and couldn't hear her.

"Stay here," Felicity told the imp, and she struggled through the tall grass, stopping under the branches of the tree.

The chair was a rocking chair. It was brown and made of wood and on the seat was a very flat red cushion with a gold tassel on each corner. It was pitching back and forth as if somebody had just stood up and walked away.

She crept a little closer and gently swept away some of the wet grass with her foot. Should she sit on it, she pondered. She shrugged and sat down. It was a chair, after all. Oddly, when she rested her hands on the wooden arms, they felt bone dry, just like Hyperion.

She started to rock to and fro. Once, twice. Wham! The blackness slammed into her making her yell out in fright. Her stomach lurched. Was she falling? But there was no howling wind, and her sandy locks still hung down over her eyes. Fear gnawed at her, making her tremble. Biting her lip, she prodded for the ground with her foot but there was no ground to prod. Gasping, she pulled her knees up to her face and wrapped her arms around her legs. What was happening?

Ghostly faces swirled around: a dorfmoron snarled at her, clawing for her neck with callused hands and a night demon hovered over her then melted away with a deafening howl. Felicity clutched her hands to her face as squealing bats with evil red eyes swooped down, then scattered in a swirl of grey mist.

Puffdolts.

Club-swinging trolls.

Goblins.

And wart-faced hags, cackling and pointing.

A pirate ship all in black, her keel charging down on her.

AND

AND – Felicity gasped and cried out. "Galibrath! Galibrath, help me! I don't know where I am. I'm lost!" But the ghost-like wizard was drifting away. "No," she whimpered. She stretched out her hand, trying to grab hold of his billowing cloak, but he was too far away. "GALIBRATH!" she screamed, and she leapt from the chair.

It was a comfy-looking room, cluttered with old leather sofas and high-backed chairs. A stuffed fish snored gently on a wall and a grandfather clock stood proudly in a corner and ticked pompously at her, out of time with the crackling of a log fire. Crouched in a corner was a polished writing desk with a quill poking out of the inkwell and a picture of a hilltop she'd never been to hung over the hearth. Oddly, there were no windows and just one dark-panelled door.

Something bumped the back of her legs. She jumped and spun around but it was only the chair, still rocking gently. Then she heard a creak and a breath of wind stroked the back of her neck. She span on her heel, her chin dropping to her chest as she stared at the wizard standing by the open door.

"Well, Felicity," bellowed Galibrath, giving her a colossal grin, "we do have a lot of work to do."

Follow Felicity Brady on her next
exciting adventure in
ARTICULUS QUEST